TO BE YOUR LAST

rae kennedy

Copyright © 2020 by Rae Kennedy

All rights reserved. No part of this book may be reproduced or used in any manner without written permission of the copyright owner except for the use of quotations in a book review. For more information, address: raekennedystudio@gmail.com

FIRST EDITION
RAKE Publishing

www.raekennedyauthor.com

978-1-7333189-5-2

To Be Your Last

CHAPTER 1

Just as I turn to leave, I see him. Sitting in the back shadows watching me.

Even though we haven't seen each other in years, I'd recognize him anywhere.

He was my first.

The first guy I went to bed with, my first love, my first heartbreak. And here we are, in a dive bar in Chicago, our eyes locked across a stage just like the first time I saw him at my sister's wedding.

Two Years Ago...

The moon is a bright white spotlight and stars are just starting to dot the expansive navy sky as I walk across my parents' back yard. The night air is warm but the breeze that washes through my thin, peach chiffon bridesmaid dress is cool, reminding me that though it's the end of May, summer is not quite here.

I make my way toward the reception, just past the barn where people are gathered in groups. Some standing, chatting, laughing, yelling over cups of beer and champagne glasses. Others sitting at tables, eating dinner by the flickering light of the tiny votive candles in the centerpieces.

Tables are scattered around the yard, surrounding the stage and dance floor in the center, which is brightly lit by thousands of string lights crisscrossing overhead. Each strand had been painstakingly put up by my three older brothers yesterday. It'd taken them all day, a case of beer, and only one almost-fist fight. Impressive, really.

I make my way to the food table—it's next to the dance floor, directly across from the stage. I peruse the buffet and my stomach grumbles, finally surrendering to hunger. I haven't had much of an appetite these last few weeks.

My mom and I made all of the food, planning, shopping, prepping, and cooking it all in our century-old, tiny farmhouse kitchen. Beef short ribs, brisket, glazed carrots, potato salad, corn on the cob, giant slices of watermelon, and buttery cornbread muffins. It all looks wonderful, but nothing sounds good to eat. Maybe I'll just wait for cake.

"How's everybody doing tonight?"

I turn toward the voice—it belongs to a guy walking across the stage carrying a mic and a guitar. Mom had made a comment about the band being "unconventional," but looking at this guy, I don't see it.

He's in a black suit, black tie, white shirt. Average height and build. His brown hair is curly and tousled back out of his eyes in a carefree sort of way, like he just rolled out of bed and ran his fingers through it. He has big dark eyes and even a little dimple in his chin. His face has a sweet, boyish charm to it, though he's probably in his mid-to-late twenties. He's cute.

He waves out to the guests and flashes a big white smile. He's really cute, actually.

"Are you ready to have some fun?"

A couple of people hoot from their seats, and the guy on stage points them out and winks as he continues. Other guys all wearing the same black suits come on stage and take their places, but I'm focused on bedhead guy and his amazing smile.

"We're Wicked Road, and weddings aren't our normal gig, but we're friends of the best man and are excited to entertain you and celebrate love." He slings the bright red guitar over his shoulder and runs his fingers through his disheveled hair. His curls look like they'd feel nice and soft between my fingers. *Wow. Chill out, Gracie.* "I'd like you all to welcome, for their first official dance as husband and wife, Mr. and Mrs. Tucker and Courtney Collison."

Everyone claps as my sister and her new husband step onto the dance floor, hand in hand. Court is statuesque as she wraps her arms around Tuck's broad shoulders and he gazes down at her, whispering something in her ear that puts a dazzling smile on her face. They're perfect together in their happiness and all eyes are on them. My grizzly bear of a father is beaming at them. The apples of his cheeks bulge under his thick, red beard in a big grin that crinkles around his eyes. My mom is tucked into his side, wiping the occasional tears she's been unsuccessfully trying to fight off all day.

They are so proud of her. The perfect daughter is now married to the perfect man, and together they're going to make a perfect life. Everything about them—perfect.

Many people might say I'm perfect too. I'm just as blonde, blue-eyed, and bubbly as my sister—maybe more so. A cheerleader. Popular. Straight-A student. And that was all true—when I was in high school.

RAE KENNEDY

Since returning home from my first year at the university last week, everything has been so hectic and everyone so focused on Court's wedding that they haven't taken much notice of me. But that will all change tomorrow.

Tomorrow, everyone will finally find out how much of a failure I, Gracie Gallagher, truly am.

The music begins to play. It starts slow, with a simple bass line and rhythmic guitar. It's familiar, but I can't quite place it.

Then the drums start in, low and then hard. I dig the beat. I glance to the stage and whoa. The drummer's arms are a blur of bright color. His jacket is discarded on the floor, the sleeves of his white dress shirt smashed up, revealing arms covered in tattoos in brilliant shades of red, orange, and green. He squints in concentration, a neon yellow mohawk on top of his head.

Okay, maybe this is what my mom meant by *unconventional?*

The man standing front and center at the mic has his head bowed. I assume he's the singer but he hasn't started singing yet and I can't see his face. He sways slightly to the melody.

Just beyond him is the bassist. He's in the same black suit and has the same dark eyes as the guitarist. But while the guitarist seems to have a partial smile while he plays, the bassist wears a scowl. He has the same brown hair, but his is shorter and slicked back. They even have the same chin dimple. The bassist, however, has a metal piercing above that chin dimple, another one in his septum, and in the bridge of his nose. Their faces are so similar, yet different. Brothers, maybe?

A deep, smooth voice pours into the air, overwhelming

everything else. Chills immediately prickle down the back of my neck and raise goosebumps on my arms.

I snap back to the front man as he sings a cover of Cyndi Lauper's "Time After Time." The tone of his voice is unique and haunting. It's beautiful. I want to close my eyes and listen to him sing, concentrate on the steadiness and clarity, the ease with which he changes pitch, but I can't look away from him.

He's in the black suit, skinny black tie. He holds the mic stand, black tattoos swirling out from his jacket cuffs, covering the backs of his hands to the knuckles. More black tattoos twist out from his crisp white collar on the sides of his neck, disappearing behind his ears.

He has black gauges and short black hair. His eyes are shadowed under heavy eyebrows, almost menacing. He has a square jaw and a square nose. His lips are pouty and pink, and so pretty.

He lifts his head and he looks out beyond the dance floor, which is now full of guests slow dancing. His eyes are surrounded by thick, black eyelashes. They are... mesmerizing. Hypnotic.

My eyes lock on his and it's like he's looking right into my soul.

Is he...is he looking at me?

Yes. Yes, he's staring directly at me.

And I stare right back. I should look away, right? Act like I'm not caught in a gooey trance watching him.

But it's like he's singing to me. Only me. Each line, word, note, is meant just for me to hear. An invisible connection. There's an undercurrent of melancholy in his voice. And desire. Need.

"Oh there you are, Gracie Lou!" Mom walks up to where

RAE KENNEDY

I'm perched against the buffet table and I jump up, quickly tearing my gaze away from the singer and his eyes.

"You look so lovely, dear," she says, smiling with that *I'm just so proud of my grown-up baby girl* look she's started giving me since I left for college. I wonder if she'll still give me that look after she finds out tomorrow.

"Thanks." I smooth down my dress.

She sort of fusses over the now-askew table cloth and straightens it out. "Oh! The potato salad is getting low. I better go get the other batch from the house. It's Tuck's favorite, you know."

"I'll go get it. You stay and enjoy the party."

"Are you sure, honey?"

"Of course."

"Oh, thank you, Gracie Lou. It's been so nice having you home again this week. You've been so helpful with all of this. I don't think we could have pulled off everything without you."

I offer a small smile.

"I feel like we just got you back and now you're leaving again." She's giving me that smile again. The proud one. But this time she looks like she might cry too.

Shit.

"Uh...yeah." My hair falls, covering half of my face as I turn and look away. I really should have told them earlier. I'd originally justified the secret so I wouldn't take any attention away from Court and her big day, but with every passing week, day, hour that I've been hiding this, I can feel the weight of it pressing harder and heavier against me.

I trudge back up to the house, across the faded wood deck and through the back door, letting the screen door bang shut behind me. Inside, the house is warm. A single lamp is lit in the corner of the living room and down the hall. Light is glowing from the kitchen, but otherwise it's dark. Dark and quiet and still. No band, no rowdy dancers or loud conversations. Not even the soft hiss of the wind—only the occasional snort or whimper from our elderly hound dog, who is currently napping under the dining room table.

I run up the stairs. The old wood planks groan and creak with each step. I flip the switch in my room and the light flickers twice before crackling on. I ignore my collection of dance ribbons and trophies, the pom-poms on my dresser, and the collage of photographs from high school on my wall—mostly selfies—to get to my phone charging on the bed.

Me: *are you still coming to the reception?*
Kyla: *Yes! I just got here, sorry I'm late...Grandpa.*
Me: *No worries. I'll be the one carrying a bowl of potato salad the size of Jupiter*
Kyla: *Do you need help?*
Me: *Nah, I'll meet you down there in a few*

On my way out, I pass the suitcase sitting at the end of my bed, ready and waiting to leave with me tomorrow.

It's empty.

I race to the kitchen. The giant-ass bowl of potato salad is, in fact, only marginally smaller than Jupiter. It proves difficult to manage while opening the door to the yard. *Maybe I do need help.*

The air outside is fresh and I'm surrounded by crickets chirping as I huff it toward the party. Kyla waves at me from the buffet table. She's been my best friend since we were awkward twelve-year-olds with braces and knobby knees. I'm glad we grew out of that phase.

She's wearing a flirty emerald green dress that is stunning

with her auburn hair and bright hazel eyes. Her shoulder-length hair has the perfect amount of natural wave—one side is tucked behind her ear, revealing a peacock feather earring that hangs to just above her collarbone.

"Hey!" She runs up to me and helps carry the bowl back to the food table.

"Hi, thanks," I say, a little out of breath.

"Gracie, I've missed you!" She pouts and squeezes me around the middle. "You look great, by the way. I could never pull off the color peach. I'm so jealous of your complexion."

I chuckle at her rapid-fire compliment. "You look beautiful, Ky. Love the earrings."

"Yeah? I love them too." She fluffs a giant feathered earring. "I saw them, and I was like, yes, these are perfect, because I'm going to be peacocking the hell out of tonight."

"Peacocking?"

"Yeah, like when peacocks display their feathers to get a mate's attention. Peacocking. It's a thing. Anyway, tonight is the night I'm going to finally get Wes to notice me."

"Tonight's the night you make your big move?"

"Yep. I mean, he's been pining over your sister for how many years? And she's now officially off the market, so he has no choice but to move on, right?"

"Right. Totally."

"But enough about Wes finally realizing we're soulmates—I'm just so glad we get to hang out tonight before you leave me again. I'm so sad."

"Um…" I need to tell someone already. "About my trip—"

"Are you so excited? I mean it obviously sounds like a lot of work, but you'll have so much fun. I'm so jealous of all the adventures you're going to have out in the world! We should celebrate tonight. Hey, there's some champagne.

TO BE YOUR LAST

Let's sneak some champagne!"

Champagne is for celebrating. "I don't want champagne."

Kyla tilts her head toward me, a little crease forming between her eyebrows. The look isn't because I turned down alcohol—that's not new—but she can read even the subtle changes in my tone.

"I need to tell you something."

She steps closer to me. "What's up, G?"

"I'm not leaving tomorrow."

"Huh? Why?"

"I...I lost my spot in the summer research fellowship."

"How? What happened?"

"My grades last semester didn't meet their requirements so they gave my spot to someone else."

"Oh, Gracie, I'm sorry. That sucks." She puts her arm around my shoulders. She always smells like citrus. "I didn't know you were having a hard time in school."

"It's not... I just... Yeah. It hasn't been great."

"And your parents...?"

"I haven't told them yet. But they'll know tomorrow. Everyone will know. It will spread through the whole town, like every other piece of gossip does, and people will be talking about me behind my back again. The worst part about failing school is it was supposed to be my way out, so I don't get stuck here."

"Hey, I kind of like it here."

"I didn't mean it like that. I love this town... I just want more. I want to see more, have more experiences. I've never even left the Midwest. But right now, what I really want is to run away."

"Ahem—" Someone clears his throat behind me.

I jolt away from the food table. *Jesus, Gracie, you're*

completely in the way. "I'm so sorry, I—" I look up and am met with dark brown, smiling eyes. Bedhead hair. The guitarist.

I glance at the stage, which is empty. The band must be on a break.

"No need to apologize." He flashes me bright white teeth that stand out against his tanned, olive skin. He's holding a plate full of food and eyeing the watermelon at the end of the table. The watermelon I had been standing so inconsiderately in front of.

"Hi!" Kyla steps up next to me, chin held high, chest proudly puffed, hand outstretched. "I'm Kyla. This is Gracie."

"Hey Kyla. I'm Logan." He shakes her hand and nods, then looks back at me. Before I know it, my hand is wrapped in his warm one. "Gracie..." He glances down briefly at my dress, and warmth rises from my chest to my ears. "Bridesmaid?"

"Yeah. I'm the bride's sister."

"Right!" He bobs his head like this should be totally obvious to him. I guess I do basically look like a miniature version of Court. "It's nice to meet you, Gracie. You too, Kyla."

It's at this moment my stomach decides to let out the loudest, gravelliest growl known to man. I'm probably red as a beet right now. *Please let it be dark enough he doesn't notice.*

"Hungry?" he asks.

"Have you not eaten yet?" Kyla looks at me with her overprotective I-will-cut-a-bitch face.

"No, I keep getting distracted by this and that."

"Shit, girl—" Logan gives me his plate so quickly I almost drop it before I realize what he's doing. "Here."

"You don't need to give me your food, really." Like,

really, this is a little weird.

"I'll get more, come on." He waves me over to where he's standing by the fresh bowl of potato salad with a heaping ladle full.

I eye the already-overflowing plate of food in my hands. "I'm good."

He gives me a scoop anyway. And adds a couple slices of watermelon for good measure.

As soon as we sit at a table Kyla freaks out. "He's hot. Ohmygod Gracie, he's totally into you. Did you see him eye-fucking you out of your dress?" Also, something to note—Kyla does not know how to whisper.

I'm trying—unsuccessfully—to get her to chill out about hot guitar player when he walks up to our table, all nonchalant and running one hand through his wavy hair.

"Mind if I join you ladies?" He flashes his gorgeous smile.

"Um..."

"Of course, yes, you can! Here, take my seat," Kyla chimes in, standing and pulling out her chair for Logan.

"Ky," I say in a low tone, and I stare at her with wide crazy eyes. She knows what the crazy eyes mean. She ignores them.

"I was just about to get up, anyway. I've got peacocking to do. I'll come find you in a bit." With a wave, and a not-so-subtle wink, she walks away.

"Peacocking?" Logan asks.

"Yep." I really don't want to expand any further than that.

He just shrugs in acceptance and starts tearing into his food. "Oh my god." He talks between bites of food, licking his fingers. "This is so good. Have you tried the ribs yet?"

"Yeah, I helped make them."

"No shit? That's so cool."

"Thanks."

"Seriously, it's so nice to have a home-cooked meal like this right before we head out. We always eat like crap on the road."

"You guys are going on the road, like on tour?"

"Yep, all summer. Thirty-one shows, all across the country."

"Wow. That sounds exciting. I've hardly been anywhere."

"This is our fifth tour, but yeah, still just as exciting as our first time."

He continues to tell me a bit about the band and their past tours as he polishes off his plate. I'm done eating—though you wouldn't know it by the mountain of food still sitting in front of me. Logan casually reaches over and takes a remaining short rib off my plate without skipping a beat in his story about when they'd played a teeny tiny venue in New Jersey and a fire broke out halfway through their set. No one had been hurt, thankfully. They finished their set outside the club in the sprinkling rain for whoever wanted to listen while they waited for the first responders.

"So," he says, leaning back in his chair. "The bride's sister. Younger, I'm guessing?"

"Yeah." That's obvious. I'm six years younger than Court, and I have a naturally heart-shaped baby face.

"You're like, what, twenty-two, three?"

"Nineteen."

"Huh. I would have guessed older. Not because you look it, just you seem mature. I don't know, like there's a depth in your eyes."

Not often have I—as a bouncy blonde cheerleader—

been called deep, but I'll take it.

"I kind of have a lot on my mind right now."

He nods knowingly. "Is that why you said you wanted to run away earlier?"

"You heard that?"

"Yup. I also heard you say you wanted to see new places, have new experiences."

"Does that make me sound lame? Like I'm a sheltered girl from a small town who hasn't seen or done anything?" I guess that's exactly what I am.

He puts his hands up in apology. "Hey, no judgments here. But you don't seem like the kind of girl who would run away."

"I'm not. Maybe that's why I want to so badly."

He looks at me for a beat, running his index finger along his jaw, a spark in his dark eyes. "You could run away with us."

"What?" I nervous-giggle, but he looks completely serious.

"Come on tour with us. We're going to leave tonight around two, heading for LA. You'll get to see the whole country. It'll be an adventure."

"Oh no, I couldn't."

"All right. Hey, I've got to go announce they're cutting the cake, but—" He pulls a black sharpie out of his pocket and scans the table. Not finding what he's looking for, he takes my hand and starts writing on my palm. "Here's my number. Text me if you change your mind."

CHAPTER 2

"Ohmygod ohmygod ohmygod, he asked you to go on tour with them? I told you he's so into you, now do you believe me? Are you going to go? I think you should go," Kyla says with wild eyes.

I drop the forkful of decadent chocolate cake to my plate. "Are you serious? Of course I'm not going."

"Why not?"

"Ky. It's crazy. I don't even know these guys. Following them on tour would be reckless and possibly dangerous. Don't you watch *Dateline*?"

"Gracie. These are the years in our life when we're allowed to be reckless. Take a risk. You don't always have to be the perfect daughter, or the perfect friend, or the perfect student. I mean, you have the whole rest of your life to settle down and be boring, so go have some fun now while you can. Plus, aren't they good friends with Tuck's best friend?"

"Yeah, that's true. I still just don't think it's a good idea."

"What's the worst that could happen? If you're not having fun, you can get a plane ticket home. I know you have money saved up that was supposed to be for your summer school program—just think of it as being used for a different kind of learning experience."

Actually, the worst-case scenario is that I get sold into some human sex trafficking ring, but I keep that thought to myself. I hate how she's actually making some sense.

"Just imagine what any one of those guys could teach you. I bet they're really good at eating pussy."

"Kyla! Oh my god!"

"What? I bet they are." She gets out her phone and types furiously. "Here, found them." She reads as she scrolls. "Wicked Road is an American rock/alternative band... Started playing small bars in Chicago... They have three albums with an indie label no one's heard of... They have a huge underground following though. And their tour this summer is sponsored by, wow, Universal. That's the biggest record label in the country. You have to go. For me."

"I'll think about it."

I look over to the dance floor where couples are dancing under the lights, the night sky a black backdrop. Wes and the youngest of my three older brothers, Eric, are chatting near the corner of the stage, both dateless.

"I'm going to go talk to him," Kyla says, standing then licking her fork clean before throwing it down to her plate.

"Good luck."

She saunters away, and my gaze drifts back to the band. They're good. Logan's fingers move effortlessly over the strings as he keeps a mischievous grin on his face. He seems like a genuinely nice guy, which is why I feel bad when I find myself staring at the singer again. His voice rolls through my body. I'm drowning in it and can't get up for air. I'm drawn to him when he closes his eyes and pours every emotion into a single note. And when he opens those eyes, they're so intense.

Then a deep green dress catches my eye. A smile breaks across my face as I watch Kyla lead Wes out to the dance floor by the hand. He puts his hands on her waist, her arms go around his neck and she's beaming as she looks up at him. Their dancing is a little awkward and they almost bump into the best man and maid of honor, Cade and Haley—who are definitely going to bone immediately after this—but she did it. She finally made her move. She took a risk.

I want to take a leap, too. Screw anyone else's expectations. I'm going to do it.

I'm going to run away with the band.

* * *

Kyla squeals and jumps up and down when I tell her.

It's almost one in the morning and everyone left over an hour ago. Kyla stayed to help me and my brothers clean up. She really is the most supportive friend I could ask for, even if she talks nonstop and has zero filter.

"Hey." Eric runs over to us as we're carrying the last of the chairs to the shed. "I'll take these for you, ladies. Thanks for staying to help. I know it's late, and you're leaving in the morning."

I just smile awkwardly and hope he drops the subject.

"I probably won't see you again before you leave, so—" He leans over and pulls me in for a hug while making a *grrr* noise. Then he ends the hug and holds me firmly by the shoulders. "I know it's a school thing, but promise you'll try to have some fun too."

"Oh, she's going to have lots of fun," Kyla says over my shoulder.

I shoot her *shut the hell up* crazy eyes. She's unfazed.

When we run inside the house, clanking noises are coming from the kitchen, where my parents are working on the dishes.

"Hey. Mom, Dad?"

They turn around with tired smiles. Mom's washing a bowl and Dad's drying a serving spoon.

"'Sup, Gracie Lou?" Dad asks.

"Yeah, so I know you were planning on driving me tomorrow, but Ky and I haven't been able to really hang out since I've been home. So…I was wondering if I could spend the night with her, and she can drive me in the morning?"

"Oh, but dear, I was looking forward to seeing you off." A dangerously deep crease forms between my mom's eyebrows.

Dad puts his giant paw of a hand gently on her shoulder. "Bev." He tilts his head and looks at her with soft eyes when she turns to him.

She momentarily frowns but then sighs and nods. "All right, honey," she says, turning back to me. "Of course that would be fine."

"Thank you!" I bounce toward them, and they surround me in a warm bear-hug sandwich.

Kyla and I race up the stairs to my room.

"Remember to call me!" Mom yells from downstairs.

I immediately rip off my dress and Kyla grabs my suitcase. I put on a pair of cut-off denim shorts, a soft white T-shirt, and my Chucks, then head to the bathroom to get my toiletries. Meanwhile, Kyla is throwing clothes into my bag in a frenzy. I walk back in and find my suitcase overflowing with possibly the most obscure clothing items I own—several shorts and tank tops, but also skirts I didn't even know I had and a little black dress I haven't worn in years. Like, I think I was fourteen, and I cannot put enough emphasis on the *little* part.

"I don't think I'll be needing this dress."

"You never know," Kyla says, digging through my top dresser drawer. "Where's your sexy underwear? These all look like your time-of-the-month underwear."

"What? I don't have different types of underwear."

She shakes her head at me with a silent, stony look on her face. "I've failed you as a best friend."

I roll my eyes.

She returns to rummaging through the drawer. "I know you have some thongs from cheer. Where are they?"

"Try looking in the back."

"A-ha!" Her hand emerges with a fistful of tiny thongs. She stuffs them in the corner of the suitcase. "Trust me. You'll thank me for that."

"If you say so." I toss in my phone charger and hastily zip up the bag.

We dash toward the stairs, giddy and giggling.

"Wait—" I say.

Kyla's already halfway down the flight of stairs when she turns.

"I just need one more thing. Go on down and I'll meet you in a sec."

I jog back to my darkened room and slip my hand between my mattress. I pull out my little leather notebook. I hold it for a moment, unsure if I should bring it or not. Finally, I tuck it into the side pocket of my suitcase.

* * *

TO BE YOUR LAST

Bright blue lights display 1:45 on Kyla's dashboard as she pulls into the dark parking lot. I rub my sweaty palms on my knees.

When I'd texted Logan earlier, he'd replied almost immediately, telling me where to meet them—followed by approximately a hundred emojis to convey his general excitement.

I'd been excited too.

In fact, my heart has been pounding the whole drive out to this motel on the outskirts of town.

There are only a few cars in the lot in front of the shabby one-story building. It has peeling mustard-colored paint and a red glowing sign with only the letters M and T still working.

At the far side of the lot is a large silver van. Three figures stand near it, silhouetted by a street light. They appear to be talking, laughing even, and passing something between them. A puff of smoke billows out around one of the men's heads and gets swept away, dissolving into the breeze.

I recognize the relaxed posture and the way Logan runs his hand through his hair.

"That's them."

"You sure about this?" Kyla asks, her voice higher than normal.

Nope.

"Yeah."

Wasn't she the one convincing me to do this earlier? It's okay, I can hype myself. Once a cheerleader, always a cheerleader, right? I'm only about to leave in a dark van from a seedy motel in the middle of the night with four men I don't know.

Am I being kidnapped?

I reach for the handle, and if I thought my heart was racing before, it's now a jackhammer against my ribs as I open the door and climb out of the car.

CHAPTER 3

"Text me every day to let me know you're all right."

"I will." I snatch my bag from the back seat.

"I want constant updates. I need to know what city you're in at all times."

"Okay."

"I mean it! If I don't hear from you I will tell your dad and brothers. And we will all hunt you down. I'm so serious."

I believe her, and it makes me smile.

"Bye, Ky. Love you."

I swear I see her wiping a tear away. "Love you, too. I'm going to stay here for a bit. Just in case."

"Thanks."

With a little nod and a big breath, I turn and walk toward the van.

I cross half the distance of the parking lot and stop. I shouldn't be doing this. This is nuts. I should just turn around and get right back in the car. And go home. And tell my parents the truth—that I basically flunked last semester, got kicked out of the summer program, will have to redo eighty percent of my classes to get back on track, and will probably—definitely—be on academic probation come fall, which will result in the loss of at least one scholarship.

The thought makes me want to vomit the entirety of my stomach contents onto the pavement. It would be mostly chocolate cake.

"Hey, Gracie!"

Logan has spotted me. He's jogging over.

It's now or never.

Turn around or go forward.

"You made it!" Logan reaches me, a bit out of breath, with a huge grin that lights up his entire face. "Come meet the guys." He puts his arm around my shoulder and steers me toward the van. I feel a bit braver, my feet moving faster with Logan walking by my side. His happy, easy energy calming my nerves.

And then we're standing behind the van with two other guys. The bassist with the slicked back hair and facial piercings is leaning against the bumper, the end of his cigarette a faint red glow. The other guy, the drummer, is not much taller than me but easily twice as wide and is holding a crinkled brown paper bag in his left hand.

"Hey guys, this is Gracie! She came!"

"Hi." I hope my smile looks natural and my little wave isn't weird. It feels weird and unnatural. Also, is that my voice?

"This is Joey." Logan gestures to the shorter one.

"The drummer, right?"

"Yeah." His voice is soft, almost a husky whisper, and he gives me a nod and a small smile. His eyelashes and eyebrows are so light they're barely noticeable, and his skin is fair and rosy with tiny, faint freckles. The freckles are splattered on every inch of his face—they even cover the hand that holds the paper bag.

"You're amazing. Seriously, you're awesome to watch. Your arms move so fast!"

He mouths the word, "Thanks," but I don't hear it before he looks down, a blush coming to his cheeks. He takes a swig of whatever is inside the bag.

"And this is—" Logan looks to the bassist.

The bassist stands, throwing his cigarette butt to the asphalt and putting it out with his shoe.

"I'm Dean." He reaches for my hand and gives it a nice, strong shake.

Up close, I can't help but look at his eyes. It's strange to see Logan's same brown puppy-dog eyes surrounded by metal balls and rods—and is that eye shadow?

"I'm the better-looking twin," Dean adds.

Twins?

"Yes. He's the pretty one, and I got the glowing personality." Logan leans closer to me and whispers, "Don't remind him that we're identical. If he knew I got all the personality and I'm just as good-looking, that'd be a real hit to his ego."

I smile and nod as he gives me the cutest wink.

"Whatever he's telling you, it's all lies," Dean says.

Headlights flash in my peripheral vision as Kyla's blue car turns out of the parking lot and heads down the street.

Joey holds the paper bag up, offering it to Logan, who takes it eagerly. He takes a big gulp, tossing his head back. Then he extends it toward me, his eyebrows up in question.

I look at it for a second. The glass lip of a bottle is clearly protruding from the brown paper.

"Umm..." What the hell? I'm already doing something crazy. Might as well go all in, have some new experiences. "Sure."

RAE KENNEDY

He hands me the bottle, and I grip it around the neck. It's heavier than I expected. I bring it up to my face and catch a strong whiff of alcohol tinged with spice and caramel. It burns my nose, and my stomach tightens with an immediate aversion. I shouldn't have hesitated. I shouldn't have breathed. But it's too late now.

I put it to my lips and take a drink. I try to shoot it down quickly, but I don't know how to do that. I taste it and it's horrible. I feel the alcohol go all the way down my throat, searing my flesh like I imagine acid would. I immediately start coughing, my eyes water, and I desperately try to keep from gagging.

"Whoa." Logan starts patting and rubbing my back in circles. "You okay there?"

"Shit, Logan." Joey opens the back of the van and retrieves a water bottle. "Always offer a lady a chaser." He hands me the water.

"Thanks," I say in a croaky voice.

"Not used to drinking it straight?" Logan asks.

Not used to drinking at all, actually.

"No shame. I prefer mixed drinks myself." Dean stretches his hand toward me, and I happily pass the bottle to him. He takes a big swig and makes a tight face, breathing through his teeth. "Yeah, this shit's awful."

I take a few sips of the water—it's not particularly cold but my esophagus no longer feels as though it's on fire, so there's that. Dean and Joey both seem to be watching me carefully. The genuine concern on their faces is sweet and surprising.

Logan is still rubbing my back. In a low voice, he says, "Sorry about that."

I shake my head and wave it off.

TO BE YOUR LAST

"No, I mean it. I don't want you to feel pressured into anything. If you don't want something, just tell us no, or to go fuck off. And we will." He puts his arm around my shoulder and leans away, regarding me with a lopsided grin.

"Let's get going—" A smooth, masculine voice calls from around the van. He steps out of the shadows and into the light.

It's the singer.

He's wearing a plain black T-shirt and jeans. The short sleeves show off the intricate puzzle of black tattoos that cover his arms and hands. I can also see more of the tats on his chest and neck than earlier when he'd been wearing the collared shirt and suit jacket. He checks something on his phone then slips it into his pocket and looks up.

He stops dead when he sees me.

His gaze fixes on me, his piercing eyes just as intense as when he was performing, like he can see right through me.

He glances down the length of my body, my bare legs. Why did I choose such short shorts? He only looks for a second, and though I'm fully clothed I've never felt so naked.

Apparently, it only took him that one second to assess me before he turns to Logan, whose arm is still draped around my shoulders.

The singer's jaw clenches and nostrils flare as he looks Logan square in the face and says, "No."

Logan removes his arm. "Oh, come on, dude. We have room, she's cool—"

The singer turns back to me, his features hard and calm, and says, "No."

It's definitive.

Deafening.

Shattering.

He directs his heated glare back to Logan. "Fuck no. She's not coming." Then he turns and walks back toward the front of the van.

My stomach churns and I'm too hot. Of course this was a stupid idea. "I'm sorry. He's right. This was dumb. I shouldn't be here. I'll call Kyla and she can come back and get me."

"Nah, it'll be fine. I'll go talk to him." Logan flashes a reassuring smile, then chases after the singer.

"Here." Dean picks up my suitcase as Joey opens the back of the van and throws it in.

"But—"

"Don't take what Colin said personally. He's just in a bad mood from having to navigate around the giant stick up his ass."

"But he doesn't want me here."

"Too bad for him, because the rest of us do want you here." Dean shuts the door and tilts his head. "So, you still coming?"

I climb in the van even though my heart is pounding.

I take the middle bench seat, Joey climbs in the very back, and Dean sits in the front passenger seat. I twist my fingers into a ball on my lap, trying to quiet the thoughts in my head telling me what could go wrong. After a few minutes, Logan hops in the van with his relaxed smile and slides into the seat next to me.

The singer—Colin, I guess—gets in the driver's seat, a scowl set on his pretty lips. He doesn't say a word, just starts up the van. As we roll forward, I steal a glance at him in the rear-view mirror, and his eyes are already on me. They shift back to the road immediately. So fast, in fact, I think I might have imagined it.

We turn onto the main road, and as we accelerate, the lights of my little town become smaller and smaller, farther away in the distance until they becomes just a speck. And then I can't see them anymore.

CHAPTER 4

THE NEXT HOURS PASS QUICKLY. LOGAN ASKS ME SO MANY questions I'm flattered and overwhelmed. It's basically twenty questions—the Gracie edition. When he asks me my major, and I say Biology and that I'm pre-med, they're all stunned silent. I move the subject along.

They all seem fascinated by the fact that I'm the youngest of five siblings, and that I'd grown up on a ranch. Well, everyone but Colin, who has done nothing but look straight ahead with a bored look on his face and sigh every once in a while. Logan tells me he and Dean have an older brother, Joey has a younger sister, and Colin is an only child. Figures. They grew up in a suburb near the city. Logan and Dean lived across the street from Colin, and they started the band when they were fourteen.

Logan recounts stories from their teenage years with fervor, practically yelling, arms flying across the seat as he dramatically acts out scenes. Joey mostly chuckles in the back, occasionally hiccupping and chiming in to say, "Hey, I was there too!" when Logan forgets to include him in the aforementioned stories.

Dean is content to listen to Logan talk, a cool smirk on

his lips, and only interrupts to correct him on the details, which Logan likes to exaggerate. For instance, he didn't break both arms and four ribs jumping off a bridge—it was a sprained wrist and bruised ribs. Also, the band wasn't almost broken up by a girl named Yoko who had kissed Logan and Colin on the same night, resulting in an all-out fist fight between the two sixteen-year-olds—her name was Megan, and Logan had only gotten a bloody lip from one elbow, which Colin maintains was an accident.

Colin remains, of course, silent on the subject.

I can't believe they all have so much energy. It's almost five a.m. and I can't stop yawning.

"Do you guys always stay up this late?"

"When we're on tour, we travel during the day and work at night, so yeah. We basically sleep all day and stay up all night," Logan says.

"Better get used to it," Dean adds.

"Yeah." I yawn again. "I can totally get used to it."

I lay my head back against the seat—just to rest my eyes, just for a minute. It's not comfortable and I don't know if I'll even be able to fall asleep.

* * *

I WAKE UP WITH THE SUN SHINING THROUGH THE WINDOWS, bright against the tan cloth seats. My cheek rests against something hard and warm—Logan's shoulder. I sit up, stretching my back. My neck is a bit stiff, but it was probably more comfortable than my head being smashed between the seat and window.

Logan's head is back, his neck arched, lips slightly parted as he breathes softly in his sleep. Joey is curled up in a ball in the back and Dean has gone with the head-against-the-window method in the front. Only Colin is still awake. Still driving. Still brooding.

I pull out my phone and see it's almost noon. I also have five texts and two missed calls from Kyla.

Kyla: *How's it going, are you good?*

Kyla: *???*

Kyla: *Update me already!!!*

Kyla: *Where are you? I'm about to send a search party.*

Kyla: *Srsly about to freak out right now you better call or text me in the next five minutes or I swear to God*

Luckily, that last one was only ten minutes ago.

Me: *Hey sorry, I was asleep. I'm fine, having fun so far*

Kyla: *Oh thank fuck. How are the guys? Are they nice? Have you made out with the hot one yet?*

Me: *Yes they're nice. No making out.*

Kyla: *Boo. I'll need to know immediately when it happens*

I send her the eye roll emoji and she sends me the kissy emoji.

I look out the window to the nondescript landscape of middle America. It's mostly flat with the sporadic patch of trees and a few land formations so far in the distance I can't tell if they're hills or mountains. Occasionally, we'll pass a farm or random outbuilding, but other than the infrequent fellow drivers and big rigs, no sign of life. Just the straight stretch of highway and an endless blue sky. I have no idea where we are. I could be one or three states over from home, for all I know.

I. Have. No. Idea. Where. I. Am. The familiar panic creeps up. Heart racing. The voice that tells me I have no control.

"You all right?"

He startles me and somehow brings me back. In the mirror, I meet Colin's eyes. His face is calm, his driving steady, and he doesn't break eye contact. I no longer feel the pull of anxiety, no longer slipping into darkness.

"I'm fine." My voice cracks. I probably don't sound fine. But I am. I'm fine. I close my eyes and take a few deep breaths. I chose to come along. I'm not here against my will. I can leave if I want. I am in control.

My heartbeat quiets, and I realize that's the first thing Colin has said the whole trip so far, and he was expressing concern...for me. Should I say thank you?

I hate this feeling of not knowing what to do, the fear of saying or doing the wrong thing. High school Gracie never second-guessed herself. Eighteen-year-old Gracie was confident, popular, and excelled at everything she tried. Perhaps I was too confident. My first experience as a small fish in a big pond and I'd fallen spectacularly on my face. That's when the stress started, the fear, the anxiety, the failure.

"Where are we?" I ask when I feel steadier.

"Nebraska. More than a third of the way there."

Okay. That feels better.

The soft *click-click click-click* of the blinker sounds as Colin pulls off the highway. We come up to a little rest stop and I'm suddenly grateful as I realize I have to pee so bad.

As the van rolls to a stop, the guys stir and groan awake.

"It's too early," Logan grumbles.

We jump out and it feels nice to move and stretch my legs. The sun is hot on my back. The air is heavy and dry and there is no cool breeze like back home.

"Fuck, why is it stupid hot already?" Joey wipes his forehead, which is already pink and perspiring.

RAE KENNEDY

After the much-needed bathroom break, we all pile back in. Logan takes the same spot next to me and whispers with a devious smirk that he likes being my seat-buddy. Dean takes the driver's seat this time and Colin lays his head to the side as soon as he lands in the front passenger seat.

It's only minutes before Logan is passed out again. I think Colin is asleep too even though he looks uncomfortable. I can't help but linger on his face—peaceful yet somber. The thick, black lashes fanned across his chiseled cheekbones are beautiful. I've never thought the word *beautiful* as many times about a man as I have about Colin.

I should stop staring at him.

I slide out my phone.

Me: *We're in Nebraska*

Kyla: *That's not very specific, you realize that's a whole fucking state, right? Any update on the makeout sitch?*

Me: *It's been an hour*

Kyla: *So?*

Me: *Nothing new to report. Promise you'll be the first to know if it happens*

Kyla: **when it happens*

As the lulling sounds of languid breathing fills the van, I lay my head back against Logan's welcoming shoulder. He smells like sunshine and fresh-cracked pepper, and I close my eyes.

* * *

"Wake up, sleepy-head."

My eyes flutter open to Logan smiling dreamily down at me. My head is still pressed into his white cotton shirt.

"Hey." I sit up yawning, not feeling embarrassed Logan

caught me sleeping on him. Everyone else is already awake. I roll my head to stretch out my neck. "How do you guys sleep sitting up without being stiff all over?"

"We've gotten pretty good at it over the years." Logan reaches over and starts rubbing the back of my neck, his strong fingers digging into my skin and massaging out the ache. "But, this tour, we're getting a bus."

"It's going to be so cool," Joey pipes up. "We get a driver and everything."

"That'll be better," I say, savoring the massage. "That feels nice."

"I'm at your service." Logan gives me a wink.

Heat rises to my cheeks.

Colin is sitting up front, looking straight ahead, but it feels like he's still watching me, aware of everything.

"Thanks." I shift slightly, and Logan eases off the massage, finally releasing my neck and laying his arm across the back of the seat.

We're off the highway now, on a side street in some unnamed town, the expanses of concrete and asphalt just as nondescript as the landscape around it.

We pull into a gas station and Joey instantly sits up.

"Yes, dinnertime!"

We're having dinner at a gas station?

"We need to restock the cooler, too." Dean puts the van in park.

Logan gives me his hand and helps me step down. Joey lumbers out after me, clapping and rubbing his hands together. "Jackpot," he says with a grin.

Jackpot? I look up at the building—it's a little fancier than the gas stations I'm used to, and the word *market* is on the front, but still, I was hoping we'd eat at a restaurant.

Joey bolts for the glass doors with Logan and Dean following. I glance back to the van. Colin is standing in the shadow of the van, filling the tank with gas. I can barely make out his profile, but he looks lean and tall, and I notice how his black shirt is stretched taut between his broad shoulders and the way his short sleeves strain against the curve of his tattooed biceps.

"Blondie—"

I snap back toward the door, thinking the voice is Logan's, but it's Dean standing there, regarding me with an amused smile.

"He's pretty to look at, huh?"

"Uh..." Shit, I'm blushing again. I swallow thickly.

"It's okay," he says in a hushed tone. "I won't tell."

We walk inside, and Joey immediately pulls me over to the small grocery section. He declares himself a connoisseur of gas station fare and proceeds to impart his knowledge on me. I'm impressed, as it seems like he's actually put quite a lot of thought into the subject. His various pointers include to avoid the hot dogs and sushi, burritos are good, nachos are too messy. Look in the refrigerated section for healthier options and get some snacks that are good at room temperature that have a lid or are in a resealable package, avoid anything that requires utensils. It's a lot.

I get a pre-made sandwich and a banana. That should be safe. A gas station banana is still just a banana, right?

"Don't forget snacks!" Joey calls from three aisles over.

"Hey!" Logan sidles up next to me, his arm brushing against my shoulder. "Let's get Slurpees."

It's the most intense Slurpee machine I've ever seen. There are sixteen different flavors. Sixteen. I walk up and down the aisle with my sandwich and banana smashed to

TO BE YOUR LAST

my body in one arm, the other holding the giant empty cup as I peruse the flavors. Cherry, blue raspberry, mango bango, piña colada, sour apple, dragon fruit... I finally decide on watermelon. Meanwhile, Logan is running up and down, giggling and filling his cup until it's overflowing. He sips it down, but it spills over again when he tries to put on a lid and stick in the straw. I grab some napkins, and we clean up his sticky hands as he licks the side of the cup. We unsuccessfully try to stifle our laughs so as not to draw attention to ourselves, but the cashier, a middle-aged woman with a crew cut, keeps glaring our way.

"I'll get this for you." Logan takes my cup and reaches for my sandwich.

"You don't have to—"

"Blondie, we need your help." Dean is waving to us from across the store.

"You go help him. I got this," Logan insists and heads to the register with our food.

I wander over to Dean and Joey, who are studying the beer case intently.

"I want to make sure we get something you like. Any preferences?" Dean asks.

I look through the glass and metal doors, clueless. Joey has half-disappeared into a fridge to retrieve a thirty-pack from the back of the cooler when I lean over to Dean.

"Can I tell you something?"

"Shoot. I'm a vault."

"I don't really drink. I have no idea what I would like."

His face remains neutral. "Do you want to drink? You don't have to."

"It might be fun," I say quietly.

"Okay." He walks over to an area where the beers have

pictures of fruit on the labels and there are brightly colored hard lemonades. "Fuzzy navels?" He points to a blue six-pack with peaches on it.

"Sure." Sounds as good as anything.

"Cool."

Joey comes back with a huge, awkward box of beer under each beefy arm. "Ready?"

"Yep." Dean grabs the pack of fuzzy navels, glass clinking inside. "Hey, since you're not twenty-one—"

"Yeah, I'll just head out to the van. Logan's got my food, anyway."

I exit the store. Heat radiates from the pavement, and the station's lights are buzzing overhead. Logan is standing by the van across the lot, a plastic bag in his hand, our Slurpee cups on the roof of the vehicle.

His back is turned and as I get closer, it's obvious he's talking to someone hidden from view. I slow, then freeze when I hear the disembodied voice from around the van.

"There's plenty of groupie pussy on tour. You didn't need to bring your own personal toy."

"I didn't bring her for that."

"Sure you didn't."

"And she's not a groupie."

"I can see that. She's a toddler."

"Col, you're such an asshole."

"I don't care what the fuck you do with her, but you invited her along, so it's your job to babysit her."

Colin's cold words sink through me.

He doesn't want you here. You shouldn't have come.

Dean and Joey are heading for us, boisterously conversing and laughing, arms full of alcohol and, not surprisingly, many snacks. They're unaware of my embarrassment as they walk up to me, yelling my name, bringing me to attention. Logan turns to me as Colin appears, both men looking directly at me, and I wonder if they know I heard their conversation.

I manage to drink most of my Slurpee but I don't feel much like eating as we drive. The landscape morphs from flat plains to rocky mountains as we travel through Colorado. I notice that Joey likes to constantly tap the steering wheel as he drives.

He called me a toddler. A toddler in need of babysitting.

There's a loud popping sound quickly followed by another as Joey says, "Whoa, holy shit!" And the van jerks and sputters as he grips the wheel, swerving out of control. The van starts to spin. I clutch at my seat and Logan throws his arm across my torso. The crunch and grind of gravel is deafening as we drift off the road and then sand and pebbles are pinging the sides of the van. We finally bump and skid to a stop several feet off the highway.

In the middle of nowhere.

CHAPTER 5

A BLOWN TIRE.

And no spare.

Because, well, they'd needed more room for instruments and equipment.

"Are you sure you're okay?" Logan puts his hand on my shoulder.

"I'm fine."

Logan and I are sitting in the open doorway of the van as Colin paces several yards away, talking on the phone. Dean is a ways down the road having a smoke and Joey is near him, hands shoved in his pockets and kicking rocks along the side of the road.

The sun is getting lower in the sky, which is still a clear cerulean blue. Other than the occasional passing motorist, it's quiet, desolate, and I'm grateful at least for the warm weather.

Colin walks over as he ends his call, rubbing the back of his neck. Joey and Dean arrive soon after for the news.

"Tow truck is on its way, but it will be at least an hour. Probably two."

Joey groans.

TO BE YOUR LAST

Logan rubs his hands together, smiling wildly. "So we've got an hour to kill and we just loaded up the cooler? Sounds like it's game time."

"Aw shit. Starting early this time," Dean says, though it seems like he says it more to himself than anyone else.

"Game time?" I'm a little lost.

"Yep. I'm the unofficial official gamemaster of our tours."

"So what's the game?" Joey asks.

"I think, in honor of our new tour-mate, and in the spirit of getting to know each other better, let's play Never Have I Ever."

Okay. I can do this. I'm cool. Logan even said so. I can play a drinking game with these guys. Whatever. Totally cool. Except now they're definitely going to find out how lame I am, because I haven't really done anything. I've never even played Never Have I Ever before.

Colin is leaned against the side of the van, one leg bent, foot up on the wheel well, arms crossed in the darkness while Logan and Dean lay down the back seat of the van and Joey rifles through the cooler.

"Perfect." Logan holds out a hand and hoists me into the back of the van. I sit cross-legged on the hard, carpeted surface.

Joey hands me a fuzzy navel, popping the top with a quiet "here."

"Thank you." I take the bottle and rest it on my knee, the scent of over-ripe peaches wafts from the open container. Joey sits across from me, then Logan and Dean climb in and we all sit in a circle—or square, I guess. Logan raps his fist against the window closest to where Colin is standing.

"Man, get your ass in here. We're waiting on you."

"Play without me."

"Dude, no."

Colin walks around to the back of the van where the door is ajar. "I'm going to wait for the tow truck. Besides, someone's got to stay sober."

"Come on. Just one beer."

He glowers at Logan for a beat, his lips set in a hard line. "Fine. One beer."

Joey fishes a dark bottle out of the cooler and Colin takes it as he climbs in and sits between me and Logan.

Logan sets his beer down between his legs. It looks like he's already emptied half of it. He claps. "All right, Gracie. Do you know how it's played?"

"Uh, yeah." I've never played, but I know the gist.

"Cool. Then ladies first." With a wink, he raises his bottle to me.

And then they're all looking at me. Expectantly.

Shit.

Okay...just need to think of something I haven't done (that won't be hard) that doesn't make me look completely lame. I look around the circle, smiling. "Um..."

Logan takes another swig of his beer, his throat bobbing as he swallows. His red guitar is propped up behind him.

"Never have I ever...been to a rock concert."

"What?" Logan shakes his head.

All of the guys take a drink.

"Well, put that down on your list of things to do, because we're going to cross that off for you really quick."

I nod.

"And since she got all of us, we have to take a bonus drink."

"Are you just making up rules now?" Dean deadpans.

"No. We've always played like this," Logan insists.

"Fine," Dean says. He's to my right so his turn is next. "Never have I ever gone skinny dipping."

Logan takes a drink but no one else makes a move.

"Really? None of you fuckers? Shit, Gracie put that down on your list too. I'm making it happen."

"Okay." I'm not sure what this list is he's talking about, but apparently now I have a list.

Joey clears his throat and says in a not-quite-steady voice, "Never have I ever had a threesome." A slight blush colors his freckled cheeks.

Dean and Logan each take sips and Joey gets redder.

"Col, I'm surprised." Logan looks at Colin, whose beer is sitting to his side. He hasn't even been sipping between turns like the other guys.

Colin shrugs. "I'm singularly focused—I wouldn't want to split my attention." His blue eyes land on mine for a second before I look away, heat rising up my neck.

Logan pauses, his bottle at his lips. "Well, if there's only one girl—"

"You had a threesome with another dude?" Joey's eyes go wide.

"Shit. I almost forgot about that night," Dean muses.

Joey's head swings back and forth between the brothers. "Really? How have I not heard about this yet?"

"We shared a girl once, a long time ago. Before I figured my shit out," Dean says coolly.

"Okay," Logan cuts Dean off. "Let's move on." He tips his head back, finishing the rest of his beer, and motions for Joey to grab him another. "It's my turn anyway." Then he turns to me, a half smile on his lips and a glint in his dark brown eyes. "I've noticed Gracie here has yet to take a drink. Let's fix that."

I swallow a lump in my throat but manage to keep a smile on my face.

He taps his chin a few times.

"Take it easy on her," Colin says quietly.

"Ha! But that wouldn't be any fun." Logan looks at me again with a huge grin. "Got it. Never have I ever given a blow job."

Colin smacks Logan on the back of his head at the same time Dean says, "Fuck, Logan, we just met her."

"Hence, why we're playing the game!" Logan pops the top to his new beer.

Colin looks right at me. "You don't have to answer that."

I don't know why I'm surprised at the serious tone in his voice. Colin is always so serious.

"No, it's fine. I can handle it." Yeah, I can totally hang. I can't decide if them knowing I've given a blow job is more or less embarrassing than them thinking I haven't. I feel the heat blooming in my cheeks as I bring my drink to my lips. I probably can't hang.

"There we go!" Logan pumps a fist in the air.

"All right, girl." Dean cocks his head and raises his bottle to clink mine. Then with a conspiratorial nod, he takes a big drink of his beer as I take a sip of my fuzzy navel. It's sweet and peachy, almost too sweet. And there's a pungent aftertaste, but it doesn't burn going down or make me gag like the straight whiskey from the paper bag.

I try not to think about my one sexual experience—a blow job behind the bleachers after a game with my high school boyfriend, the small-town football star. It's so cliché. The cheerleader and the football player. He dumped me the next day when I told him I didn't want to go all the way. So there's that.

"You're up, Wolfe." Logan tips his bottle toward Colin.

"Okay." Colin looks at the drink in my hand, then up to my face. Not smiling. "Never have I ever run away from home."

Did he just call me out? He just called me out. I want to come back at him with something clever, but the only thing I can focus on is my heartbeat pulsing in my ears. And then his lips start to curl at the edges as we continue this staring match. So I do all I can—I take a drink.

"Does the time I ran away when I was eight count?" Joey asks, his cheeks still flushed.

"Yeah, sure."

Joey makes a big, toothy grin and takes a drink. "Man, I hid in the neighbor's yard for, like, three hours and no one even noticed," he continues, mostly to himself, shaking his head and taking another swig.

It's my turn again. Shit. I should have been thinking of things to say during everyone else's turns. The guys are all drinking and laughing at Joey's story—except Colin. He's holding his mostly full beer in his tattoo-covered hand and looking out the window. With his head turned, I steal a glance at the tattoos on his neck and exposed throat. There's a small block of text—a verse, maybe—surrounded by black flames, roses, and a skull. He turns back to the group circle and I look away before I'm caught.

I clear my throat.

"Never have I ever"—their eyes are all glued on me now—"gotten a tattoo."

Again, all of the guys drink.

"That'll be two drinks again," Logan says.

Of course Colin and Joey have a ton of tattoos, and I've noticed a few small ones on the insides of Dean's wrists, forearms, and the back of his neck, but I haven't seen any on Logan. I wonder how many he has and where they are. Maybe by the end of this summer I'll get to find out.

"Hey, isn't our third show in Vegas? We're gonna stop by Tyler's shop, right?" Joey asks.

"We definitely are. That's an awesome idea." Logan turns wild eyes to me. "Do you want a tattoo, G? Because if you do, Tyler is the absolute best, and he'll totally hook you up."

A tattoo? Like a real, permanent one?

"I don't know. Maybe. I mean, it'd have to be something I could live with on my body for the rest of my life."

Did I really just say maybe I would get a tattoo?

Of course I'm not going to get a tattoo. What would everyone think? Why do I care so much about what everyone thinks? Kyla would tell me to do it. I ran away to do something a little wild, a little crazy, and forget expectations. Maybe Crazy Gracie is the type of girl to get a tattoo?

I completely miss Dean's turn, but no one says anything about me not drinking, so I'm probably safe.

I swear a tiny smirk crosses Colin's lips for a split second.

We go around the circle a few more times. Joey seems to be trying to up the kinky sex factor with each of his statements. He's as red as a beet at this point, I don't know if it's just the alcohol or all of the sex talk—maybe both. Dean drinks for every one of them, though. Either Dean is exceptionally experienced or Joey just isn't creative enough.

Logan keeps trying to come up with things that will make me drink, but he's been unsuccessful. Spoiler: I haven't done anything worth bringing up in a game like this. But I've been drinking my fuzzy navel throughout the game anyway and by the time we're back around to Logan, I'm warm and happy. I've been giggling a lot and am a bit wiggly.

Am I buzzed? I think I'm buzzed. I've never been buzzed before.

Dean offers me another drink and I happily accept, even though I can feel Colin's eyes on me as I open it. He's still nursing his original beer.

"Hey! I've got it. I've got it. I've got it this time!" Logan hunches down, a mischievous grin directed toward me. "Never have I ever been to a frat party."

No one drinks. I kind of shrug and shake my head at him.

"Really? You went your whole first year at college without going to a frat party?"

"Yep. I was too busy studying." And secluding myself, not making any friends. A lot of good that did me. I practically flunked out anyway. "I decided to spend my freshman year being lame, and I didn't partake in any college pastimes, really." I realize I'm rambling but I don't really care and I keep on going, counting on my fingers. "I never went to a frat party, or any party, actually. I never got drunk, I never tried weed, I never had sex—"

"You're a virgin?" Joey blurts out.

Dean practically chokes on his beer as he tries not to spit it across the back of the van.

Logan smacks Joey across the shoulder. "Dude!"

"Sorry, I just..." Joey's shaved head is as bright as a fire hydrant.

My face is so hot, I'm afraid it's the same color as his. I don't know why I admitted that just now. Stupid tasty fuzzy navel. I take another drink and close my eyes, willing time to rewind over the last two minutes.

"You were a virgin when you were nineteen, too, so shut the fuck up," Colin says to Joey. Everyone is quiet. Colin turns his hard stare to me. I don't know if it's with pity or disdain. He turns away, dismissing me like a child, and downs the rest of his beer.

Maybe he was right—I am a child. A toddler he doesn't want here.

Colin's phone buzzes. He pulls it out of his pocket and looks at the screen.

"Game's over. The truck is almost here."

CHAPTER 6

It's almost three in the morning by the time the tow truck gets us to the next town with a service station.

"They open at seven. Switching out the tires shouldn't take long—I reckon you'll be back on the road by eight," the friendly tow truck operator tells us as he climbs back in his cab.

We are left standing in the empty parking lot of the repair shop. The entire town seems to be asleep and dark except for a few buildings on this strip of road.

"Fuck," Colin says.

"We'll make it to LA in time," Dean assures him.

Logan is looking intently at his phone.

"Let's get some food." Joey motions toward the yellow Denny's sign glowing in the distance.

"I have a better idea." Logan holds up his phone. "There's a public pool less than a mile from here. Who's up to cross skinny dipping off their list?"

Again with this list.

"Are you trying to cross breaking and entering off your list, too?" Colin asks flatly.

"You need to lighten up. We're not hurting anyone."

"And you need to grow up. You're not a twenty-year-old kid anymore."

Logan and Colin stand silently until Dean interrupts.

"I'm in."

"Yes!" Logan turns to Joey. "How 'bout you?"

Joey looks between Logan and Colin. "Uh...I don't know. Pancakes sound pretty good."

"You do you, bro." He turns to me with a raised eyebrow. "And what about you, Gracie? Pool or pancakes?"

I hesitate, looking between Logan's smiling face and Colin's cold one.

He wants to sneak into a public pool and jump in without swimming suits? I would never do that. Correction, Old Gracie would never have done that. The same Gracie who had no fun at college, has no stories, and barely gets buzzed during a game of Never Have I Ever. I don't want to be her anymore. Not this summer, not on this trip, anyway. I want to be New Gracie. Fun Gracie. Carefree Gracie. Exciting Gracie. Fuck-the-Consequences Gracie.

"Let's do it."

* * *

"It's right over there," Logan says as we round the block.

The pool is across from a large community park. It has a small outbuilding and is surrounded by a tall metal fence and a few sapling trees. The water looks deep and dark, only the bright moon reflecting off its glassy surface. The elevated lifeguard chair sits empty under a red and white striped umbrella. It's eerily still.

Logan and Dean start scaling the fence like freaking twin monkeys. They turn at the top, holding out their hands to help me up, and I have a sudden moment of panic. The image of Colin's face when I started walking away with Logan and Dean flashes in my mind. It was clear he didn't approve. He'd almost looked disappointed as he rubbed the dark stubble along his jaw. For some reason, it had made my stomach sink.

Fuck him. He argued Logan wasn't a twenty-year-old kid anymore. Well, I am (almost) and this is my time to do stupid stuff like this, right?

I grab the guys' hands and easily scale the fence, leaping over the top and landing nimbly on the other side.

"Wow," they say in unison.

"I was a flyer in cheer."

"Mmm, I always had a thing for cheerleaders," Logan says with a devious smirk.

I put my hand on my hip and roll my eyes. I'm so over the cheerleader label. "You like cheerleaders? How predictable."

"Predictable?" Logan's eyebrows shoot up.

"Yep. Just like every other hormone-fueled American male. What part do you like most? The uniform, the short skirt, the bouncing up and down? Or is it the enthusiastic cheering for sweaty, aggressive guys who are most definitely overcompensating for their tiny dicks?"

Logan's mouth falls open.

Dean coughs from behind Logan. "Shit, she bites and I like it."

New, exciting Gracie is sassy, and I like it too.

"I'm predictable, huh?" Logan smiles as he tears his shirt off over his head.

"Uh huh."

"Okay." He unbuttons his jeans, never breaking eye

contact. "What am I about to do now?" His jeans hit the concrete. "I'll give you a hint. You'd better undress fast unless you want to get your clothes wet."

"Logan..." I shake my head as he prowls toward me in just his black boxers. "Okay, okay!" I toe off my shoes. He comes closer. "Wait!" I pull off my shirt and toss it to the ground. It's probably a good thing I'm going too fast to overthink it. I shimmy my jean shorts down just in time before Logan picks me up by the waist and hauls me into the pool with him.

We hit the water with a deafening splash and I go under in a tangle of limbs. It takes a second to find my bearings and we both pop out at the same time. My hair drips into my face and my teeth are chattering but I'm smiling and Logan is laughing as we tread water, just looking at each other.

"Hey. I thought we were supposed to be skinny dipping."

We turn to Dean, who is stripping down at the edge of the deep end. He's shirtless, undoing his belt. I can see that he has pierced nipples and a couple more tattoos on his ribs.

"If I'm not mistaken, you two are both still wearing clothes." Then he pulls down his pants, and either he goes commando or his underwear went down with them because he's buck ass naked. It's dark and I turn away quickly, so I don't see much. No, I saw it. I totally saw Dean's penis. It was just for a second but the unmistakable glint of moonlight on metal is all I needed to see to know that he's pierced down there as well.

Water cascades over us as he jumps into the pool with a crash, and we bob up and down as waves undulate through the pool. We swim around for a bit, but mostly tread water.

I'm finally acclimated to the temperature when Logan gets a scheming look on his face and dives into the water. I can barely make out his dark figure under the surface as he heads straight for me. He swims between my legs and his fingers wrap around my knees as he pops up under me. I'm now straddling his shoulders as he breaks through the water.

I'm exposed to the cool air and instantly freezing in my bra and panties. Good thing it's dark. Even though I've always been active and fit and never self-conscious of my body, I've also never been mostly undressed in front of two hot rock stars either. Day two and they've already seen me in my underwear. I guess Kyla did know what she was talking about. But I'm also grateful I'm not wearing one of the tiny thongs she packed.

"Ready?" Logan asks.

"For what?"

"Three, two, one!"

Logan launches me up in the air and I let out a surprised scream. I fly halfway across the pool, flipping in the air and landing sideways back in the water. I come back up, wiping wet hair out of my face and dripping water from my eyes. Logan wades over to me and we smile at each other. I move a little closer.

"Hey guys." Dean points toward the street where a car is passing. "I'm pretty sure that's a police cruiser. Maybe we should call it."

"Yeah, okay."

We climb out of the pool. Shivering, we run to where our clothes are scattered around the pool deck just as the car turns this direction, the bright headlights shining directly on us, the overhead light bar unmistakable.

"Shit."

We scramble to grab our clothes and shoes. We run to the other side of the pool, away from the cop, and throw our stuff over the fence. Logan jumps up, giving me his hand as Dean gives me a boost from below and we go toppling over the fence, Logan landing on his back with a thud and me falling on top of him.

"Ope." I awkwardly giggle as I place both hands flat on his chest—his damp, naked chest—to push myself off him.

Logan smiles at me in the dark and I forget for a second how cold I am.

"Let's go," Dean says as we get up.

We snatch our clothes again, hugging them close to our bodies, and we run.

We go behind the pool building and down the street, behind dark buildings between alleyways and parking lots, staying in the shadows. I don't even notice that I'm wet and freezing or that I'm not wearing shoes on dirty, uneven pavement. We finally stop, hiding between two dumpsters behind a chiropractor's office, and my heart is beating so fast. But I'm smiling. We all break into nervous laughter as we catch our breath and get dressed.

I see way too much of Dean's ass as he hops into his jeans, and Logan gives me his shirt to dry off with.

"Thanks." I hand him back his damp shirt and quickly get on my T-shirt and shorts.

My feet sting as I slip them into my shoes but we're finally all dressed—except for Logan's shirt. I see dark tribal patterns just above the waistband of Logan's jeans.

"Oh my god, Logan, you have a tramp stamp?"

He shrugs and chuckles a little. "Yeah—"

The beam of a flashlight sweeps over the alley near us.

"Shit."

Logan reaches for me. "Come on."

We run up the street holding hands, Dean just behind us. I'm simultaneously panicking and the most excited I've ever been. The thought of being caught is scary and thrilling, and I'm smiling so wide my cheeks hurt. I've never felt so wild. So free.

"This way."

We follow Dean, sneaking alongside a few houses to a little grassy clearing that's nearly invisible from the road. It overlooks a valley beyond the town, and we sit, exhausted and out of breath. All of the blood and adrenaline pumping through my body has me feeling hot, but I'm still shivering. The boys notice and each scoot closer to me so that I'm shoulder-to-shoulder with both of them in a twin sandwich.

"Well, we can definitely cross skinny-dipping off the list now," Logan says.

"And trespassing...and running from the cops..." Dean adds.

"Yeah, this list rocks."

I smile at Logan. "You keep talking about this list like it's a real thing."

"It should be. You wanted to run away and have an adventure. See and do new things, right?"

"Yeah."

"So, let's write it down. What do you want to experience this summer? Let's make it happen."

I look out in the distance where the sun is starting to peek over the majestic rock formations that dot the landscape. The sunrise is beautiful, and we sit and watch as yellow rays of light kiss the ground and the sky is painted a soft lilac.

"You'll have to help me come up with the list. I'd hardly know where to start."

"I think we can manage." Dean bumps me playfully with his shoulder.

As the sun gets higher, I can already feel its warmth on my face. This is going to be the summer of Fun Gracie, and it starts right now.

CHAPTER 7

"OH MY GOD, YES!" I'M ALREADY SALIVATING AS WE OPEN THE to-go boxes Colin and Joey got for us from Denny's. We dig in, sitting on the cold, hard concrete curb in the parking lot of the car repair shop at seven in the morning. I don't even care that the food is lukewarm. It's freaking amazing. My entire container of pancakes, eggs, and bacon is covered in maple syrup and I scarf it down with my plastic spork greedily. It's the most I've eaten at one sitting in months.

When the food is gone I wish there was more. It's amazing to have an appetite again.

Colin comes out of the shop at around seven-thirty and says the van is just about ready. He's changed clothes, now wearing a charcoal gray T-shirt that looks super soft and black ripped jeans.

By eight, we're ready to hit the road again. Joey opens the back of the van for me so I can get to my bag. I slip out my little notebook from the side pocket, feeling the worn, buttery leather in my hand. It's pink with gold embossed polka dots and my initials, GLG. I'm so distracted by my favorite notebook that I don't even realize until the engine turns over that Logan is in the driver's seat. And I have slid up next to Colin in the middle seat.

He's looking out the window, his tattooed hand resting lightly on his knee. He's taking no mind of me—I'm insignificant. But his energy is huge. It takes up the whole seat and I feel like I'm sitting too close. Too late to move now, though.

I flip quickly through my notebook, skipping over pages covered in my little scribbles, musings, and scratched out verses. Colin glances my way, eyeing my notebook, and I hurry to a blank page, not wanting him to see any of the words I've written.

I swallow hard and grip my pen. "Okay, guys. What should I put on my summer bucket list?"

"Nah, not a bucket list. That makes it sound like you're dying. It's your fuck-it list," Logan says from up front.

I write *Gracie's Fuck-It List* on top of the page and make several bullet points. I write *skinny-dipping* and *running from the cops* and then cross them off. Then I write *go to rock concert* and *get tattoo*.

Logan and Dean shout out ideas, most of them silly, but I write down a few. *Smoke a joint. Get drunk. Kiss a stranger.*

"You want to get anything pierced?" Dean asks.

"Hmm...maybe."

I write it down.

I read over the list. Satisfied, I close it, secure it with the elastic band, and tuck it under the seat. The thought of doing half the things on the list is terrifying, and it feels strangely exhilarating. Liberating.

I can't wipe the smile off my face. I'm tired and happy and my belly is full. The morning sunlight streaming in through the windows reminds me I've been awake over sixteen hours, and my eyelids are heavy. I roll to my side and rest my head against the seat, careful to face away from Colin and give him as much space as I can. Even out of my sight, I can sense his presence, and I swear I can feel his eyes on me as I curl up and try to sleep.

* * *

My face is pressed against soft cotton and I'm surrounded by warmth, an arm wrapped around me and the unmistakable rise and fall of a broad male chest beneath my cheek. Logan is being extra cuddly, I guess. I nuzzle deeper into the space between his shoulder and pec. He smells good.

He smells...different.

I blink against the light. I'm clutching a dark gray shirt, Colin's heavily tattooed arm wrapped across my shoulders.

Holy shit. I'm lying on Colin. I move to sit up, but his arms tighten around me and he lets out a breathy whimper. His eyes are closed, brows furrowed in his sleep. I lay back down on his chest and his hold eases, his face softening.

I hold still. How the heck did we end up like this? Colin is partially reclined, his head and shoulders propped against the seat and armrest. I'm on my side, somehow wedged between him and the seat. It's actually the most comfortable I've been while trying to sleep in the van this whole trip. My back doesn't ache and my neck isn't stiff.

I carefully slide my phone out of my back pocket. It's almost one in the afternoon. I haven't even been asleep for five hours yet. I should try to go back—but do I sit up? Change positions? I glance up and Logan is sleeping in the front passenger seat while Dean drives. I catch Dean's eye in the mirror and he gives me a knowing smile with a shrug

I don't move. I just listen to the sound of Colin's steady heartbeat at my temple until it lulls me away.

* * *

Buzz buzz.

The quick vibrations against my rear pull me out of my hazy white dream world and back into the hot van. I'm still lying across Colin, my hand rests on his stomach and I can feel his hard abs under his thin shirt.

Buzz buzz.

Oh yeah—my phone.

I don't want to move, though. I'm so comfortable actually lying down. Not quite as cozy as earlier—and I realize it's because Colin's arms aren't wrapped around me anymore. I glance up at him and I. Am. Horrified.

He's awake.

He's not looking at me, but at his phone in his hand, his other arm bent behind his head.

I sit up quickly and smooth my hair out of my face. Dean is still driving. Logan is curled up in the front, and Joey is snoring in the back.

"Sorry," I say. "I would have moved."

Colin's gaze shifts from his screen to my face, which is now heating exponentially with every second his dark blue eyes are on me.

"I wasn't going to wake you up. It's fine." He turns back to his phone, face unreadable, and pays me no more attention.

I pull my phone out of my pocket to see it's after four in the afternoon.

Kyla: *Girl. If you think I was joking about hunting you down then all our years of friendship have been a lie*

Gah. I ask Dean where we are.

Me: *Sorry! I'm fine, we're in Nevada*

"We'll be getting into LA late, or early if you want to be technical. Then our first show is tomorrow night," Dean adds.

"Wow, so soon?"

Dean nods. Soon, Logan starts stretching and yawning as he blinks awake and we stop at the next town to eat. The boys are all so cute. Logan gives me a hand out of the van and opens doors for me, Joey grabs me the last "good" gas station burrito, and Dean buys me another pack of fuzzy navels along with a couple of books of crossword and sudoku puzzles for when I'm bored. Colin is outside pacing the sidewalk, on the phone with their manager, Rick, probably explaining why we're getting into town the morning of their first show instead of the night before as planned.

After gassing up, Joey gets in the driver's seat and I jump in the middle after Logan. Colin finally walks over after finishing his call. He opens the door next to me, stepping up and then halting when he sees Logan in the seat with me. I swear, for a second annoyance flashes on his face. But then it's stoic once again and he shuffles to the back seat.

After several hours, it's getting dark outside. During a lull in conversation, Logan claps his hands.

"We've been so cooped up. Let's have some music! Wolfe, can I borrow your guitar?" Logan turns behind us to Colin. "Please?"

Colin lets out a sigh but reaches behind the seat. "Fine." Behind Logan's red electric guitar case is a bigger black one. He opens it and gingerly takes out a black acoustic guitar and hands it to Logan. It's decorated with beautiful wood inlays in an intricate geometric pattern.

Logan touches the knobs and plucks a couple of the strings.

"It's tuned," Colin says flatly.

"Okay, okay. Just checking."

Logan nestles the guitar in his lap and plays the first unmistakable chords to "Sweet Child O' Mine" by Guns 'n' Roses. Joey taps out a beat against the steering wheel and we all join in to sing the lyrics—except Colin, who's inexplicably quiet with his arms folded. Logan and Dean aren't terrible singers, but they definitely can't hit the high notes. They just end up yelling those lines and laughing hysterically afterward. I finish singing one of the verses by myself while they're busy chuckling, holding a particularly long note.

Logan, still strumming the guitar, smiles lopsided at me.

"You have a really pretty singing voice, you know that?"

"Yeah, thanks." I've always loved singing. "I grew up singing in church and I was Maria in our eighth grade production of *The Sound of Music*, so…"

Logan continues to play, filling the car with music as Dean and Joey call out requests. I sing along to the songs I know, but he also plays many I've never heard before.

"Hey, you haven't sung to the last few. You pick the next one."

Suddenly, I know no songs. Like, can't even conjure up one tune. My mind blanks on anything cool. Shit. I listen to a lot of country music—they probably don't. I refrain from requesting Taylor Swift.

"Hmm… Maybe something by Adele?"

Logan scratches along his jaw, thinking. "I don't know—

"

"I got it." Colin's deep voice cuts in from the back.

He takes the guitar from Logan, and looking down with intensity, begins to play. Then quietly he sings the first lines of "Rolling in the Deep." I'm staring at his mouth as the words pour out of him. His voice is at once soothing and heartbreaking, gorgeous and raw. Chills move down my spine to my toes. And then I sing with him, soft at first. He raises his head and our eyes lock as we sing the chorus together, our voices combine, getting louder, stronger. My voice is saccharine to his grit. Perfectly balanced.

I'm out of breath when he strums the last notes.

"We're coming up on it, guys," Joey says and we all look forward. As we crest a hill the black expanse outside the windshield gives way to a seemingly endless tapestry of lights. They blanket the valley and climb up the surrounding hills. Lights emanate from tall buildings and move across extensive freeway systems like blood coursing through veins and arteries, feeding the giant city.

Los Angeles.

"Wow," is all I manage to say.

* * *

It takes almost two hours to get to where we're supposed to meet their manager. Correction—where *they* are supposed to meet him. I am to stay hidden away in the van after Colin reminds all of us I'm not supposed to be here. Their meeting lasts over an hour, and I'm tired but too nervous to sleep alone in the van while parked in downtown Los Angeles. I text Kyla to let her know we made it. Honestly, the book of sudoku puzzles Dean got for me comes in quite handy.

"Let's get to the fuckin' bus!" Logan says as the guys all clamor back in.

It's at least another hour of driving—most of it sitting in traffic—until we get to the venue of tonight's show, where the bus is already parked around back.

A couple of burly dudes in tight black shirts come out of absolutely nowhere and help unload the van, moving bags and suitcases to the bus and taking any equipment and instruments inside with them.

The bus is enormous. The outside is black and silver, and the interior is cream-colored leather and funky patterned carpet. Inside is tight with a small kitchenette and a little table surrounded by banquet seating. Everything is accented with black and this marbled faux-wood and lit with rows of lights along the floor and ceiling. The driver's cab is completely blocked off for privacy, and the back of the bus is the sleeping quarters. There are six bunks stacked, each with their own little window and privacy curtain. The bunks look small, not even as wide as a twin mattress, but we're all exhausted, and after sleeping in a van for three days, we might as well be in a five-star resort.

We all sleepily claim our bunks and pass out on the cool, dark bus.

* * *

"Hey."

I peek one eye open to see half of Logan's face peering at me from where he's peeled back my privacy curtain.

"Sorry, you can go back to sleep. I wanted to let you know we're heading out. We have to go do a rehearsal, then some media interviews, then sound check before the show tonight." He hands me a badge with my name under the words *Wicked Road VIP*. "This will get you in anywhere you want. There's also a shower you can use back by our dressing room."

"This is so cool, thank you. I'm excited for the show." Not going to lie, I may be more excited for the shower.

"I'm actually a little nervous to play tonight, knowing we'll be taking your rock concert virginity. I feel pressure to make sure it's good for you." He gives me a little wink and I promptly feel myself blush.

"I'm sure you'll be great."

He smiles, his hair perfectly disheveled, his brown eyes warm. "Doors open at seven-thirty but we should hit the stage about nine. Make sure to find us backstage before the show—I'm going to save you the best spot in the house."

CHAPTER 8

The back hallways are a dimly lit maze, but I keep following the sound of the music. Logan was right, this pass literally gets me through any door, and the shower was magnificent. I'm wearing skinny jeans and a black tank top—am I underdressed? Should I have found some scissors and cut slits into the shirt or something? Do girls actually do that or am I just recalling stuff from movies?

Large men in black polos nod as I pass, showing them my badge. Other people rush around talking on phones and radios without giving me a second glance.

The music is louder. I can feel the bass, hear the drums. A big metal door with BACKSTAGE written on a plaque stands between me and the bands. I grip the cold metal handle and turn. It doesn't move. It's locked. Should I knock?

I knock.

I knock again harder. I'm sure no one can hear me—the music on the other side of the wall is too loud.

I feel so stupid, standing here alone. I'm not even sure how to get back out to the bus from here.

The door opens with a metallic screech before me. A tall guy with biceps the size of my head stands in the opening. I hold up my pass. He narrows his eyes.

"Gracie!" Logan runs up behind the massive guy and I breathe out a sigh of relief.

He ushers me in. The backstage area is cramped. Everything is black—the floor, the walls, the ceiling, the curtain separating us from the stage. There are all sorts of equipment, speakers, and scaffolding around the space.

I follow Logan up a short set of steps and then we are on the stage, just behind the curtain.

"Guys, she made it! We're just about to go on. I was getting worried."

I smile at him as we meet the other three.

Joey's mohawk is styled so it sticks straight up, his *My Little Pony* T-shirt has the sleeves cut off so his colorful arms are on full display. Dean is wearing a black mesh tank top and I'm definitely not staring at his nipple rings through it. He has more metal in his face than usual. Small hoops cover the outside curve of his ears—he has extra rings and barbells and studs in his nose, eyebrows, and lips. He has rings on all of his fingers, his nails painted black.

Colin is standing the farthest away. He's all in black, a long-sleeved Henley shirt and the same black ripped jeans from earlier.

"They're wrapping up," Colin says, looking beyond the curtain.

Then I realize the music has stopped. There's screaming and clapping on the other side of the curtain and a guy yells to the crowd, "Have a good fucking night."

Dean and Logan grab their instruments. Joey twirls his sticks and Colin gives them all nods.

"You ready for this?" Colin asks them.

They all grunt and put their foreheads together and I

can barely hear Colin's next words.

"We're gonna kill it. Love you guys."

They grunt some more, hitting each other on their backs.

Then guys are piling in from the stage—the opening act, I presume.

"Let's go scope out tonight's pussy," one of the new guys says to his bandmate. He's tall and lanky, his shirt drenched in sweat. Then he sees me and immediately strides over. "Who do we have here?"

Logan and Dean are instantly at my side. Joey stands behind me and Colin steps right in front of me, standing between me and Sweaty Guy.

"She's with us." Colin is eye-to-eye with him.

"All of you?" Sweaty Guy raises an eyebrow.

"Shut the fuck up," Logan says.

Guys dressed in black are moving all around the stage, quickly switching out equipment and stealthily setting up speakers.

The rest of the other band, five in total, come to stand around Sweaty Guy, and my guys seem to close in around me. It's sweet, actually, but it's also making me a little claustrophobic.

I step forward and Colin side-steps, letting me pass. I don't really want to touch Sweaty Guy, but I put my hand out to him anyway.

"I'm Gracie."

"Jace."

Jace shakes my hand. The smirk on his face is probably supposed to be cute or flirty, but it makes me feel weird.

"Are you going to be with us just tonight, Gracie?" He says my name slowly.

"She's traveling with us all summer," Logan says. He looks weird, standing all upright instead of his usual casual stance.

Jace seems delighted by this news, complaining no one informed him they were keeping permanent groupies now.

"She's not a groupie," Colin and Logan say in unison.

The opening band's name is apparently Donkey Lips—I don't get it either. They all tell me their names while looking with various degrees of obviousness at my breasts. One of them goes by Boner, and there's no way I'm going to remember the rest of their names after that, so they will hereby be referred to as Boner One, Boner Two, Boner Three, and Boner Four.

"You're up," a woman with a headset calls from somewhere out of my eyesight. Colin looks toward the stage, then back between me and the five guys from Donkey Lips, his jaw clenched.

"Here, real quick!" Logan places a light hand on my back and shows me to a little stool sitting off to the right. The guys from Donkey Lips walk off, disappearing in the dark hallway.

The stool is lined up perfectly so that I can see the entire stage, and I admire how the bright lights reflect off Joey's iridescent drums. I sit, completely concealed behind the curtain. I can see about half of the crowd, which seems to be getting restless. It's not a huge venue, but it's packed.

Joey steps on stage to applause as he sits behind his kit, inspecting the surfaces and cracking his neck. Dean walks toward the front next, and the roar from the audience grows. Then Colin strides up front and center and the crowd goes crazy. People hoot and yell, women scream in the front row, and more push their way through to get closer.

"See, best seat in the house." With a wink, Logan runs on to the stage to join the other members of Wicked Road.

Their set is a blur. I don't register where one song ends and another begins—I only feel the music, the energy of the crowd, the rhythm of the bass, the melody of Logan's guitar, Joey's masterful beats, and Colin's voice. On stage, he's truly enigmatic. He's constantly moving. At times he hunches over to belt out guttural notes, neck veins straining, screaming, growling, his face twisting as he emotes the lyric. Then other times, his voice is soft, smooth, and beautiful as it comes out of his perfect mouth, his face serene.

The audience eats it all up, shouting out the lyrics, dancing, moving, moshing. I see more than one pair of breasts flashed throughout the show. A little over halfway through their set, Colin pulls his shirt over his head and wipes sweat off his forehead before tossing it into the crowd. Women scream. Like, *bloody murder* scream.

He takes a sip of water from the bottle on the side of the stage. His stomach flexes as he gulps it down, and I take in all of his lean muscle and the giant chest tattoo of an eagle, wings spread across his chest.

And then it's over and the guys are hustling off stage. Logan grabs my hand and I'm whisked down the hall with them to a small lounge where the boys from Donkey Lips are already hanging. There's a table off to the side of the room with bottled water, little bags of chips, and sub sandwiches. The guys are practically yelling at each other as they shove chips in their faces and drink from forty-ounce beers. Not water drinkers, apparently.

"We'll be right back." Logan steers me toward the food table.

The sandwiches don't look particularly special, but I'm starving so I eat two of the turkey avocado ones, hoping that if my mouth is full I won't be expected to talk to Jace or any of the Boners. Luckily, they're preoccupied getting drunk, and I stay mostly off their radar until my boys come back in. They're all freshly showered and changed.

Logan walks over to me with a smile and soon the table is wrecked, food devoured.

"Ready for this?" Dean asks.

Joey grabs the remaining two bags of chips, stuffing them in his pockets. "Ready."

Colin sighs and heads toward the door. "Let's get it over with."

We all follow him out. I have no idea where we're going. The halls are all so dark and there are so many turns, like why? We're joined by several big guys in black and the lady with the headset again. We're walking fast and she's talking to Colin but I can't hear. Donkey Lips guys are too rowdy.

"Hey, after-party in our room! You coming?" Jace yells over our little caravan. The other guys all seem stoked on this idea.

"Sure," Joey says.

"Maybe, I like to keep my options open." Dean plays with his tongue piercing, twisting it with his teeth.

"Hell yeah, I'm in," Logan calls over to Jace. He turns to me. "You want to come?" We're still walking briskly, being ushered closer and closer to the exit.

I'm a little out of breath. After-party? This is what I signed up for, right?

"Sure."

Logan tells me to stick close to the security guys, and the one with the enormous biceps gives me a little nod in acknowledgment right before the big metal doors open and we are swept outside.

It's dark outside and cars whiz past on the street. The air is cooling off and smells faintly of cigarettes and asphalt. There's a small crowd of twenty or thirty people outside the back door—lots of women. Biceps security guy hovers by me and keeps me near the building, staying between me and the fans.

The guys go up to the crowd. I can't make out individual conversations over the ruckus and occasional screams. Girls reach out to touch the guys and grab their shirts. There are lashes batted and body parts exposed for the guys to sign—and they sign every stomach, boob, and butt like this is an everyday normal thing.

Jace and the Boners take special attention of some of the girls, whispering in their ears and touching their shoulders. Logan is his normal, outgoing self, giving out high fives and winks to everyone. Joey stands a little back, shy and pink-faced the whole time. Dean has disappeared. And Colin is signing some girl's hip and then he smiles at her.

He smiles.

Like, a real smile with teeth and everything. I already feel this gravitational pull around him, like a moon orbiting a planet, but when Colin smiles, he's the sun. He gave it so easily you'd think he smiles all the time. All I've seen him do these last few days is brood in dark corners and look bored or annoyed. What did she do to earn a smile?

"Come on." Logan waves me over with a huge smile and I scurry over to him.

The crowd is starting to disperse and he lays a protective arm around my shoulders. Several girls are plucked out of the group by Jace and the Boners (that really should have been their band name) and we all start moving down the street.

"Where are we going?"

"Hotel, just over there."

"Hotel?"

"Yeah. We'll sleep on the bus on travel days—which will be most days—but our show tomorrow night is only a couple hours away, so the label's paying for a hotel tonight."

We're surrounded by people—Joey is near my right and I recognize Jace in front of us walking with two girls, an arm around both of them. We're a tiny, noisy swarm as we cross a five-lane boulevard and reach the hotel. It's in a tall building and it looks fancy.

Everyone runs and giggles and shoves into the elevators, getting stern looks from the front desk. We ride up to the sixth floor, becoming a loud mob in the corridor. Then Colin is walking toward us from the other direction.

"Hey! Wolfe!" Jace gives him a high five, which Colin glumly returns.

As we walk by, he catches my eye and jerks his chin away from the group. "Can I talk to you for a minute?"

I look over to Logan, who's being carried away by the group. Literally swept down the hall like a wave. He glances back to me, calling out to go to room six-seventeen, before he and Joey are swallowed up and they turn a corner.

I turn back to Colin. The buttons at the top of his shirt are undone and I find myself staring at the tips of the wings that are inked along his collarbone.

He crosses his arms. "I just need to know if you need your own hotel room or if you're wanting to share."

Share? Is he asking if I want to share a room with him?

"Share?" I'm confused as fuck.

He rolls his eyes. "Were you planning on sharing a room with Logan?"

He says it like it should have been obvious. Should it have been?

"Um..."

He uncrosses his arms. "Look, I don't give a shit either way. You're an adult, do whatever the fuck you want. I just need to know if we need to get you a room or not."

"I'll have my own room. But I can get it—I mean, I can pay for it."

Flustered, I take a couple of steps back toward the elevators, then realize I turned in the wrong direction.

"I'll take care of it for now and when you check out, you can have them charge it to your card if you want."

"All right. But I will pay for it," I say, keeping my head raised proudly.

He's unimpressed. "You go have fun." He gestures down the hall in what I presume is the correct way to room six-seventeen.

"Okay, thanks." I turn down the hall as he puts his hands in his pockets and goes the other direction but then I stop. "Colin—"

He turns back to me, his thick, dark lashes almost completely obscuring his blue eyes.

"Are you... Will you be coming up to the room too?"

"Have I given you the impression that I party?"

"Uh, no."

"That's because I don't."

"Oh. All right, then." I tuck my hair behind my ear as I look away to keep it out of my face, and I can feel his eyes on me, discerning any tell or hint of emotion I betray.

"But I might stop by later," he says, his voice low and casual before he walks away.

It's not hard to find room six-seventeen. I just have to follow the sound of the loud voices and laughter.

Boner One opens the room for me. He isn't wearing a shirt. Everyone else seems to be dressed, though. One of the Boners, I think Boner Three, is hardcore making out with a girl in the corner, and Jace has a girl on his lap, a beer in one hand and her ass in the other. Joey is sitting on one of the beds, Logan lounging next to him on his side, telling Boner Four a story, when he spots me and waves me over to sit with them.

Joey offers me a beer and I take it. It's gross. I sip it anyway as I listen to the rest of Logan's story.

"Hey, how'd you like the show?" he asks.

"It was amazing. I loved it."

Logan makes an exaggerated relieved face. "Now I can sleep tonight." He smiles at me and takes a drink of his beer. "If we were ranking items on your Fuck-It list, how'd it compare to skinny dipping?"

"Definitely right up there, but with less cardio."

"For you, maybe."

We chuckle and then Boner Two hands Logan something. Logan puts the little blunt to his lips and closes his eyes as he takes a drag. He turns to blow the smoke away from us, nodding his head in appreciation. I've never seen pot before, but I lived in the dorms so I know what it smells like. He takes a second puff then holds it out to me.

"Want a hit?"

I'm unable to speak for a moment. Do I want a hit? Not really. It is on my list, though.

Fuck it.

RAE KENNEDY

I take the joint in my two fingers, staring at it. I have no idea what I'm doing. You just put it to your lips and suck, right?

Wrong.

Whatever I just did, it was wrong.

I'm coughing, my throat burns, smoke is billowing out of my nose and I'm afraid I'm going to be hacking up this taste for the rest of my life.

Warm fingers touch mine, slipping the joint out of my hand. I look up and Colin is standing there, his hard stare on me as he brings it to his lips. He takes a long pull, never breaking eye contact.

"Wahoo! Colin came to party. Old times, bro."

"No." Colin passes the joint along to one of the Boners. His eyes are still on mine and I'm glad he didn't hand it back to me. "I just came to give her this."

He pulls a key card out of his pocket and hands it to me. The envelope it's in says room eight-eleven.

"Thanks," I say quietly, my throat feels raw.

Colin looks at me, his face unreadable. "I can show you where your room is, if you want."

"Nah, dude. I'll walk her to her room when we're done," Logan says.

Colin glances to Logan, his expression the same but somehow harder, before returning his gaze to me, waiting for my response.

"I'm okay, thanks." I mean, does he think I can't figure out how room numbers work? I hold my mostly full can of beer up with a reassuring smile.

He tongues the inside of his cheek but doesn't say anything. Then he turns and leaves the room.

It's starting to really stink in here. Thankfully, someone

opens a window. The girl with Boner Three in the corner of the room definitely has her hands down his pants and the possibility of them having sex in the room with us seems quite high. Jace has moved on to girl number two, sharing the joint with her while Joey tries unsuccessfully to get girl number one's attention.

I sit and listen while Logan and Boner Four trade tales of late-night drunken shenanigans. They're entertaining, but I can't really relate, nor do I have any stories to contribute to the conversation.

I drink more of my beer. It still tastes bad.

I look toward the door and realize Colin was giving me an out. And I wish I'd taken it.

CHAPTER 9

Checkout is at two in the afternoon. I insist on paying for my room and then we all pile on the bus. Though he was inexplicably absent last night, Dean shows up on the bus, wearing sun glasses and complaining about how "way too fucking bright" it is outside.

Note to self: Dean may actually be a vampire.

He goes straight to his bunk.

Logan and Joey also climb into their beds with half-closed eyes. When they said they sleep all day and stay up all night, they meant it.

Colin sits at the little dinette table, looking intently at a small black book opened in front of him. I feel pretty awake, but I don't want to disturb him, so I get in my bunk too.

I close my privacy curtain and slide the one covering the window open to let in the light. The bus lurches forward and I watch out the window as we move through the city.

I slide my little pink notebook out from under my pillow and turn to my Fuck-It list. I cross off *go to rock concert* and *smoke a joint*. Okay, so I didn't successfully smoke a joint, but I'm counting it.

I'm about to close my notebook when I flip to the

TO BE YOUR LAST

front pages instead. I haven't read through it in a while. Haven't actually written in it for much longer. I glance over my words—my scribbles, half-finished poems, little haikus—and I find myself smiling as I read. For the first time in months, an idea bubble rises to the surface. It's delicate, barely there, but I can feel it.

I get out my pen as fragments of words whisper to me, threatening to blow away and be forgotten in an instant if I don't write them down.

I step to the edge
And take the leap.
The water is cold—
It awakens my soul
And I feel reborn.

I write down a few more lines, trying to convey the beauty of a lilac sunrise, a haunting voice, and a breathtaking smile. Not happy with any of it yet. I scratch down one line but the rest escapes me.

He is the sun.

* * *

THE SECOND SHOW IS IN A MUCH SMALLER VENUE. IT HAS A bar upstairs, and the guys all want to get drinks there after the show. I get let right in with the band and no one cards or questions me.

We end up squeezing around one long table—all twelve of us (as the Boners have acquired female companionship at some point in the night). The drinks don't stop coming.

RAE KENNEDY

Colin seems to be nursing the same beer most of the night, but Logan and I take watermelon shots and he orders me a vodka Sprite with his Long Islands. Joey is trying to go shot-for-shot with Jace and some questionable tequila. He's quickly red in the face, and before we know it he's offering to give piggy-back rides to everyone, including the older women at the table next to ours and our male bartender.

It's not long before Joey is quietly moaning and Colin walks him out to go back to the bus and sleep it off.

This leaves vacant chairs that are soon filled by more girls, who the members of Donkey Lips are more than happy to entertain.

Now Dean's not in his chair and I look around, finding him at the crowded bar. He's standing close to a man who's sitting on one of the stools. Dean's whispering in his ear and the man has his hand on Dean's forearm and nods with a smile.

They look exceptionally friendly.

"Is Dean gay?" I ask Logan in a hushed tone.

Logan looks at me, straw between his lips as he finishes off his second Long Island, and shrugs. "I don't think he identifies one way or the other. Dean is just Dean. But does he like fucking dudes? Yeah."

Hmm. All right.

And with that, it's just us and the Donkey Lips guys, who are getting rowdier by the second. Logan and I order more shots. He teaches me how to throw darts, which I'm convinced I'd be excellent at if I were sober. At one point, he and I end up on a table singing to a Joan Jett song, and we end up stumbling into the bus giggling at three a.m.

The next day I can easily cross *get drunk* and *have a hangover* off my list.

* * *

I stay on the bus when we arrive in Vegas while the guys to go their mic check before the show. I feel like resting and nursing this hangover a bit longer. I have one of my dreaded phone calls with my mom where she makes me feel guilty for not calling her every night and then proceeds to ask questions about how the program is going. I try to keep the conversation vague and as short as possible so I don't have to lie too much.

Then I text Kyla to let her know I'm still alive and that we're in Las Vegas. She replies that if I don't send her a selfie with a bunch of male strippers then it doesn't count.

I doze and write a little bit. Being out here in the desert is so different from home. Home is green and lush and surrounded by hills—or corn. Also, a lot of corn I've felt so trapped and suffocated by those hills the last few years, but here the landscape is vast, expansive. It's wide open and, in spots, barren, intimidating, dangerous. And in others, beautiful, a limitless canvas for the sun to paint with color. I try to capture what I mean in words. Of course I can't do it justice.

"Hey." Joey smiles as he steps onto the bus and holds up a white carry-out bag. "Tacos?"

"Oh my god, yes."

"Figured you'd be hungry."

He sits across the small table from me and we eat the most amazing street tacos I've ever had. He insists on walking with me to the concert house.

The show is amazing, again. Now that I've seen it a few times, I'm starting to remember the songs and catch some of the lyrics, and I appreciate the work and artistry that goes into each one. Even the Donkey Lips' set is okay.

After the show, Jace and the Boners have already accumulated several female groupies by the time we get backstage. More than one girl per guy, actually, and a few of them keep hanging all over Logan, more than subtly hinting they'd be into a ménage. Another girl, who had been sitting by Jace originally, is now practically glued to Colin's hip. Smiling coyly at him and giggling at everything and complaining it's so loud she has to lean in even closer to speak in his ear. Her name is Marnie, and she has curly dark hair and a great figure. She's wearing a shirt with slits all cut along the sides—so I guess that really is a thing. He isn't talking to her. And he doesn't smile at her. Somehow, that makes me feel better. But can't she see he's totally not interested in her? He totally isn't.

"We've got the next couple days off and we're spending them in Vegas, baby!" Jace shouts, a bottle of some sort of clear liquid in his hand. "Party starts at the club and ends in my room. Who's joining?" He looks over to us.

"Sorry, man. We have plans tonight," Logan says.

"We do?" I say.

"Yup." He grins.

"We better get going, actually." Colin gets up, leaving Marnie alone. She looks comically forlorn, moving back to sit next to Jace.

* * *

WE'RE ON A SIDEWALK A FEW STREETS OFF THE STRIP AND EVEN though it's the middle of the night, it's still almost eighty degrees outside.

TO BE YOUR LAST

"You ready?" Logan asks with a wild glint in his eyes. Oh no. That's the *hey, let's go skinny dipping* look.

"Ready for what?"

He just smirks and then we come up on a shop. The windows are blacked out and a bright neon light glows on the door that says CLOSED.

Colin walks on in anyway. We follow and are greeted by a young woman at a tall counter with maroon hair, black lipstick, thick winged eyeliner, and silver ball piercings in the dimples of her cheeks.

"Hey guys!"

"Leah, babe!" Logan bellows and she comes out to give him a hug.

"Wolfe! My man." A short guy with a buzzed hair, head tattoos and thick black glasses walks up to us. He and Colin shake hands and clap each other on the backs. "I'm going to go finish setting up. Come on back when you're ready."

The shop is small with black walls that make the large framed photos of brightly colored tattoos pop. There are several stations set up with black leather chairs and tables in the back.

"Do know what you want to get?" Logan asks me.

"Um...no." Shit.

"Here, you can look through our book for some ideas." Leah pulls out a thick three-ring binder and sets it on top of the counter. "There are some cute little flash tats near the front you might like."

I open the huge binder. There are so many pictures.

"I do piercings and Skillet is here to do ink work for you guys," Leah adds as I stare hopelessly at the book.

"No, it's her first one. Tyler's going to do it," Colin says flatly from behind me.

I didn't realize he'd been standing there.

"I thought he was going to work on your back piece?" Leah asks Colin.

"We can work on it after."

Leah just smiles, her dimples deepening. She and Logan start talking about music while Joey goes off to talk to a large guy with mutton chops—I'm guessing Skillet? Dean is standing next to me as I flip through the pictures.

He leans in. "You don't have to get one if you don't want to."

"I do want to get one." And not just because of the list, I think. "I just don't know what I'd want on my body for forever. I mean, what if in a few years I'm totally different and I hate it?"

"That's the beauty of tattoos." Colin steps closer to us.

I didn't think he was close enough to hear.

I swallow to clear my throat. "How so?"

"The fact that we do change but the tattoos don't. They're a constant reminder. You can look at a tat you got years ago and remember just where you were, what was going on in your life at that moment. Sometimes the memories are good ones, nostalgic. Sometimes they remind you of when you were being an idiot—but even that lets you know you've grown, changed, gotten better."

Wow. That's literally the most words I've heard Colin string together at once this entire trip.

"Thanks." I look away from Colin so I don't get too flustered. Just his closeness, his attention, his scent makes me feel hot and nervous.

I glance to Logan and smirk at him. "So, what does your tramp stamp remind you of when you see it?"

Everyone erupts in laughter. I think even Colin chuckles

quietly.

Dean gives me a low-five and says under his breath, "Savage, girl."

Logan, unperturbed and smiling, says, "It reminds me that I'm a badass who never backs out of a bet."

If Logan doesn't even regret a tramp stamp, maybe there is something to Colin's logic. I think about his words. *Something that represents me at this moment. Who am I? What the fuck am I doing?* I think about the poems I've been writing and why I even ran away in the first place.

"I got it. I know what I'm going to get."

* * *

Slipping my bra off under my shirt is embarrassing enough. Having it laid out on the table next to me where all the guys are gathered around is even more so. Then lifting my shirt so Tyler can place the stencil on my ribs just behind my right breast makes me blush. He places it, then rubs it onto my skin with a gloved hand. I chose this spot because it will be hidden even in a skimpy bathing suit—not that I need to hide it. I just want it to be private, just for me.

But now, as I stand, looking in the mirror with my shirt held up to approve the placement while trying not to flash the guys too much side boob, I'm realizing I didn't think this placement through logistically.

"That's going to be killer," Dean says.

"Badass and sexy," Logan agrees.

"How does it look?" Tyler is sitting a few feet away, filling a tiny cup with black ink.

I'm actually doing this. "Good," I say, walking back to the chair, nervous laughter bubbling up in my throat.

I lie down on my side and raise my arm over my head so Tyler can lift my shirt over the stencil. He's careful not to expose any more skin than necessary, and I'm grateful for that. He's being completely professional and I'm only slightly shaking.

The guys are crowded around, loudly discussing what they're going to have done. Logan wants something with a tiger. Dean wants a new piercing but will apparently need a private room for it. Joey has a piece on his arm that needs a color touch up, and he also wants more tacos.

Tyler turns his machine on. It's loud, vibrating, buzzing, menacing. I close my eyes.

"Why don't you guys go talk to Leah and Skillet about what you want? It's on me tonight," I hear Tyler say.

The guys excitedly shuffle away, their voices dying down as they go. Now all I can hear is the tattoo gun. I squeeze my eyes shut tighter.

"Just relax." Tyler's voice is calm, completely cool.

I try to relax. I really do. But my heart is pounding and I feel a cold sweat all over my skin. My hands are balled in fists and I don't think I've taken a breath in a while.

"All right, here we go. The ribs are a sensitive spot, but this won't take long, okay?"

I nod my head, keeping my eyes clamped shut and willing my body to hold still as I feel Tyler lean over me, his gloved hand on my skin and the tattoo gun louder, closer.

The first touch is a razor blade to my flesh, sharp and burning.

I let out a whimper.

Then a warm hand slips into my cold fist, large fingers gentle but firmly holding on.

"Just breathe," he says in a deep, quiet tone. His voice

a soothing caress.

My eyes shoot open and Colin is sitting right next to me, my hand in both of his, leaned in close, blue eyes locked on me.

He encourages me to take a few deep breaths with him and I do. Colin is freaking holding my hand. And I feel better? Yes. I'm still literally being repeatedly stabbed by a needle right now and it really hurts, but I'm okay.

"It's not even the pain, really. I just hate needles so much." I try to smile but tears are starting to well in my eyes. "Dumb, right?"

He shakes his head and I cringe when Tyler hits a spot with absolutely no fleshy cushion, just skin and a rib bone.

"I'm terrified of heights," Colin says.

All I can do is grimace, so he continues.

"I freak out about flying. It's not so much the flying, but the falling part that scares me. When I was five, I climbed into a tree to try and save my neighbor's cat. The cat just scratched the hell out of me and then jumped out of the tree. But I couldn't climb down. It looked so much higher from up there than it had from the ground. I was so scared I couldn't move. I stayed in that tree, frozen, for three hours until my dad came home and got me down. I had scrapes on my knees and cuts on my hands from where I was gripping the branch so tightly." He pauses and looks down, like he's still affected by the story, and squeezes my hand a little tighter.

"All done," Tyler says, knocking me out of Colin's story.

"Really?"

Tyler nods, wiping lotion on my reddened skin, and gives me some after-care instructions.

Colin leans in closer. "You did great," he whispers, the

heat of his lips so close to my ear I can almost feel them.

I can't force any sound out, so I just mouth the word, "Thanks."

I get up to see it in the mirror. It's perfect. On my ribs, in low, dragged-out cursive are the words *take the leap*.

* * *

Logan and Joey show me around Vegas the following afternoon. I can't go into the bars or gamble in the casinos, but we do other touristy stuff, like see the fountains at the Bellagio, take our picture in front of the Vegas sign, and eat dinner at In-N-Out Burger.

I send Kyla the picture of us in front of the sign to prove I am, in fact, in Las Vegas. She's unimpressed by the lack of male nudity in the photo.

"You ready for the game tonight?" Logan stuffs no fewer than five animal-style fries into his mouth.

"Is there a baseball game or something?"

"Oh no. I've been slacking on my gamemaster duties so far this tour, and tonight we're going to fix that."

"Another drinking game?" I'll have to do a better job at pacing myself.

"Nope." He smirks.

"Will there be more girls than last time?" Joey asks, sauce dripping from his burger down his chin.

"Yeah. Jace says the girls from last night are in and they're bringing a few more friends."

More girls? "What are we playing?"

"Spin the bottle." Logan winks.

* * *

I chug my fuzzy navel while Logan and Dean take shots.

"Okay, I think everyone's here. Game time," Logan says.

I sit on the green carpet in the hotel room, my cheeks hot.

"Dean, come sit here." Logan pats the spot on the floor between him and me. "I can't sit next to Gracie."

Dean comes to sit by me, smelling of whiskey.

"Why not?"

"It's bad luck to sit next to the person you're hoping to kiss," he says to me, his dark eyes sparkly.

Oh.

My ears feel hot, and I try to suppress nervous laughter.

Jace, a couple Boners, and four chicks sit on my other side, already drunk and giggly. The girl from last night's show sits directly next to me on my left.

"I'm Marnie." She smiles and holds out a manicured hand.

"Gracie." We shake and even in the poorly lit hotel room, this close, I can see she's wearing more makeup than I probably own, but there's no denying she's pretty. And her eyebrow-shaping skills are amazing. I might have to ask her for pointers later.

"So, Gracie." She moves in, lowering her voice. "Are you *with* one of the Wicked Road guys?"

"With? Oh, no." I let out a strange giggle I've never heard before. "No, I'm just friends with them."

"So...none of them are taken, then?"

"Not that I know of."

"Perfect!"

I turn back to the circle as Joey squeezes in between two of the groupie girls, apologizing as he bumps them.

"Didn't think you were joining us," Logan says loudly, and I turn just as Colin sits down on the other side of him.

He's dressed all in black again, his square jaw tightening as he ignores Logan's comment.

"Okay, so for the rules—" Logan starts.

"No choice rule," Colin cuts in.

He and Logan face each other, locked in a silent argument.

"What does that mean?" I whisper to Dean.

"Usually when we play spin the bottle, the rule is the spinner gets to pick where the other person has to kiss them."

My eyes widen. Oh.

"Fine," Logan finally agrees after a minute. "Lips only this time. But the bottle rule is still in play. So everyone make sure your drinks are open. You can't spin it until it's empty."

"Start us off, brother." Logan says to Dean who immediately starts chugging his beer.

Oh shit. I better finish mine quick too.

Dean sets his bottle in the middle of the circle and spins. We're all smashed tightly together, watching the bottle spin on the ugly carpet, and it's so quiet I think everyone is holding their breath.

It slows after several seconds and then comes to a rest, the neck of the bottle pointed squarely at Colin.

"Ah, spin again," Boner Two says, waving his beer in the air.

"That's not how the game works," Logan says.

Three out of Four Boners' jaws drop.

"Grow the fuck up," Colin says, rolling his eyes. Then he leans into the circle as Dean crawls on all fours toward him.

"Seriously, though, no tongue this time."

"You're no fun." Dean sticks his pierced tongue out at him.

They meet in the middle of the circle and their lips meet for only a second, but the sight of Colin's pouty pink lips pressed against Dean's metal lip ring stirs something low in my stomach.

Dean sits back next to me with a smug smile on his lips. "You're up," he says to me.

I chug the last few gulps of my drink then place the bottle on the floor in what feels like slow-motion. Blood pumping. Hand trembling as I spin it.

I will the bottle not to stop. I just need it to keep spinning until I can calm down, maybe another twenty minutes or so. But it stops spinning after only about three rotations and lands on one of the groupie chicks. I don't even know her name.

We put our hands in the center of the circle and kiss quickly to the appreciative hoots of several of those around us. Her lip gloss tastes like berry-flavored rubber. I guess I can cross *kiss a stranger* off the Fuck-It list.

Marnie goes next. Her bottle also points to another girl, but they decide to put on more of a show. Kissing over and over, flashing tongue and touching each other's arms. Joey's eyes are wide like a deer in headlights as he watches.

Jace hollers for them to keep going. He, however, is less enthusiastic when his bottle spin lands on Boner One. They keep their eyes screwed tightly shut as their lips touch for the briefest of moments.

"Dude, your lips are really soft," Boner One says.

"Fuck off." Jace downs his beer.

We go around the rest of the circle until the last two

spinners are left—Colin and Logan.

Colin takes his turn and I watch the bottle turn. My pulse is racing so fast, but every time it passes me my heart stops. My breathing is quick and shallow.

I can't take it.

The bottle starts to slow down...slower...slower...and then it's just about to stop as the neck of the bottle points toward me. It goes just a couple degrees further so it lands between me and Marnie.

Heat pulses under my skin as all the blood in my body pounds through my veins. *That's definitely closer to me, right?*

I look at Colin. He's already looking at me. His eyes hooded by his thick, black lashes. His lips are parted and he licks them, his chest rises, his breathing just as fast as mine.

"Yay!" Marnie moves to the center of the circle, smiling big at Colin.

His eyes flick to her then back to me. "I don't think—"

But she's already moving on him. She wraps her hand around the back of his neck and plants a kiss right on his closed mouth, holding it for several seconds too long, in my opinion, and ending it with a loud smack of her red lips.

She has a pleased smile on her face as she retreats to take her spot next to me. After she stole my kiss. Colin is expressionless.

I don't even notice when Logan spins the bottle for his turn, but now it's slowing and when it comes to rest, clearly pointing directly at me, I don't feel any of the excitement I did a few moments ago.

Logan's smile is huge, full of genuine happiness. It lights up his whole face from his puppy dog brown eyes to his adorable chin dimple. I return the smile and Dean whispers, "Go get it girl," from behind closed teeth with a nudge of his elbow.

Logan meets me halfway in the circle, still smiling, still cute. But I can't help but glance past his shoulder to Colin. His face stony, unreadable, hard.

Logan leans in and then his lips are on mine. They're warm, the kiss gentle, his hand lightly on my cheek. Nice. Holding my face, he deepens the kiss, moving his mouth against mine, but he doesn't try to slip in any tongue.

Someone whistles and I end the kiss, feeling my face get hot.

Logan wraps an arm around my shoulder. "Game's officially over, guys."

"Strip club?" Jace asks.

"Hell, yeah," yells Boner Four.

Everyone starts to get up from the circle.

Logan tilts his head toward me. "Want to hang out with me a little longer?"

"Sure," I say, not thinking much of it.

He steers me toward the door, his arm still slung across my back. We pass Colin, standing with his hands in his pockets, his gaze fixed on me. To anyone else, his expression would look like one of indifference, but being on the other end of his sharp stare, his blue eyes like daggers, I know he's anything but indifferent.

* * *

Apparently, "hang out" meant alone, in Logan's room, sitting on the bed and watching a weird movie together. Logan talks through most of it, though. He asks me questions about growing up and he's absolutely fascinated with the fact I live on a ranch and know how to saddle a horse and rope calves.

"Honestly, I don't do much ranch work. I'm the baby of the family, and by the time I was old enough to work, my brothers were already teenagers and my dad didn't really need my help. So I tended to help my mom inside more. I liked cooking and especially baking."

"So if I visit you on your ranch, you can show me how to ride a horse *and* bake me a pie."

I chuckle. "Yeah, I guess."

"Cool."

He's been in a semi-reclined position with his legs crossed a few feet away from me but now he's sitting up and scooting closer to me. He's only a few inches away, his arm brushing mine, his body turned toward me, looking at my face, my mouth.

"So, Gracie…" He swallows, his voice abnormally quiet. "I enjoyed our kiss earlier."

"Yeah. Me, too." For some reason I can't bring myself to look up from my hands clasped in my lap.

"Can I kiss you again?"

"Um—" I look at him, my throat tightening and my pulse quickening. "Yeah, okay."

He closes the space between us. The kiss is slow but firm. He slips an arm around my waist as he presses against me, his lips moving more greedily. His tongue invades my mouth and I don't know what to do with my hands. *Where should I put my hands?*

Logan is a good kisser. It's not too wet or too dry. And he's super cute and super nice. *But what the fuck do I do with my hands?* I end up sort of clinging to his shoulders while trying not to rub against him with my boobs or let him inadvertently touch the tender spot on my ribs from my tattoo.

He's leaning harder into me so I have to push back against him to stay upright. I think he mistakes this for enthusiasm because he tightens his arm around me and lays me down on my back.

Nope.

I pop up, eyes wide.

"You know, my ribs still really hurt. I probably shouldn't… I'm going to go, I'm sorry—"

Logan sits up too, running his hand through his hair. "No, I'm sorry. That's totally fine. I didn't mean to move too fast—"

"I'm fine. I mean, I'm good. It's—thanks."

"I'll walk you to your room."

"That's okay. I'm right across the hall."

"All right." Logan nods.

He gives me a small smile and I awkwardly wave as I walk to the door.

I close the door behind me and turn toward the hall. Colin is walking by with an ice bucket and our eyes meet as I stand here, my hand still on the door handle to Logan's room.

His mouth is tight and then he says, "Might want to fix your shirt."

I look down. My shirt is completely askew, the side seam twisted to the front at the bottom, my black bra strap also clearly visible.

Ohmygod.

But I can't move and just watch in horror as Colin walks away, his face still blank.

CHAPTER 10

Me: *I made out with Logan*

    Kyla: *OMG I've waited my whole life for this moment tell me everything*

    Me: *It's been one week*

    Kyla: *Right. A lifetime long week. Now. Tell. Me. Everything. When did this happen? Where were you? How was it?*

    Me: *Last night. In his room. It was nice. He's a good kisser.*

    Kyla: *Were you on the bed?*

    Me: *Yes*

    Kyla: *Squeeeee!!!!! Please tell me you were wearing the sexy underwear*

    Me: *It didn't get that far.*

    Kyla: *Boo! Why not?*

    Me: *Let's just say that when I left the room, my "sexy" underwear was very dry.*

    Kyla: *I'm deceased.*

    Me: *What should I do?*

    Kyla: *Shit, there are like three other guys in the band, right? See if one of them does it for you*

    Me: *Not helpful. I mean, what do I say to him?*

    Kyla: *Just be honest, it's not like you guys were dating and* you've only known each other for a week, I'm sure he'll get over it

Me: *But what if it gets awkward now?*

Kyla: *If things get weird and you don't want to be there anymore you march right off that bus and don't get back on. Send me your GPS location and I will drive through the night to get to you*

Me: *Thanks Ky*

Kyla: *Love you G.*

Kyla: *Srsly tho, sample as much hottie Rockstar dick as you can. It's basically your duty as my best friend so I can live vicariously through you*

* * *

We have to check out and be on the bus by eleven to head north to the next show, which is in Salt Lake City. I've never been and Logan tells me it's beautiful there, but everything closes at six pm and the beer tastes like beer-flavored water. As he's telling me this, we're sitting at the dinette table on the bus, his arm around my shoulders. It seems his arm has been glued to this spot all day.

Dean and Colin are napping and Joey is listening to headphones, rocking out on the little couch across from us. He's impressively skilled at the air drums, air guitar, and lip syncing.

This would be a good time to tell him, right? I rehearse what I want to say in my head but nothing sounds right.

I really enjoyed kissing you last night, but I just want to be friends.

I like you, I just don't like like you.

You're so nice and I can tell you like me, but I think I

actually have a thing for the guy who only frowns at me and doesn't even want me here.

Oh, boy.

"Hey, Logan?"

"Yeah?" He cocks his head toward me with a lopsided smile, his chin dimple out in full force.

But then Dean walks out, rubbing his eyes and I hastily abort said talk. I slip out from under Logan's arm and force an unnaturally big smile.

"I'm actually going to go nap for a bit before the show." And then I scuttle away to my bunk.

During the show, Logan keeps glancing back to my spot just offstage. Smiling, winking, waving. He even blows a kiss at one point.

After the show, the Donkey Lips guys complain that there aren't any bars to go to so they invite us back to their bus to smoke some weed.

Logan initially accepts their offer, but when I say I'd rather chill on our bus, he says he'll join me instead.

The next two days are travel days as we drive to Oregon. I'm literally only feet away from him on the bus at all times. His presence is constant, which means I should have ample opportunity to talk with him. But the other guys are constantly here too, which means Logan hasn't gotten me alone. Good news: he hasn't tried to kiss me again. Bad news: I keep putting off the talk. What if, when I tell him, he goes from following me around like a sweet puppy to treating me with cold indifference? The way Colin treats me.

The longer I don't have the discussion with Logan, the worse I feel, the bigger it feels, the harder it feels to do. It's my school situation all over again.

* * *

It's day three after the abruptly ended makeout session. After sleeping all day, we stop to fill up and get some food just before nightfall. I hang back a little as the guys all run ahead into the store. I've started to lose my appetite again.

I make my way slowly to the glass doors when I hear a voice from my left.

"You should tell him."

I glance over and Colin is standing near the corner of the building, almost hidden away.

"Tell who what?" I walk over to him.

"Logan. Tell him you're not interested."

"Who says I'm not?"

He looks at me for minute with hard eyes. "Are you?"

I hold my head up. "That's none of your business."

"If it has to do with my band or is happening on my bus, it's my business."

He doesn't want you here.

I cross my arms, and when I don't reply, he continues, "You went back to his room with him the other night—"

"I'm an adult, not a *child*. I can do whatever or whoever I want." My face feels hot, my heart is beating a hundred miles a minute, and I have no idea how he managed to get me so worked up so fast.

Colin, on the other hand, is still calm, completely unaffected. "I think I already told you I don't give a shit about what you do. You can do whatever you want."

Guess he wasn't jealous about me kissing Logan. Just despises me.

Colin lowers his eyes to me, his dark lashes casting

shadows on his cheekbones and he says, quieter, "He didn't try to get you to do something you didn't want to do, did he?"

It takes me a moment to register what he's insinuating. "What? No! We just kissed." It comes out all in a rush. "What would make you think that?"

"You haven't been yourself since. You haven't been eating or talking much. You haven't smiled."

He's noticed I haven't smiled?

"It's nothing like that."

"Good." He steps closer and I have to look up as his tall figure looms above. "Now tell him you don't want to do it again."

I swallow hard. "Why would I do that?"

His voice is a hoarse whisper. "Because it's true."

"Fine. But I was going to talk to him, anyway. I'm not doing it just because you told me to." There. Take that.

Shit, I *do* sound like a defiant child.

Colin's lips don't move but somehow it still looks like he's smirking at me. "You're stressing yourself out over it— you don't need to. Logan will be just fine, trust me."

And then he walks past me toward the doors without a glance back.

Shit. Now I've really got to do this.

* * *

I BUY A BOTTLE OF WATER AND SOME APPLE JUICE. THE IDEA OF eating any food right now makes my stomach turn.

"Hey Logan."

He stops in front of the bus and turns around to me. The other guys all climb on, carrying their bags of snacks and drinks.

"Can I talk to you for a second?"

"That sounds serious." He sets his bag down on the ground and follows me around the back of the bus. "What's up?"

"Uh." *Deep breaths, deep breaths.* "I just…it's just that… There's no privacy on the bus so I haven't had the chance… I wanted to talk about the other night…after spin the bottle…"

Bah, take a breath.

Logan nods along with me, but the little crease forming between his brows definitely means he's either confused or concerned or both.

Gracie, strap on your lady balls and say it already! I pause for a second then finally push it all out in one breath. "Logan, I really like you, but, like, as a friend, and I really want to just stay friends, if that's okay with you."

I finally let out a breath and his face breaks into a wide grin as he chuckles.

"Yeah, sure, that's cool with me."

That's it? "Yeah?"

He laughs a little harder. "Of course. I'm a little bummed. I think you're super hot. But I also think you're pretty awesome and fun to hang out with and I'm glad to have you as a friend."

He gives me a playful elbow nudge and his easy-going smile as we get on the bus. And true to his word, he doesn't treat me like anything less than a cherished friend after the talk. Logan decides we should play poker and breaks out the cards. We start with five card draw. Dean is amazing at shuffling and dealing. Joey can't bluff for shit—even I can tell he's lying when his forehead immediately starts to sweat. Apparently, Logan never folds. Even when he really, really should. And Colin is just stupid good at poker. I don't know why that would be surprising—he only practices his poker face every day of his life.

They teach me how to play Texas Hold 'Em and I get by mostly on beginner's luck. We laugh and joke, and Joey and Logan share their stash of junk food with me, which I happily dive into, my appetite finally returning.

After the show the next night, we decide to go out and eat our weight in seven different kinds of chicken wings rather than to the club where the Donkey Lips guys are going. And while plenty of beers are consumed, it's nice to just hang out with my four guys doing something low-key and laughing until my stomach hurts.

The next afternoon, before the second Oregon show, my stomach legitimately hurts. Sonofabitch, I'm not prepared for this. Literally—I only have two tampons. *How the hell did I forget to pack tampons?*

When the guys go off for their pre-show stuff I walk down to the corner and get my feminine things. Then I go back to the bus, lie down, and text Logan that I'm not feeling well enough to go to the show.

I curl into a ball in my bunk and nap.

I'm woken up by the sound of heavy feet and whispers and rustling bags. When I pop my head out of the curtain, all four of them turn to look at me and ask me how I'm feeling and apologize for waking me. They have an array of snacks. Logan offers me an extra pillow and blanket. Joey even brought me hot broth from the Vietnamese restaurant across the street. It's all so sweet.

Then Colin hands me a little bag. "I don't know what your favorite is, but here." He looks at me expectantly, his hands in his pockets.

I look in the bag and there's a family size bag of peanut butter M&Ms and a bottle of ibuprofen. "Thank you, this is...perfect."

He gives me a little nod before going to sit next to Dean on the couch. At first I expect they're going to leave to do their after party thing, but they don't leave. They stay on the bus with me all night. I sit between Colin and Dean on the couch while Joey and Logan sit on the floor. When I sit down, Colin doesn't move all the way over on the couch but stays close enough that his knee keeps touching my leg.

We watch silly videos of cats and kittens and puppies. And puppies with kittens. And kittens with bunnies. Soon we're in a spiral of cuteness so deep we don't come out until the sun starts rising in through the windows.

The next couple days, we drive north into Washington, and by the Tacoma show, I'm feeling much better. I sit just offstage watching their set. By now I have it memorized. I find myself singing along with some of the lyrics, wishing I was out in the audience so I could experience the full energy of the show. If I was out in the crowd, would Colin's eyes find me, lock on mine like they did at the wedding? Would he sing the songs like they were each meant for me?

Maybe I'd just imagined that moment at the wedding. Maybe there was no connection. He probably doesn't even remember. Maybe he never saw me at all.

The next day, we head to Seattle and before the show we explore downtown. We go to Pike Place Market and eat fish and chips near the water and walk to the Space Needle. The view from the top is spectacular.

"Can we get a picture?" I ask, pulling out my phone.

"Sure, Blondie."

I stand in front of the windows excitedly and the guys gather around. Colin stands next to me. "Here." He holds his hand toward my phone.

I give it to him and he holds the phone up with one long arm as the other one wraps lightly around my back.

His side is pressed against me and he smells just as good as I remember from when I woke up on top of him. Logan is on my other side, and we all squeeze in as Colin takes the picture. Then he's away from me as quickly as it began. His hands are shaky when he gives me back my phone. He stuffs them swiftly in his pockets.

"Are you all right?" I ask.

"Uh, yeah." His eyes flash to the window then back to me. "We're just... It's really high up here."

Oh right. He's afraid of heights.

"Hey, let's go get some food. I'm starving," I say to the guys.

Joey is, naturally, immediately on board, and the twins start heading to the exit yelling something about getting lobster with their butter.

As we leave I glance to Colin and he gives me the tiniest of nods.

Later on the bus, I look at the picture. Logan and Dean have almost the exact same smile. Joey's eyes are half closed. Colin's not smiling in the picture like the other guys, but I can see his tattooed fingers curling around my hip and I can't stop staring at them.

I send the picture to Kyla as further reassurance I am, in fact, in Seattle and alive.

Kyla: *Damn girl, you look great, like you're glowing*

Kyla: *Also the one with the tattoos, idk is that the singer???*

He definitely needs to be your next conquest

Me: *Ugh, he doesn't even like me*

Kyla: *Could have fooled me, but honestly that's even better, HATE FUCK!*

Me: *OMG I'm not going to have my first time be a hate fuck*

Kyla: *Ok, ask him to do you real nice the first time THEN hate fuck*

Me: *No*

Kyla: *Please*

* * *

"Need help with your technique?" Logan raises his eyebrows at me.

"Nope. I'm good."

He shrugs and racks the balls. "You break."

I place the cue ball in the center of the red felt. I have to lean over to get a good angle for the break. I'm keenly aware that Colin and Dean are sitting at a table directly behind me and I'm wearing my very short cut-off jean shorts again. I line up my shot and with a deafening bang and clapping of balls, I sink several into the pockets.

"I'll take solids." I walk around the table, and I can feel Colin's eyes on me, following my movements, lingering.

I'm definitely, most likely, probably just imagining this.

Logan still has four balls on the table when I bank shot the eight ball for the win. He insists on best two out of three. He has five balls left when I win the second time.

"My turn, Blondie." Dean saunters over, chalking up a new stick.

At the end, we're both going for the eight ball but I

manage to get it in first.

"Damn, girl. You're good. I'm going to try my luck with darts." Dean walks across the bar to where Joey, Logan, and a couple Boners are playing darts and drinking pitchers of beer.

Colin stands from the table. He's tall and lean, and the harsh light plays with the contours of his face. His white shirt is so threadbare that I can see the black eagle wings spread across his chest through it. He takes a step toward me and my stomach flips.

Be cool. I give him a small smile. If he wants to play, I can beat him too.

But then Jace and Boner One are at the table. Jace grabs a stick with a crooked grin. "I want a go with you, Gracie," he says my name in the weird, slow way he likes to say it.

I glance back to Colin, but he's already walking to the back toward the restrooms.

Hate fuck in a bar bathroom? Shut up, Gracie. That's definitely not how I'd want my first time.

"I'm ready for you," Jace says.

"I'll let you break."

He's terrible at breaking.

Jace and Boner One make ball jokes and snicker the whole time we play. I'm trying to end the game fast, but when they start making jokes about who has the bigger stick and gesturing with said sticks between their legs, I'm out.

I look around the bar. I don't see Colin or Dean. Joey and Logan are still playing darts but now a couple of girls have joined them. Logan is standing behind a cute girl with curly dark blonde hair. His face is at her cheek, one hand on her hip while the other one guides the dart in her hand, showing her how to throw it.

I tell Boner One to finish the game and I walk straight out to the parking lot and onto the bus.

* * *

"There you are."

He says it like he's been looking for me.

I glance up from my notebook, shutting it quickly.

The little light over the dining table where I'm sitting is on—otherwise the bus is dark and only the silvery light shining in from the moon illuminates Colin as he walks up the steps.

"What are you writing?"

"Oh it's nothing, really." I push my notebook to the side and tuck a lock of hair behind my ear.

"Is that a diary or journal?"

"Um, no. It's just where I sometimes write little notes, thoughts. Poems mostly."

I look at him standing there, his white shirt partially tucked into his black jeans, revealing the waistband sitting low on his hips. He's half-painted in blue shadow and shimmering moonlight, the skin of his arms highlighted as it peeks through the black ink. He's all contrast.

"It's dumb, really." I wave it off with a small smile.

He cocks his head. "I doubt that." He disappears toward the back of the bus and reappears after only a moment. "I'll show you mine if you show me yours," he says, the look in his eyes deviant, but playful.

"Show you my what?" I'm confused.

He holds up a black journal. "You can read mine if I can

see yours."

"You write poetry?"

"I write songs, so that's kind of the same thing, yeah?" He sits across from me and hands over his book. It's thick and slightly bent, curling at the edges. Some pages stick out farther than others, slightly askew as they've gotten loose.

The urge to take it and read through it is overwhelming. To get into Colin's head.

But then I'll have to give him mine.

He's still holding it out to me. He glances down to my pink notebook and back to me, amusement in his eyes at my hesitation. Then it happens. He smiles at me. It's too brief.

"You don't have to."

And suddenly, I want to.

I've never shown my writing to anyone, but in this moment, on this dark, quiet bus with no one else around, I can feel the connection again. Something that tells me he'd understand.

I silently slide my book to him and take his in my hands.

He opens mine immediately and I watch him read. His face is downturned so I can only see his thick lashes. He stays on each page for a long time, laser-focused on my words, and it makes my chest ache. He turns each page delicately.

I open his. It's all in black pen. Some pages are covered in words, going in all directions, paragraphs with words and lines crossed out violently, notes vertically up the margins. Some of the writing is neat, some all caps, some so slanted and angular it's like he was writing in a furious frenzy. Some pages just have a few lines and some are entire songs. Some pages are half-nonsensical words and random doodles. I recognize many of the lines and lyrics in the front of the notebook from their songs.

> *Everyday*
> *I must keep it at bay*
> *At bay*
> *At bay*
> *At bay*
> *It's made of black and smoke and nightmares*
> *Everything ugly, everything that scares*
> *He's inside me*
> *Always waiting, always ready*
> *He wants out*
> *I must keep him at bay*
> *At bay*
> *At bay*
> *At bay*

"What's this one about?"

He looks over to where my fingers are splayed on the page.

"Addiction," he says matter-of-factly.

"Oh." I'm a little flustered. I didn't realize I was asking about something so personal, private.

He doesn't look upset, but maybe he's just that good at concealing his emotions. He keeps looking at me, almost as if he's waiting for me to ask another question. I do want to ask him more. *Is it about your addiction? What kind of addiction? Drugs? Alcohol? Sex?* But when I don't say anything else, he drops his focus back to my notebook.

I do the same. I keep turning. Keep reading. I don't know how, but I can feel the emotion in each word as if I was sitting in the room as he wrote them. Anger, heartbreak, sadness.

As I go further into the book, I can tell the writing is newer, the ink blacker, fresher. The last page before they go blank screams frustration. Nearly every line is crossed out so many times I can't read what's behind them. But I make out one of them.

I can't have her.

I want to ask him about that line. But I don't. I already feel like he's sort of letting me in, letting me catch a glimpse of his soul. I don't want to take too much.

"These are all amazing," he says, closing my book.

I look up at him. "Really?"

"Yeah. The way you describe things in so few words but with such richness—it's fantastic. You're really talented."

"Wow, thanks." I hand him back his journal. "I'm sure you already know how talented you are. Everything in here is really cool and authentic."

He runs his teeth over his lower lip as he slides my notebook back to my side of the table. "I have a new song idea I've been working out in my head for a little while. It's different than our usual stuff. Maybe you could help me with it sometime?"

"Okay." The word just comes out. I think my brain has stopped functioning.

* * *

The next night, Logan invites the girl from the bar to the concert. Her name is Christine and she's very nice. It's totally fine and not weird that I'm sharing my special spot backstage with her to watch the show. Not weird at all.

"Game time!" Logan yells, after the show. He's standing in the middle of the living area on the bus, swaying as we ride to the hotel, one arm around Christine to keep his balance and a bottle of tequila in his other hand.

"What are we playing, babe?" Christine asks in a sugary sweet voice.

"King's cup."

"What's King's cup?" I lean over and ask Dean.

"Sort of a card game. Basically a way to get drunk real fast."

I don't know if I feel like getting drunk tonight. It's been a week and a half since the game of spin the bottle, and that got a little weird. I'm especially hesitant as we're walking up to Logan's room and the Donkey Lips guys join us, hyped up on their post-concert high, already yelling, and they have no groupies with them tonight. I repeat, only two of us have boobs and Christine's are currently glued to Logan's side.

"You playing with us tonight, Wolfe?" Logan asks while trying to unlock the door to his room. It takes him three tries.

"I'm playing if she is." He cocks his head toward me.

Me.

He only wants to play if I do?

Now everyone's eyes are on me and I can feel heat rising to my cheeks as they all wait for my response.

"Yeah, I'll play."

I'm nervous as I sit with my beer to play. Is Colin going to start paying me attention? Is he interested in me? Maybe it was reading each other's writing last night. Maybe he's feeling this attraction too.

I can't even focus, and I don't notice until it's too late that Boner Two and Boner Three sit on either side of me—closer than necessary, I'll add—and Colin might as well be across the room.

As we play, he doesn't talk to me or even make eye contact. The only thing he seems to take notice of is when I open my second beer.

Then I realize it. He's babysitting me.

Now that Logan is preoccupied with another girl, he's taken it upon himself to watch out for the toddler. Was that what he was doing on the bus too? Did he even care about reading my poetry? He probably thought it was silly and immature, like he still thinks of me.

I chug my beer, just to test this theory. It definitely grabs his attention. He doesn't say anything, but his jaw is clenched, and his eyes follow me as I reach for another one.

On a side note—I don't know how long it takes to acquire a taste for beer, but it hasn't happened for me yet.

"Let's do some shots!" I say, fisting the cheap bottle of vodka instead.

If he wants to be Mary-Fucking-Poppins, I'll give him something to worry over.

It's probably a good thing the vodka is so shitty because in the last two hours I've only been able to stomach one and a half shots of it. I'm feeling a decent buzz, but I think I'd puke before I'd be able to get drunk off this stuff. Everyone—except Colin, of course—has joined in and now the bottle is officially empty.

Colin is standing moodily against the wall while Joey and Dean play a game of quarters with Boners One and Four. Logan and Christine are connected at the mouth on the chair in the corner. I'd tell them to go get a room already, but we're in Logan's room so...

Currently, Jace and Boner Two and Boner Three are arguing over top of me about some sort of video game. I'm thinking it's probably time to call it a night and head to my room but then they're directing their comments to me. I have no idea what they're talking about so I just sort of nod and smile.

Jace steps a little closer.

I glance around him. I don't see Colin. Did he leave?

"Hey Gracie, you want to keep the party going back in my room?"

A stare at him for a second, frozen in a mixture of confusion and shock. "No thanks." I make a move to step away but all three of them are around me and they don't move.

"Okay," Jace says with a shrug. But he still doesn't move.

I look over to Logan. He's still making out with Christine. She's now fully in his lap and they're practically tearing at each other's clothes.

"I thought you liked to party," one of the Boners says.

Both Boners take a step in.

"All partied out." I move toward Joey and Dean, who are too focused on their game.

"Where you going?" Jace asks.

"I think she said she's done talking to you." Colin's low voice from behind me sends a cool wave of relief through my body.

"I didn't hear her say that, did you?" Jace says, straightening his shoulders.

"Take a fucking hint."

The Boners slink away with wary expressions, but Jace

doesn't budge.

"I don't see your name on her. How about you let her speak for herself?"

I glance between the two men. Colin's hands are fisted at his sides, his forearms flexed. I don't need his misguided protection.

"You know what? You're both right." I look at Colin. "I can speak for myself." Then I turn to Jace. "And I am definitely done talking to you."

I stomp toward the door, feeling for my room key in my pocket.

"Wait—" Colin reaches a hand out for me. "Can we talk?"

I turn on him, my arms folded. "I don't really want to talk to you, either."

He has the audacity to look taken aback, his blue eyes wide. He steps back and we stand there face-to-face for several beats.

"Please?"

I tighten my arms across my chest. "Fine." I wait for him to go on, but he doesn't.

"In private?" He tilts his head toward the door.

I'm not in the mood to get criticized about irresponsible choices, but I do want out of this room, so I follow Colin out and to his room down the hall.

He shuts the door behind us then runs his hands over his short hair.

"Listen, what you need to know about those guys is that they've been on the road for almost the last two years straight, and there are two types of girls that travel with a band. Girlfriends and groupies."

"But I'm not—"

"I know. I've told them that and to leave you alone, but I can't get it through their heads. Frankly, that's not the body part they think with most of the time."

That's obvious.

Colin continues, "In their minds, if you're not fucking one of us on the regular, you're fair game. They're not going to stop hitting on you."

"I can handle myself. I don't need you to be my chaperone. I'll be more careful around them in the future. Thanks for the lecture, but I'm going to go." I head for the door.

"Gracie, wait—"

I snap back at the sound of my name on his lips. "What?"

"I'm not trying to lecture you." He sighs, rubbing his temple. "I don't like those guys, but I have to play nice with them. The label is signing us, but the results of this tour will determine how good our contract is. This could be our one chance, our big break. They're watching everything—not just the sales numbers but also our behavior. They want to know we're a good investment and aren't going to be the next internet scandal."

"Okay... What does that have to do with me?"

He drags his fingers over his scalp, grimacing as he speaks. "Because, if I have to watch them try to get on you for the rest of the tour I'm going to end up in jail for beating one or more of them into a bloody pulp."

My pulse races, the pounding in my ears obliterating any rational thoughts from forming as he continues.

"Gray, will you please let me tell them you're my girlfriend?"

CHAPTER 11

"What? You can't be serious."

"I am."

"I still don't understand why—"

"They're a bunch of morons, but they understand the unspoken rules. You don't mess with a band-mate or tour-mate's girlfriend."

My head is still swimming from his proposition. Pretend to be dating...Colin?

"This whole idea is ridiculous and I don't even think it will work. I mean, it would make more sense coming from Logan. Maybe he would be interested—"

"Do you know what Logan is doing right now?"

Oh yeah. "Christine."

"Yup. Logan likes to have fun, especially on tour. We wouldn't want to spoil his fun, now would we?"

"What about you? Wouldn't pretending to be tied down ruin your fun too?" I ask.

He rolls his eyes. "No."

"Really? You wouldn't feel like you were missing out?"

"If you mean missing out on pussy, no. I don't fuck groupies. I don't hook up with random women on the road, and I don't have one-night stands."

"Okay." That checks out. "But I don't think anyone will buy it—you and me, together."

He steps closer to me. "Then we will just have to convince them."

He's looking down at me, his lips parted. His stare is heavy on my skin.

"We can start right now," he says. My breath quickens as his eyes flash to my mouth. "Stay the night with me."

My eyes widen. "Excuse me?" I stutter.

He points behind him, an amused glint in his eyes. "There are two beds."

And, yep, there are two queen beds in this room.

"I'm only asking you to pretend," he says.

"You want me to pretend to be in a relationship with you?"

He nods.

Okay. I tilt my head, studying him. "And in this pretend relationship, I'm staying the night with you already?"

"Spending the night together doesn't have to mean we had sex—"

Ohmygod Colin is talking about us having sex—hypothetically, I realize—but still. I can feel the blush in my cheeks.

"—we could have just been cuddling all night," he finishes.

I burst out laughing. "Oh yeah, because that's believable."

"What? I fucking love cuddling."

I remember waking up on top of him in the van. He was so comfy and…yup, cuddly. He was holding me while he slept and didn't want to let me go when I moved

Holy crap. Colin Wolfe really does love cuddling.

I smile at the thought. "I don't know. This seems like a pretty extreme solution to a minor problem." Though, the more I think about it, having Colin pretend to be into me wouldn't be too bad.

"I don't think your safety and my sanity are minor things." He shoves his hands in his pockets. "It would really save me a lot of worry."

There it is. Why he's doing this. And my blood is boiling again.

"You know what? This whole thing is pretty messed up. They're not entitled to me just because I have a vagina. And if you don't want to have to worry about me, here's a tip. Don't. I'm a big girl. I'll deal with it. Contrary to what you may think, I do not need a babysitter."

"You're right, I'm sorry. I'm sure you can handle it." He rubs the back of his neck as he looks at the floor then back to my face. "You know the term, sex, drugs, and rock and roll? Well, I was nineteen when I started to understand its meaning. You don't really know the depravity of it until you're in too deep to get out. I wish someone had been there to look out for me."

"Look, I appreciate the sentiment, but I'm going to have to pass. Goodnight, Colin." I walk toward the door with my head held high.

"Night, Gray."

* * *

I'M THE FIRST ONE IN THE LOBBY THE NEXT DAY TO CHECK OUT. Of course the first person to come downstairs is Jace. He walks over with a smug look on his face.

"I'm still bummed we didn't get to hang out more last night." He tilts his head as he leans against the reception desk. "You and I could have a lot of fun together this summer. I could rock your world."

Gag me. "Does that line actually ever work for you? No, thanks." I step away, looking down the hall to the elevators, praying one of my guys will appear so I don't have to talk to Jace alone any more.

"Why not?" Jace asks, and I think he's genuinely mystified as to why I would decline his invitation to rock my world.

"I'm not interested." I back up a step.

"Oh, that's just because you don't know me very well. Luckily, we have time to get to know each other better. I think you'll find I'm very charming." He's closer again.

Fuck.

Boner Three emerges from the hallway headed for us. It's going to be just like last night again. Am I going to be stuck in some type of endless time loop of this? Cornered by Jace and Boners. So many Boners.

"You'll see," Jace says, completely cocksure.

No. No no no no no.

I think about Colin's proposal last night. Maybe he was right. Maybe he is the solution. Maybe just one tiny lie would do it.

I lower my voice. "Fine, I wasn't going to say anything because we've been keeping it quiet, but the real reason is Colin and I are seeing each other. Don't tell anyone, please."

Boner Three comes to stand next to us just as Logan and Christine walk out, holding hands.

Jace regards me with squinted eyes. "You and Wolfe? Are together but you're keeping it a secret?" He looks to

Boner Three. "What do you think?"

"Sounds weird to me."

"That's what I thought. Are you lying to me, honey?"

The rest of the Boners enter the lobby.

"No." My voice squeaks. I'm a terrible liar. "We just haven't told people yet, so if you'd keep it down—"

Logan and Christine join us with tired smiles and messy hair. I don't think they've gone to sleep at all yet.

"Yo, Logan"—Jace gestures toward me—"your girl Gracie here, her and Colin hooking up?"

"What? Of course not." Logan laughs off the idea.

Jace and Boner Three look at me for an explanation. All of the Boners are here now and Logan is looking at me in confusion.

Is it hot in here? I'm sweating.

Colin, Joey, and Dean are now walking toward us.

"Great, now we can clear this up. Hey Wolfe!" Jace shouts across the lobby.

My heart is pounding in my throat. Colin doesn't know to go along with this and I'm going to be found out as a liar and probably look pathetic too.

Colin already looks annoyed as he joins the group, his arms flexing under his black tattoos as he folds them across his chest and avoids eye contact with me.

"So what's the deal with you and Gracie?" Jace asks.

"The deal? What are you talking about?"

"Yeah, what are you talking about?" Logan joins in.

Jace looks at Colin. "She says you two are *together*." He says together with air quotes.

Now they're all looking at me with expressions that all very clearly express *what the fuck?* Except Christine, she looks pretty lost and chimes in that she's hungry.

Colin is staring at me unblinkingly. I try to plead to him with my eyes *help me* but he just looks at me stoically, contemplating. Maybe he's not going to save me. Maybe he's upset I turned down his idea last night. Maybe it was a one-time offer or he decided it really was a bad idea and doesn't want to do it anymore.

But then his hard mouth and blue eyes soften ever so slightly and he stalks toward me, never breaking eye contact.

"Yeah. We're together," he says matter-of-factly.

He reaches his hand out as he comes to me. He touches my cheek and then his fingers slide down and around to the back of my neck, pulling my hair away from my face. And I gape at him as he leans down, the whole thing in slow motion. I can feel the heat of his lips and breath as he whispers in my ear.

"This is a surprise." Then he presses his lips ever so softly to the side of my cheekbone.

He lingers there for a second. My cheek is warm where he kissed me. I've forgotten how to push breath out of my lungs or form words.

"For me too," I finally manage to say in a throaty whisper.

He gives me the tiniest of smirks as he straightens and slips his hand into mine, interlacing our fingers. He holds it the whole time we check out and as we exit the hotel. Logan keeps looking at us with a furrowed brow. Dean gives me a wink and a quick thumbs up as we walk, and Joey seems to have accepted it indifferently and joins Christine in championing the idea of going for food.

We'd normally go straight to the bus, but since checkout was at noon and the buses don't leave until three today, we walk across the street to a little Greek restaurant for lunch.

RAE KENNEDY

Of course I'm sitting next to Colin in the booth. Like, he scooted right up next to me, his arm slung on the back of the seat behind me, and his entire side is rubbing against mine. I repeat, *the entire length of Colin's body* is touching mine from shoulder to hip to thigh. The hot afternoon sun shines bright through the tall storefront windows and everyone else is busy in conversation, but I can't concentrate on anything else.

Colin is looking at the menu and saying something about falafel and splitting a hummus plate but I'm having a hard time listening. I'm just sitting here with my hands balled between my knees hoping I'm not being too obvious about how weird this feels.

After we order, he drops his arm down around my back, lightly stroking my bare arm with his fingertips. He does it so casually I wonder if he even realizes he's doing it. Because I do. Every touch, every circle and line he draws on my skin has my body on high alert.

He keeps his arm around me the whole time we eat. The guys talk about the small break we have after the next show and how excited they are that they're going to do some recording.

Colin leans in so his mouth is at my ear. "You're not eating. Are you okay?"

"I'm fine." I reach for a pita chip but don't turn to look at him so I don't turn into a hot pink mess.

"Is this too much for you?" He gently squeezes my arm so I know what he's referring to. "I can back off if you want."

No! "No, it's okay." I turn to him as I whisper the words and then we're face-to-face, so close I'd only have to lean in an inch to taste his lips.

His eyes flicker down to my mouth for a split second

and I wonder if he's thinking the same thing.

"Good," he says. Then he puts his lips back to my ear, our cheeks touching. "It would be okay if you pretended to like it. Or even return some affection, if you want."

"Oh. Yeah." Right. He's been acting super we're a couple this whole time and I've been sitting here like a cold fish.

Colin sits back up and I realize there's a lull in conversation and all eyes are on us.

"So." Logan looks between us. "When did this start?" He doesn't look mad or sound accusatory but his eyes give him away. Normally half-hooded and relaxed, now they are focused, unblinking. He's suspicious.

Colin looks at me, not at all rattled by the question. Guess I'm up.

"Not long." I try to keep the shakiness out of my voice. "Just since Seattle."

"Yeah, Seattle," Colin agrees, nodding as he turns back to Logan. "It's been a bit longer for me, though."

I'm not even sure what that means but it's making my heart thump wildly. He's so much better at this than me. I look up at him as he takes a sip of water, admiring the black tattoos that go right up to his square jaw. The other side of his neck is a rose and skull, but this side is a guitar and roses. I kind of want to touch them. I mean, I could. That would totally be a girlfriend thing to do, right? But reaching up and touching his neck or his jaw or his lips... I can't.

I'm going to just rest my hand lightly on his thigh. That's an affectionate thing that I can do. It takes me a second to work up the nerve to move my hand. I smile sweetly at him then awkwardly pat his leg before resting my hand there. I think I landed a little higher than I meant, but it's okay, I'm cool.

Colin looks at me from the side, his eyebrows raised in surprise. I glance down at my hand and it's much higher than I thought and the tips of my fingers are touching *not* leg.

Not leg.

Not.

Leg.

I snatch my hand away with a half-yelp-half-scream and cover my face with my hands. Heat rushes to my skin from my ears to my chest. I can't believe I touched his—I am mortified.

I peek between my fingers. I'm getting curious looks from around the table and when I turn to Colin, he's biting his lip to hold back his smile.

"What's going on over there?" Dean asks.

Colin lets go and lets out a laugh, low and melodic, his face is alight and beautiful. I lower my hands and smile because I don't know what else to do. All too soon, he's done laughing, but he's looking at me, his eyes still bright and happy. I made Colin Wolfe laugh.

"Private joke," Colin answers Dean, his eyes still on me.

I try to mouth *I'm sorry* to him but he wraps his arms around me and I'm in a tight embrace, my nose pressed against his firm chest. I breathe in the scent of him, his heartbeat steady against my temple.

"It's okay," he whispers against my hair.

And I feel warm and safe and like he doesn't think I'm a completely awkward and embarrassing virgin. But as soon as I'm no longer in the comforting cocoon of Colin's arms, I can't stop reliving the moment and I can't look him in the eyes.

We hold hands as we walk back to the bus but once

we're on, I go straight to my bunk.

* * *

It's dark when I wake up. I didn't close the curtain covering the tiny window all the way, and inky blue-green pine trees flash past as we speed by. I open the curtain wider to see the misty mountains glow gray and blue against the black night sky in the distance. The occasional passing car temporarily splashes the whole scene with blinding white light.

Then I hear the voices. So low I almost didn't notice. I'm awake so I pull back my privacy curtain to get up and join them when I hear the words and they make me freeze.

"You are such a hypocrite."

I don't have a good view of the seating area at the front of the bus, but I strain my neck just enough to make out two partial figures at the table. No lights are on and they sit shrouded in shadows. But I know who they are.

"I just don't get it," Logan says. "How many times did you remind me that she's still a teenager and the whole thing was a bad idea? Were you just pissed I brought her along because you wanted to fuck her yourself?"

"It wasn't like that." Colin's voice comes out like a growl. "And don't talk about her like that."

"Or were you just mad that I saw her first?"

There's a short pause and I imagine they're staring each other down, arms crossed, angry but restrained.

"You didn't see her first." I can barely hear Colin's words.

"What does that mean?"

"I saw her. At the wedding, during the first song. She was standing across the dance floor in her little peach bridesmaid dress and I sang to her. There was something between us. It was weird. But I think she felt it too."

More silence.

"Why didn't you just tell me you were into her? You know I would have stepped aside."

"Maybe I should have, but I wasn't going to act on it."

"But then you did." It's not a question.

"Yeah, I guess I couldn't help it."

One of them moves as if he's about to stand up. I pull my head back into my bunk and cover my face with my pillow to quiet my breathing.

I can't stop replaying the conversation in my head.

How much of what he said was a lie and how much was true?

CHAPTER 12

When I wake up a few hours later, it's quiet. Safe to get up. I grab one of the crossword puzzle books Dean got for me and head to the dining table.

Colin is sitting there, his black notebook open on the table in front of him. His eyes are closed holding a black pen between his teeth. I should go back to my bunk so I don't disturb him, but his eyes shoot open just as I start to shuffle backward.

"I'm sorry. I didn't mean to interrupt—"

"Come sit." His eyes on me are more intense than normal. I can almost see the storm swirling in them as he comes back from wherever he was just a moment ago, lost in his head.

I take small steps to the table and sit across from him.

"Are you writing?"

"Yeah. Well, trying."

I hold up the crossword puzzles. "I'll just be here working on this puzzle I started three days ago, silently berating myself for still not knowing the answer to four down. I'll try not to distract you."

"Don't think that's possible," he says, gazing at me. I

can't tell what he's thinking but he's biting the inside of his cheek. "I'm glad you're here, actually. This is the song I've been working on that I wanted your help with."

"Really?" I hadn't been sure he was serious about that.

"Yeah. I mean, if you want to. Rick says the label will want a ballad for the album. That's not the sort of thing I usually write."

"Um, sure, I'll look at it. I don't know how much help I'll be, though."

"Don't do that."

"What?"

"Sell yourself short. You've got a lot to offer. Own it."

He slides the black book across the table to me.

About half of a page is written in his neat black lettering, some lines crossed out and rewritten. The rest of the spread is blank, pristine, waiting.

I drowned the truth in her lies and ignored all the signs
And with each goodbye I took more of the blame
So she found it easier and easier to just slip away

I notice Colin across from me, fidgeting with his hands on the table and rubbing his face.

"Do you want something to drink? I'm going to get something to drink." Colin gets up and opens the little fridge in the kitchen area.

"Sure."

"Water or juice? I assume you don't want a beer."

"Juice is good." I give him a small smile.

He sets a bottle of orange juice for me and a water for him on the table. Then, instead of sitting where he was before, he slides in next to me and the cushion lets out a little sigh.

"Is this about your last girlfriend?" I hate the idea.

"Sort of. It's actually kind of about my last three relationships." He leans closer. "I want it to be about broken trust and betrayal. But I also want it to be about moving forward and being vulnerable to love again." He looks away. "I don't know. I need help with that part."

"I think it's great. I'm in."

He looks at me and his eyes look like they're smiling—even if his pouty lips haven't moved.

"I have a basic idea for the melody, something like this—" He taps out a short beat pattern with his finger on the table and then hums a mixture of rising and falling notes, short then drawn out. Beautiful. Being this close to him, I can almost feel the vibrations in his chest and it gives me goosebumps.

"Morning. Or whatever the fuck time it is." Dean walks out in a torn T-shirt and sweatpants, rubbing his eyes.

Logan follows, yawning and scratching his side, his shirt pulled up just enough to reveal tanned skin and a spattering of dark hair just below his belly button.

They come to sit across from us just as Colin closes his notebook and opens my book of crossword puzzles to the last one—my nemesis.

He slides closer to me, his arm going around my shoulder. *Play along, Gracie. But don't be weird!* I lean back against him, my shoulder into his chest, and try to relax in the feel of his warm body against mine. He welcomes the contact, immediately molding around me. He wraps both arms across my front and presses the lightest of kisses to my shoulder before resting his chin there. His warm breath is at my cheek, the stubble on his jaw lightly tickling my neck.

I take a sip of orange juice in hopes it will calm the flush I feel all over.

"Slinky," Colin says.

"What?"

"That's the answer to four down. Slinky."

* * *

The key card doesn't shake in his tattooed fingers, nor does he fumble with the door handle. He's not nervous about it at all, so why should I be?

Colin opens the door to our hotel room—our, as in his and mine, together, sharing—carrying his duffle bag on one shoulder and rolling my suitcase behind him.

The curtains are pulled away from the large picture window, afternoon sunlight filling the room. The curtains are a pretty cerulean blue along with the throw pillows on the beds, but everything else is white or cream or beige. In the corner is a little countertop area with a sink, small fridge, and coffee station, which is good because we're going to be staying here for a week. Yep. Colin and I are sharing a room for seven days. He made sure to get a room with two queens and obviously, I'm cool with it. I'm cool with all of it. Obviously.

"I'm going to go take a shower and then we've got some stuff to do before the show tonight. Do you need in the bathroom first?" Colin asks as he sets our bags down between the two beds.

"No, go ahead."

He reaches over his head and pulls the back of his shirt, removing it in one fluid motion so he's all thick arms and flexing abs and smooth skin covered in ink. If I took my shirt off that way I'd end up twisting my arms like a pretzel around my head and be trapped.

I don't know why I'm staring—he ends up shirtless by the end of every concert, it's not like I'm newly acquainted with a shirtless Colin. But this time feels different—he's not on stage in front of a crowd of fans and he has to know I'm watching. An audience of one.

He walks away from me toward the bathroom. He has tattoos up around his shoulders and neck, but most of his back is clear, smooth skin and long, sinewy lines that lead down to two dimples just above his waistband.

I turn on the television so it doesn't look like I've noticed he's left the bathroom door open a few inches. But I totally notice. The water is running and he leans over the sink to shave before getting in the shower. No big deal. He's literally naked on the other side of the wall, but I'm fine. Totally cool.

He sings in the shower.

It takes me a minute to realize he's singing the words to "Time After Time". Our song. Can fake relationships have songs? Well, ours does. And he's singing our song. While he's naked in the next room.

He comes out of the bathroom in just black boxer briefs, drying his hair off with a fluffy white towel, water droplets still glistening on his chest.

Okay. Maybe I'm not cool. I'm not cool at all. In fact, my skin might as well be on fire, and how am I going to handle this for the next seven days, let alone the rest of the summer?

I avert my eyes and end up fixating on a little dent in the wall next to the dresser to avoid watching him while he dresses. I try to think about anything else. My mind wanders to last night, and the conversation I overheard between him and Logan.

"I was thinking that maybe we could tell the guys about us, so that we only have to lie to Jace and the Donkey Lips guys."

"I thought about that—"

I hear the rustle of jeans, but I still don't look at him.

"—and we can tell them if you want, but in my experience, the fewer people who know about a secret, the better. If we tell one of the twins, the other will basically know immediately. I don't know how it works, it's like osmosis. And Joey, well, he can't keep a secret to save his life. Get a drop of alcohol in him and he'll tell anybody anything."

"Oh. All right. It's just that I'm a terrible liar and I hate keeping things from people." Funny, I've been doing a lot of that lately.

"That's a good quality to have." He comes to stand in front of me. "It's best to keep any lie as close to the truth as possible and keep it simple. That way you don't have to stress about who you've told what or how to act in different situations. So"—he dips his head down to make eye contact with me—"let's just keep it simple. When we're in this room, we're just you and me. And when we're out there, we're *us*."

"Okay." *Us*. Simple. Right.

He leans in closer and his knuckles press into the mattress on either side of my knees. "But if you want to end this, just tell me. I'll give you the most amicable break-up ever."

I give him a small smile.

"You want to come to the pre-show stuff with us? It probably won't be that exciting but it'll be better than staying here alone, unless you wanted to rest or something."

"Um, sure." I look down at my old jeans and varsity cheer tank top. "Should I change?"

He stands and steps toward the door, holding his hand out in invitation. "You look perfect to me."

* * *

Colin is doing this thing where he holds my hand everywhere, and whenever we have to separate, he kisses my cheek and gives my hand a little squeeze. He does it when they have to go in for a radio interview, before their meeting with the stage manager, before mic check, and before he gets ready to go on stage.

The venue is tiny. The crowd is packed tight and extra wild tonight and Colin's performance is even more intense than usual. The music feeding off the frenzy of the crowd, the crowd devouring of the energy of the music. He loses his shirt early, throwing it into the audience who screams in return. At one point he turns to me, our eyes locking as he sings the lyrics. I can see the words etched in black, slanted letters in his notebook:

> *My little monster wants to come out and play*
> *but I have to keep him at bay*
> *at bay*
> *at bay*
> *at bay*

His eyes are ravenous. He bites his lip before turning back to the crowd.

After the show, I hang back by security as the guys are rushed by fans. They sign shirts and hats and arms while making small talk and thanking them for coming to the show, it's like whack-a-mole. One fan retreats and two more pop up.

Jace is kneeling on the ground in front of a girl with her skirt flipped up revealing a neon pink thong as he signs her right butt cheek.

No one bats an eye at this. I look over at Colin—he's still half naked having literally lost his shirt during the performance—holding up his fat black marker just as a woman pulls down the front of her shirt to reveal a breast to him. Nipple and everything.

He glances over his shoulder to me and I quickly turn away. I don't want to play the role of jealous girlfriend. I can't be jealous. I'm literally not his girlfriend. But I look back when I hear him tell her to cover up. He autographs near her collarbone while she pouts.

* * *

"Sorry about that," he says when we get back to our room.

He fishes through his bag to find a shirt so we can meet up with everyone for dinner.

"It's fine. We're not actually dating. I'm not jealous or anything."

"I didn't say you were. But outside this room, we're together, remember? Out there, I'm going to treat you like I would a girlfriend."

He puts on a dark gray shirt and I watch it cascade over his chest and abs as he comes to me.

"If we were really together, would you care if I was looking at anther chick's tit after a show?"

I don't know how to answer. I look up at him, worrying the inside of my lip, and he comes closer still.

"It's not a trick question, Gray. If I was your boyfriend, would that bother you?" The tips of his fingers brush gently along my arm to my elbow.

"Yes."

"There you go. That's why I wouldn't do it." His fingertips trail softly down to my hand, slipping between my fingers. He squeezes my hand as they interlock. "Ready to go?"

* * *

THE NEXT SEVERAL DAYS ARE PRETTY LOW KEY. WE SLEEP IN late and then go to the recording studio. The recording studio is fine—it's basically a tan room with no windows and I end up sitting in a spinning chair for several hours with my knees tucked up, twirling in the corner.

I manage to get Logan alone when we both go to the vending machine in the hallway outside the tiny room on hour four of day two of recording. I awkwardly try to ask him if we're still cool and explain the Colin thing happened really fast and out of nowhere.

Keep the lie as close to the truth as possible, right?

He insists that we are totally fine, our friendship not in danger. He offers me one of his peanut butter cups and I just want to hug him. Then he steals half my Skittles. So, yeah. We're fine.

Colin is laser-focused on the music. Every tweak or suggestion gets another take. And each time he sings with the same amount of emotion, the same power in his voice. I can tell he's exhausted every night when we leave the studio. But once the music business stuff is over, he puts all of his focus on me.

It's weird.

It's wonderful.

He's almost always right by my side. Always touching me. Usually, it's holding my hand or an arm around my waist. The quickest of pecks to my cheek. My favorite is when we're sitting next to each other at dinner and he runs his hand up and down my arm. Touching me in the softest, most innocent ways seems like second nature to him.

I, however, am still awkward as fuck about it. When we sit together and his arm is wrapped around me, I try the hand on the leg thing again. But this time I make sure my hand is as low as it will go—like, basically his knee—and it's working. Sort of. It's a work in progress.

All the other guys go out partying at night, but Colin and I go back to the room, where absolutely no touching occurs. He hums while he brushes his teeth and sings in the shower and sleeps in only tight boxer briefs.

On the last day of recording, I'm in my usual spot in the back corner, not paying much attention. The guys are all standing in a circle with the two sound guys that work here and apparently Rick, their manager, is on speakerphone.

"Rick, we don't want to do it that way."

Colin is bent over the table, his brow creased and shaking his head. The voice on the other end of the phone is hard for me to make out, but whatever he's saying makes Colin clench his jaw and start rubbing the back of his neck. Everything about his posture is hard, tense. I think of how soft his finger strokes are against my skin and I want nothing more than to walk up to him and wrap my arms around him. Hold him against me, comfort him and feel his body relax against mine.

I mean, a girlfriend would totally do that. But I'm not his girlfriend. He probably won't want me to interrupt. He's working and I'll just be in the way.

But for some reason I'm getting up from my chair. And my feet are moving toward him. I come up behind him and extend my hand to touch his back but hesitate. What if he tells me to go back to my seat? What if—

Without even turning around, as if he senses me, he reaches back for me. Welcoming me. Wanting me.

I place my hand on his back as I close the space between us. I wrap myself around him and he holds me tight against his chest. He lets out a long exhale, and I can feel the tension in his muscles ease as I rub lightly up his back.

He kisses the top of my head and whispers into my hair, "Thank you."

* * *

The mirror is still half fogged up from my hot shower as I braid my wet hair. All of the guys are waiting on us. Colin is waiting outside the door for me. It's our last night before going back on the road and Logan convinced us to go out tonight. They've gone to this bar the last couple of nights and he assures me I won't get carded if I walk in with them.

My fingers don't seem to be working right and my thick hair is not cooperating. The longer these two damn braids take the more nervous I get. I don't know why I'm so nervous. Maybe it's because I sent off all of my jeans to the hotel's laundry service and all I have to wear tonight are skirts or that teeny black dress Kyla packed for me.

RAE KENNEDY

I put on the high-waisted denim skirt and a floral crop top. It's probably my longest skirt but it still only comes to mid-thigh. It's fine—my cheer skirt was way shorter than this and I walked around with all the confidence in the world. I was the shit. But my legs aren't as toned as when I was cheerleading every day either.

Knock it off. You are the shit. The. Shit. Own it.

Colin stands from his perch at the end of the bed when I step out. He looks tall standing there in his dark jeans. His black V-neck shirt dips low enough to show off the fierce eagle tattoo on his chest.

He touches one of my braids, sliding down to the end and twisting my hair in his fingers.

"These are cute," he says and he almost sounds mischievous.

"Thanks."

It seems like he holds on tighter to my hand as we walk through the bar to our table in the back. It's a huge round table, half surrounded by a shiny mahogany-colored booth. The other half has extra chairs pulled around it to fit our whole party. Colin and I are snug together in the middle of the booth and everyone just barely fits. But after rounds of various appetizers, entrees, beer and cocktails later, the guys have accumulated more guests.

Jace comes back from the bathroom with a girl on his arm. Logan invites a couple girls from the bar to come sit with us, and even Joey—emboldened from several Jack and Cokes—is chatting up a girl near the hostess stand.

When he comes back with her and there's literally no room to even pull up a stool, Colin grabs me by the hips and lifts me onto his lap to make space.

It's fine.

Just sitting on Colin's freaking lap.

I instinctively grip his thighs to steady myself. They're firm and strong in my grasp and I try not to squeeze them. I just sip my mojito. No big deal.

He rests his head on my shoulder, his hands lightly on my hips.

I'm going to need another drink for this.

Logan ends up buying several bottles as the night goes on. He regales us with many stories. The girls from the bar are enthralled. I've heard most of them before. Joey has turned bright orange and giggly—sure signs he needs to call it a night soon.

Colin is mostly silent. I'd forget he was there if I couldn't feel his body hot under mine. Dean is sitting next to me and I try to talk with him, but he keeps getting distracted looking at the bartender across the room.

"Does he keep looking over at me or am I imagining things? Do you think he's interested?" Dean asks, becoming bolder and making eyes at the bartender in the tight white shirt, shaved head, and bushy beard.

"I don't know." He seems to just be working to me.

Colin's hands slide down from my hips to rest on my bare thighs. Still low, just above my knees.

"Maybe you should go talk to him," I offer to Dean, my voice sounding higher than normal.

Warm fingertips sweep in easy circular motions along my legs, lightly, just like he does on my arms. Heat sizzles under my skin and my inner thighs are tingling. Whatever.

I guzzle down my drink and immediately order another.

I smile at Dean, who is still grappling with the idea of engaging the bartender in probatory conversation when Colin's fingers touch the edge of my skirt.

I finish my drink and my skin feels entirely too hot.

His knuckles graze my thighs as he plays with the hem of my skirt, and my heart is pounding. I can hear it beating in my ears and feel the pulse between my legs. It's a throb and an ache and I squeeze my thighs together. As I squirm on his lap I feel it—hard against my rear. The unmistakable feel of Colin's erection.

Oh my... oh holy fucking shit. Why don't I have another goddamn drink in front of me right now? I don't know what to do with myself. It's still firmly pressed against my ass and I try not to move. It's probably nothing, really. He has a female sitting on his lap—it's more than likely only physiological.

But when I reach for my drink in hopes I can suck any remaining booze from the ice cubes, I inadvertently rub up against it. He immediately grips my hips, holding them firmly as if in warning. I can still feel him big and hard under me and the throbbing between my legs just wants to be subdued. A big smile crosses my face when I think about how good it would feel...

I roll my hips against him deliberately, a soft gasp escaping my lips.

His fingers dig into my hips and I feel a deep rumble in his chest at my back. Is he mad?

But then his lips are at my neck, laying hot kisses on my sensitive skin. He nips at my ear as I rock back against him again. His hands on my hips don't stop me, in fact they move with my hips, encouraging me to grind on his dick faster.

"Do you like this?" he asks in my ear, his voice low and hoarse.

"Mm hm." I bite my lips to keep from panting. My heart

is racing and my breathing is fast and shallow.

Dean turns to me, grinning after having made some sort of successful eye contact with the bartender. One look at my face—which is probably flushed—and my death grip on the edge of the table and his smile turns impish.

"You two look like you're ready to head back to your room." He gives me an approving nod.

"Sounds like a good idea," Colin says, voice still husky at my neck. "You want to go back to our room, Gray?"

CHAPTER 13

"Yes."

It comes out more of a quivering moan than anything. But I mean it. I want to go back to the room with him. I want him to touch me more, in private. And I want to feel him too. I don't know if I've wanted something more.

The hotel is only a couple blocks away from the bar and Colin keeps his hand on my lower back the whole way. Our steps hurried. Eager.

My insides are a frenzy of jumbled nerves as we ride the elevator to the third floor in palpable silence. My hands are sweaty, my heart doesn't know whether to pump like crazy or stop altogether as I wait for Colin to open the door.

As soon as we're in, his touch is gone. His face is in his hands, rubbing up and down with his palms and around his eyes.

"Did I embarrass you or make you uncomfortable?" he asks, looking pale.

"What? Why would you think that?"

"You said you wanted to come to the room so we could take a break, yeah?"

What? Wait—go back to the room is code for stop?

When did we establish this?

Outside this room we're us, inside we're just you and me. No. No no no no no.

"It was good timing, actually—" Colin paces in front of the foot of his bed, massaging the side of his neck.

Thankfully this means he can't read the horror and disappointment that's surely written on my face.

"I was getting carried away and you had a bit too much to drink," he says.

I want to remind him that I told him I liked it, and that I wasn't lying. But my throat is tightening up. Maybe he wasn't enjoying it as much as I thought. Maybe he really was pretending.

"I'm not drunk, and you didn't make me uncomfortable. It's fine."

Relief washes over his face. "Good. I'm sorry. I don't want you to think I was trying to take advantage of our arrangement."

I try to muster up all of the conviction I don't feel.

"Of course not." My voice is small. *Don't let your smile fall.* Of course he wouldn't dream of taking advantage of the little girl. "Excuse me."

I go to the bathroom and shut the door, unable to hold the mask on my face anymore. The door is cold and hard against my back, my fingers clutch tight to the knob and I squeeze my eyes closed.

This is all just pretend. It isn't real. He doesn't want to be with you.

I don't think I've been standing here long but then his deep voice breaks through the sounds of my breathing.

"You okay in there, Gray?" He's close, just on the other side of the door.

RAE KENNEDY

I step gingerly away from the door and turn on the faucet, letting the water crash into the sink.

"Yeah, just getting ready for bed."

I let the water run until it's pleasantly warm, trickling over my palms. I wash my makeup off my face and then take out my braids, combing my fingers through my hair as it falls in loose waves.

When I come out into the room, Colin is lying on his bed, propped up on his side, his black notebook spread open on the cream damask duvet.

He looks up at me. "Hey. Are you wanting to go to bed right now? I can go hang in one of the guys' rooms and let you sleep."

It's almost one in the morning, but that's still quite early according to Rockstar time.

I hesitate for a second.

"Or...we could hang out and watch a movie...if you want," he adds.

Colin wants to...hang out?

"Were you working on something there?" I point to his notebook.

"Yeah, I got a couple more lines for that song. Do you want to see?"

I sit cross-legged on the bed in front of him and he slides the book to me. He comes closer to lie next to me as I read, the side of his stomach brushes my thigh.

Every time it replays in my mind, the knife in my back
How she smiled to my face and took everything I have
But still, I'd give more to you
If you wanted me to

My heart stutters in my chest when I read it and I can feel the tension rippling off him. Every word raw. I don't know why it feels so personal to me. It's not like it's about me.

"This is about your last few relationships?"

He nods.

"They all lied to you?"

"They all cheated on me."

"Oh." Wow. "I'm so sorry."

He runs his hand over his short, black hair, looking down at the bed. "It's pretty common, I guess, when you're on tour months at a time. Guys cheat on their girlfriends on the road, and the ones left home get lonely. It's almost expected. Accepted. Probably why I've just stayed single for so long."

"Did you ever cheat on them?"

He looks at me, blue eyes steady. "No."

"And the relationships were all pretty serious?"

"Yeah. Well, I thought so."

"You really don't do casual hook-ups do you?"

"Nope."

For some reason, it feels like a little flicker of hope is snuffed out. Good.

Knock that shit off, Gracie. Nothing is happening between you and Colin.

"The worst part," Colin continues, looking off, lost in thought, "about being cheated on, isn't even the break-up—it's the embarrassment. The humiliation that you weren't enough for the person and everyone knows it."

I have the urge to take his hand, to comfort him. But I don't.

"Being betrayed and humiliated by someone you cared

for, trusted is the worst. I know all about it," I say.

He tilts his head, a small crease forming between his brows. "Tell me."

I hate talking about this. But he's been so open, I want to reciprocate.

"My last boyfriend"—I've only had two, but whatever—"he broke up with me after I told him I didn't want to have sex yet. Then he told the whole school how much of a prude I am, and how it took months for me to even go down on him." My cheeks heat as I think of the next part. I almost don't continue. "He told everyone that when I finally did, I was awful at it. It was a small high school, so when I say everyone heard about it, I mean everyone. From the freshmen to the teachers…"

I have a hard time meeting Colin's gaze. But when I do, it's soft. He shakes his head slightly.

"He was a fucking idiot. You know that was all about his ego and had nothing to do with you, right?"

I nod. "Yeah, I know." Sort of. "But, I mean, it was the first"—and only—"time I've done… that. I probably was horrible at it." I didn't think it was possible for my face to feel any more flushed, but here we are.

"Nah."

I look at him with a tiny smile. "You can't know that."

"Yep. I can. I've been a teenage boy and trust me, a girl putting her mouth anywhere near or around his dick is the complete opposite of horrible. In fact, it was probably the highlight of his pathetic little life up until that point. I bet he blew his load pretty fast."

I look down, letting hair fall across my face. "Um, yeah. He did."

When I look back up, Colin's staring at me. He grazes

his teeth across his bottom lip and it makes my heart thump.

After a few beats of uninterrupted eye contact, I let out a high-pitched giggle. "So... the song?"

"Oh. Yeah."

* * *

It's back to the bus, back to the tour. Without the refuge of our hotel room, I feel like I'm constantly glued to Colin's side. Sitting with him at the table while I do a crossword or on the little couch just talking with the guys, close, always so close. I'm finding it easier to lean into his touch, to wrap my arms around him, hold his hand. I look forward to his little hand squeezes and the light kisses on the cheeks when we part.

He and I work on the song—usually right after we first wake up, before the rest of the guys have stumbled out of their bunks. The bus is quiet except for the sounds of sleep and the soft purr of the engine below foot. It's funny—I keep finding myself waking up earlier and earlier to walk out to the common space, and he's always there waiting. I don't know why he keeps saying he needs my help, he's written almost every word. Mostly, we just talk about the images and emotions he wants the song to evoke. I'll say something fairly unextraordinary and he'll look at me and say, "Hmm," then he'll write down a line that's amazing. He's much better at songwriting than me. I suppose that's to be expected.

Every line has a rhythm, a cadence that pulls me in when he recites them. And when he starts to sing them, even though his voice is barely louder than a whisper, it feels like I'm melting from the inside out.

RAE KENNEDY

We don't work on the song when the guys are around, though. Logan, Dean and I have been playing a fair share of poker. They're trying (unsuccessfully) to teach me tricks and techniques to winning. It still seems like mostly luck to me. I've also been teaching Joey how to play Sudoku. He spent the better part of four days squinting at the little squares in distrust, like it was a trick or something. But he now has the hang of it, mostly. He can complete the majority of the easy puzzles but says he's not ready to move on to the medium level ones yet.

I don't spend much time in my bunk other than sleeping, but I sometimes look out the little window and try to write. I want to finish this poem about gravity and tidal waves, the sun and the moon—but the idea behind it isn't solid enough and the words keep dissolving like mist.

I text Kyla every day and send her pictures to prove I'm still alive and not a catfishing kidnapper. I haven't told her anything about the Colin arrangement. I don't want to lie to her or answer a billion rapid-fire questions. Her suggesting I "carpe the dick" almost every day is enough.

The last several days have been nothing but shows and travel and random gas station stops so I'm ecstatic that the next two shows are in neighboring towns and we get to stay at the same hotel for a few nights in a row. It's nice to not always be moving.

* * *

"You in?" Logan yells at me from across the table.

The restaurant is crowded and noisy. People are packed around tables, having loud conversations, standing over by the bar, jumping and shouting at the game on the giant television screens, and the sound of dishes clanking, glasses tinging, and silverware scraping fill in all the gaps.

"For what?" I practically scream back.

"Poker game. Jace's room."

"Nah, man, we're out," Colin calls back, his arm tightening around my waist so that we're hip to hip.

Logan pushes out his bottom lip in an exaggerated pout.

"I'm totally in," I yell.

He smiles and gives me the thumbs up. He turns to Joey to his left. "How 'bout you?"

Joey turns a bright shade of salmon and shakes his head.

I reach for my drink and I can feel Colin glowering next to me before I even look at him. His mouth is set, jaw tight, eyes trained on me, unblinking.

I roll my eyes at him as I sip from my straw.

"What? You can go be a downer in the room all you want. I'm going to go have some fun." Like, bye, Felicia. I came here to be Fun Gracie, remember?

His face stays calm and controlled. "Can we talk about it, at least? In the room?"

"Fine." But if he starts dictating what I can or can't do, I'm going to have to put in a request for that amicable break-up. Hey, if he's going to be a dick, I don't even care about the amicable part.

I stuff my hands in my jean shorts pockets as we walk back to the hotel and I'm pleased to notice Colin's frustration when he goes to hold my hand and can't.

I stand in the room with my arms crossed and my hip popped as I wait for him to speak.

He latches the door and stands in front of me. "I'm

sorry I spoke for you. I just… I don't know. I didn't think you'd want to do that."

I scrunch my face up in confusion. "Do what? Play poker? Why would you assume I wouldn't want to do that?" I'm more flustered and annoyed than I was two seconds ago before he opened his mouth.

He scratches along his jaw. "Do you know what kind of poker they're playing?"

"Hopefully Hold 'Em—"

"Strip poker," he says, and it seems like he's standing closer to me now.

"Oh." I missed that part of the conversation. Strip poker. I definitely haven't done that before, but it could be fun. New. I could put it on my Fuck-it list. And he didn't think I'd want to play.

Of course not. Not innocent, prude little Gracie Gallagher.

"Well, you were wrong. I want to play. I think it will be fun." I stand tall. "And if you're this controlling as a boyfriend, I think that's something you need to work on."

He quirks an eyebrow at me. "Controlling?" He takes a step toward me. "You're free to do whatever you want." Another step. "I wouldn't dream of stopping you." Another step closer. "But if you were actually my girlfriend, I wouldn't be too keen on the idea of you stripping in front of other guys." His eyes are spearing into me as he closes the space between us so we're standing so close I have to tilt my head up to look at him, his chest is almost touching mine. "And if I was your boyfriend," he says it low and slow, his eyes flickering to my mouth, "I hope you'd only want to strip for me."

My chest is heaving with shallow breaths. Holy crap.

Are my clothes still on? Because I swear the heat in his stare could easily melt them right off. I swallow hard to stifle the little whimper trying to escape my lips and maybe steady my heart-rate.

"Good thing I'm not actually your girlfriend, then. Because I'm going to go."

"Okay." He dips his head and steps aside so I have a clear path to the door.

I throw the door open and huff into the hall. The door clicks behind me and I turn to see Colin standing there.

"What are you doing?" I ask.

"If you're going, so am I."

CHAPTER 14

I SLAM MY CARDS DOWN. MY PAIR OF SEVENS DOESN'T CUT IT. Crap.

After several rounds of play, I'm down to my bra and shorts. I guess I'm faring just as well as Logan and Jace who, are both in their T-shirts and boxers, and better than Boner Three and the other two girls who are playing with us. He's only in ill-fitting boxers while the girl next to him is in bra and panties and the girl sitting between Logan and Jace is only in the tiniest of thongs. I think her name is Sheila, and she is not shy at all about sitting there, boobs out. In fact, she's not shy about telling us how much she paid for them either. They are pretty nice. Not too big, perky.

Oh my god, I need to stop staring at them.

"That's another item off." Logan smiles as he passes the half-drunk bottle of tequila to Sheila.

Here goes. I stand up, fingers grasping at the button of my shorts. Colin is watching from the floor next to me as I slide down the zipper and shimmy them down my hips. He's fully dressed, of course. But he looks away as my shorts fall to the carpet, staring at the bottle of beer sitting between his legs. And when I sit back down next to him, he puts the dark bottle to his lips and guzzles it down, slinging his head back until it's empty. Muscles flexing in his jaw.

He avoids looking over at me as we play. He also doesn't seem to be looking toward Sheila either, who is happily telling Logan all about her favorite type of yoga pants. She's so worked up about them she's actually bouncing. She's bouncing but her boobs totally stay in place. Fascinating.

I've got this one. It's down to Colin, Logan, and me. I lay down my cards—a pair of fives and a pair of Jacks.

"Dammit!" Logan lays down his hand with a pair of Kings then takes his shirt off. He winks at Sheila and she giggles as she scoots closer to his side.

"You won." Colin puts his cards in a little stack and quickly stuffs them into the deck.

"Hey, why didn't you show your hand? What did you have?"

"Doesn't matter, you won." He pulls his shirt over his head and then he's sitting there all bare-chested and I forget what I was about to say.

"Let's take a break," Logan says in his gamemaster voice.

"Who wants to smoke?" Jace stands from the circle.

"Hell, yeah!" Boner Three says, hopping up.

I stand, stretching my legs, and Colin is up next to me, lithe as he moves closer, backing me up to the wall. His hands go to the wall on either side of me, his whole body sort of caging me in, making my breath hitch.

"Having fun?" his voice is low, raspy.

The scent of beer is faint on his breath and his skin smells like soap and male musk. I dare to reach out and trace the curve and dip of his obliques with my fingertips. I've touched him so many times these last couple weeks, but not this much bare skin. It's warm and smooth and raises into goosebumps at my touch.

"Are you?" My voice is equally as hoarse.

"Not really." But he tries to hold back a shiver when my fingernails rake over his ribs.

"Are you just standing here like this to hide my body from everyone else?"

"Maybe," he says with the tiniest smirk.

"I don't think you need to worry about it. They were definitely all looking at Sheila, not me."

His tongue briefly flicks out to wet his lips. "Trust me, they weren't." And then he gazes down my chest to where my breasts are heaving almost out of my bra. He's not even being subtle about it.

Oh.

"Are you ready to go back to the room yet?" he asks.

I glance past him to where Jace is standing by the large dresser with rolling papers set out next to a little plastic baggy full of green clumps of marijuana. Next to it is an even smaller baggie with a white, powder substance. I've never seen hard drugs in person, so I'm not sure what it is, but definitely something I'd rather not stay to find out.

"Yeah. Let's go back."

"Thank fuck." Colin immediately picks our clothes off the floor and helps me dress like he can't get my clothes on fast enough.

Boner Three hoots at us as we head for the door. "Yeah, Colin's going to get some!"

Colin ignores him, slings his arm around my shoulders, and walks us out the door.

He lets out a sigh when we get back to our room. "Thanks for leaving with me."

"I don't know why you think it was such a big deal. It

was just some fun."

"You might not have thought it was so fun when it turned into an orgy."

I roll my eyes. "It was not about to turn into an orgy."

He sits on the foot of his bed to take off his shoes. "Well, they weren't about to put all their clothes back on and watch The Weather Channel."

"And you think I couldn't have handled it?"

He doesn't say anything, just gives me a look that basically says, "Pretty much, yeah."

"Why? Because I'm a virgin? Well, I'm not a virgin because I'm afraid of or averse to sex. I'm a virgin by choice, because I've set boundaries and I know how to say no. If I had been uncomfortable I would have left. I don't need you chaperoning me."

I don't know how he gets me so heated so quickly, without hardly saying anything.

He rubs the back of his neck, tilting his head back so he's looking at the ceiling. "I don't think you realize how close you are to being in over your head." He lets out a breath. "You're so young and naïve—"

And there it is. What he really thinks of me. What he's always seen me as.

"Get out."

His face twists in confusion. "What?"

"I want you out. Go sleep somewhere else. I don't want to be around you right now."

"Are you serious?" He stands up, hands falling to his sides.

"Do I look fucking serious?"

I must look fucking serious because he picks up his bag and goes to leave. "Shit, Gray, I'm sorry. I didn't mean to—"

"I don't want to talk right now, either." I'm upset and frustrated and maybe about to cry and don't want him anywhere near me. I don't want him to know how much his opinion of me hurts.

He gives a slight nod, his dark lashes silhouetted against his cheeks.

When the door latches, I realize my hands are fisted in little balls, and when I open my hands they ache.

If he thinks I'm too young and naïve, I'll just have to show him what I'm capable of.

* * *

When Colin texts the next day to ask if I'm coming to the show, I reply only one word: No.

I'm flooded with texts from all the guys around the time the concert lets out but I'm too busy getting ready for the after party. The real show.

I have to lie down on the bed to squeeze into the itty bitty black dress Kyla packed for me. I can barely breathe and it pushes my boobs way the heck up there, but yeah, I'm going with it. I put on extra mascara so my lashes look longer and darker against my light blue eyes and lipstick the color of merlot on my normally bubble gum pink lips. Quite the task to make the lips look good when you're slightly inebriated and wobbly.

The hotel room door bursts open and all four of the guys barge in. Logan and Dean are in front. Logan calls, "Gracie," the same time Dean says, "Blondie?"

I smile sweetly at them.

"Are you okay?" they say in unison, coming to me, Logan pulling me in for a hug.

"I'm fine."

"We thought you might be sick." Joey pokes his head up between Logan and Dean's shoulders.

"Nope," I say, still smiling.

"Yeah, you definitely don't look sick." Logan looks me up and down with an appreciative thumbs-up, and Dean whistles.

Colin is standing back, leaning against the door with his hands in his pockets, eyes downcast.

"Oh, Honeymuffin," I singsong to him.

He lifts his head up, a curious furrow to his brow.

"Are you going to come see me?" I open my arms, holding them out for him.

He pushes off the door. He stalks toward me cautiously, hands still in his pockets.

When he reaches me, he doesn't hesitate to wrap his arms around my waist and hold me tight against him, cheek to cheek, his skin warm against mine.

He feels and smells so nice I almost forget my objective.

He pulls back so we're nose-to-nose. "Are you still mad at me?"

"Why would you think that?" I keep my voice light, saccharine.

"You didn't come to the show."

"I was tired."

His gaze flashes to my mouth, lower to my cleavage. Just for a split second.

"You're drunk," he says.

"I was thirsty. Minibar." I shrug, my arms still encircled loosely around his neck.

"This dress is tiny."

"It's child-sized. Should fit just right."

He rolls his eyes then moves in closer, our bodies pressed together. "Gray—" He turns his head back toward the guys. "Go on ahead. We'll be right behind you." Then he looks back to me and lowers his voice. "Can we talk for a minute?"

I shake my head. "I want to go. I'm starving. Haven't eaten all day."

"You heard the lady. She's starving. Let's feed her!" Logan yells, heading out of the room.

I follow, pulling Colin by the hand behind me.

* * *

Colin watches as I pull out a tiny minibar-sized bottle of huckleberry vodka out of my purse and add it to my sprite. It's quite delicious and I don't pay him any attention, even as his hand flexes on my hip. I press closer to his side as I continue to sip my drink, smiling and chatting with Dean and Joey.

"What is this? What are you doing?" Colin whispers in my ear.

I turn to him, giving him as much of a wide-eyed innocent look as I can muster. "What do you mean, Sweetie Pie?"

"That. What's going on?"

I bat my lashes at him. "You know me so well and what's best for me. Surely you can figure it out."

He darts his eyes over my shoulder to where I see Dean straighten in his seat, hardly holding back his smirk.

The server arrives with our food and Colin drops the subject. As I eat with one hand, I place the other on Colin's leg. Mid-thigh. None of this knee bullshit. I'm feeling bold.

Confident. I'm feeling sexy and, if I'm being honest, drunk. But that's beside the point. I may have come off a rough year where I experienced a hit to my self-esteem, but I am not a delicate, timid wallflower.

I slide my hand higher up his leg. The denim is rough against my skin. His thigh is hot under his jeans, hard and muscular. I move my hand so slightly, so slowly that I don't think he'll even notice. But at the exact moment my fingers move upward, he stops drawing lazy circles on my arms. He only stops for a beat—but it's enough.

We keep eating our dinner and he keeps stroking my arm, perfectly relaxed as I keep my hand glued in place to his thigh.

I move my palm farther up. We're firmly in upper-thigh territory now.

His breath hitches.

I pretend I don't notice and just keep chatting with Dean to my right.

This time when my hand slides up to just below his crotch, I squeeze.

He chokes on his bite of food.

All eyes at the table turn to him.

"You all right, man?" Logan asks.

I pat him heartily on the back. "What happened, Love Bug?"

He coughs a couple times into his fist and takes a drink of water. He clears his throat and assures everyone that he's fine until they resume their previous conversations. His grip on my hip loosens and he slides his hand up my side. He stops at my ribs, this thumb rubbing in a circle as he pulls me in closer.

His voice is almost a growl, vibrating against my ear.

"What's your endgame here?"

I shrug, turning into him so my breasts drag along his torso. "You tell me."

He shifts his hips and I bite my lips as I watch him try to discreetly adjust himself.

I lift to my knees on the booth seat and lean to him, giving him a great view of my cleavage and letting my lips drag lightly along his neck up to his ear. "Oops, did I do that?"

"Gray—"

"I had no idea that would happen. I mean, I'm so young and inexperienced…"

I swing a leg over, settling down on his lap, our faces close. He glances around behind me, probably to the other people at the table, but I don't care who's watching. His hands are on my hips, fingers massaging into my flesh. He licks his lips, his breathing quickens. My skirt is so short and tight I can barely spread my legs enough to straddle him, and if he lowered his head, he would surely be able to see the tiny strip of black fabric that is my underwear. But he keeps his eyes on my face and I appreciate that.

I roll my hips forward, just enough to create some friction between. Just enough so that I have no doubt what I'm doing to him as I feel his hard length along the sensitive skin of my inner thigh.

His grasp on my hips tightens. "You've made your point. Can we go back to the room now?"

"I don't want to go to the room. I'm having fun here. Aren't you having fun? Because"—I grind against his erection again—"it sure *feels* like you're enjoying yourself."

His eyes roll back at the contact between our bodies but then they snap back to me, darkening. He grips my upper thighs hard, holding me still and away from the bulge under his zipper. He's touching me just below where the hem of my skirt is shimmied up, his thumbs on the inside of my thighs. So high up. His touch sends tingles up to my center and I realize my panties are soaked through. So much that I can feel my arousal, slick between my legs. If he were to move his thumbs up just a bit, he'd surely be able to feel it on my thighs.

"How far are you going to push this?"

"Hmm..." I try to rock forward again, but his hold is on me is firm and I only manage to nudge forward an inch. Just enough movement that his thumbs slip under my skirt, and the second he feels how wet my skin is, his eyes widen.

"Fuck," he says under his breath and his lips are slack, his breathing shallow, his pupils are so large his eyes are almost entirely black.

He rubs tiny circles on my skin with his thumbs, warm and slippery, the extent of my arousal obvious to both of us.

I twist my fingers in the hem of his shirt, my knuckles brushing against the hot skin just above his waistband. And we stare at each other, practically panting, my heart pounding so hard I can't hear anything else.

After a few minutes I break the silence. "Let's go back to the room now."

* * *

His hand lingers on my hip when we enter the room. "Can we talk now?" he asks.

"All right." I take a couple steps back so we're face-to-face and wait.

"I'm sorry I upset you yesterday. What I said came out wrong. I don't know why I feel such a strong desire to protect you." He rakes his fingernails over his head, through his hair, and down the side of his jaw. "It's just that you're so…"

Young. Inexperienced. Ignorant. Naïve.

"Good," he finishes.

Oh.

"And I hate the thought of you putting yourself in compromising positions."

"Well, the whole point of me running away with you guys was to get a little compromised."

He nods. "Right. And that's your decision to make. I won't get in your way." He takes a step closer to me. "But will you promise me something? If you want to get compromised, I don't care what it is—you want to get wasted or snort cocaine off someone's ass—will you make sure I'm there with you?"

I smile. "I don't plan on snorting anything off someone's ass, but yeah. Okay."

He smiles too, just for a second, then he's closing the space between us. "And one more thing—" His expression is serious again, eyes hooded, and he's so close I can smell his sweet manly musk. "If you want to get compromised *with* someone, you can come to me."

CHAPTER 15

My foggy, alcohol-laden mind has trouble making sense of what Colin just said. Did he just say I can come to him for sexual favors?

The whole idea is absurd and I burst out in a fit of laughter. "Like, what? You want me to come ask you to give me my first orgasm?"

Colin's eyebrows shoot up.

I didn't—why the fuck did I just say that? *Vodka, I thought you were my friend!*

"You've never had an orgasm?" He tilts his head, a curious curve forming on his lips.

"That's not what I said."

"Yes, actually, you did."

I stand there, mouth open, unable to speak. I can't lie about it—my hot cheeks have already given me away.

"Let me guess." He reaches out to lift my chin and look up at him. "You went down on your boyfriend and he never returned the favor?"

I shake my head slowly, afraid to blink.

"Shame." His gaze falls down to my lips, down to my dress and back.

RAE KENNEDY

This dress is way too small. I can't breathe. And I'm too hot. Why is it so freaking hot in here? My chest is heaving with my quick breaths and I'm afraid my boobs are going to pop right out the top or rip the dress altogether.

"And…you've never given yourself one?" he continues.

Holy hell. What the fuck is this conversation? But he's speaking softly, his expression sweet and sincere, not like he's judging, just curious. It makes me want to answer. Not that I seem to have any filter at the moment anyhow.

"No. I mean, I've tried a few times. But… I don't know… Nothing really happened. At least, I don't think it happened. I'd probably know, right?"

He nods as he chews on his lip. "Yeah, you'd know."

We stand, silent for several beats. Hearts pounding. Words unspoken. An electricity in my skin. An overwhelming urge to take his hand and pull him to me. To touch my lips to his and feel our bodies shudder against one another.

"I'd like to help you with that." His voice is hoarse. His hands are at his sides but his fingers flex, like he wants to touch something.

"Uh…" I swallow hard. *Don't let me down here, vodka.* "You want to give me my first orgasm?"

He licks his lips and closes his eyes and lets out a barely audible moan. When he opens his eyes, I see a flash of what looks like pain before he steadies his expression again. "No."

No? Dammit, vodka! I want to curl up and die. I turn away from him, determined to go lie on my bed in the fetal position and do just that. But he hooks his fingers around my elbow and stops me.

I don't want to look at him. My face is burning in humiliation.

"Gray…" His tone is gentle. "I want to help you give

yourself your first orgasm."

All the air in my lungs rushes out in a whoosh and I can't form words.

"You shouldn't have to rely on anyone else to give you the pleasure you want." His grasp around my elbow slides down my arm to take my hand. He snorts. "Especially from guys your age. Most of them think they can get a girl off if they fuck her hard enough during penetrative sex."

"And...they can't?" My voice is all throaty.

"Not usually, no. Most women won't come without direct clitoral stimulation."

My cheeks grow even hotter and he looks like he wants to sink his teeth into me.

"Oh." I'm still not sure what he's proposing. And does he want to do it right now? "So you want to... what? Watch me"—I can't bring myself to say the word *masturbate*, even with vodka mostly in control of my mouth—"touch myself?"

He swallows thickly. "I don't have to watch. I could talk you through it, help you figure out how you like to be touched, offer suggestions and support. I could do it over the phone if you want."

"Col, I—"

He closes the last inches between us, our foreheads touching. He squeezes my hand, our interlocked fingers, holding on tight.

"Don't decide anything right now. Let's talk about it later, when you're sober."

And so we don't talk about it anymore.

I listen to him hum and sing quietly to himself as he gets ready for bed.

I can't sleep. I toss and turn and then finally lie awake and watch Colin in the bed across from me. Just enough light seeps into the room from around the edges of the curtains to highlight the angles of his face and his lashes against his cheeks. He hugs a pillow close to his body while his chest rises slowly, perfectly timed to his soft sounds of sleep.

* * *

We're sitting on the bus the next afternoon, waiting for the rest of the guys to check out of the hotel. I'm surprised when Colin hoists me onto his lap. He wraps his arms around my middle and nuzzles his chin into the crook of my neck as I work on a crossword puzzle. It's so nice and comfortable. I like the feeling of him wrapping me up too much. And the idea that he isn't doing this for show, that he may like it as much as I do, has me imagining what we would be like if we were really together. Visions of us just like this on a lazy Sunday morning, walking hand in hand as much as possible, tangling our bare legs in the bed-sheets...

"Gray? Did you hear me?"

"Huh?"

"Sixteen across—it's arctic."

"Oh right." I focus back on the puzzle. "Thanks for the help."

"I'm good at helping."

I immediately think about what he offered to help me with last night and my face warms. A hand moves to touch my hip and I yelp at the contact.

"Are you ticklish?"

"No."

But then he squeezes my hip and I start giggling and squirming on his lap because, dammit, it does tickle. He holds me tight with his other arm so I can't wiggle away. I laugh so hard I snort. He chuckles behind me, making me bounce on his lap and then Joey and Dean climb onto the bus.

We both look up, the tickling ceased but out of breath.

"Where's your brother?" Colin asks.

"Fuck if I know. I don't get paid enough to keep track of him," Dean says.

Colin pulls out his phone. "We're going to be late if he doesn't show up soon." He lets out a sigh as he hits dial and holds the phone to his ear. Logan doesn't pick up. "I'm going to go check in the hotel." He slides over and lifts me off his lap. "Sorry." He kisses my cheek before he gets up to leave.

At just that moment, Logan strolls onto the bus, his hair even more disheveled than usual. His eyelids are droopy and the whites of his eyes bloodshot, but he smiles his mega-watt smile and says, "Hey! I'm here!" like nothing is out of the ordinary.

"Dude, you look like shit," Joey says.

"Have you slept at all yet?" Dean asks.

"That's why there are beds on the bus." Logan's words are a little slurred this time.

"Are you still wasted?" Colin asks.

Logan just shrugs. "I'll be fine by show time." And he meanders back to his bunk, where it sounds like he literally falls into it.

And he's right. Come show time, no one would guess he had been anything other than bright-eyed and bushy-tailed earlier. His fingers move magically over the strings and he hits all of his riffs while smiling to the audience.

But I watch Colin mostly. How couldn't I? He's

beautiful on stage, under the lights. His voice resonates above everything else—the music, the crowd, the noise. I'm entranced. He throws off his shirt and I watch his muscles move and flex under his inked skin. He's a work of art—a masterpiece. If someone had asked me to sculpt the perfect specimen, I wouldn't have even come close to capturing the imperfect perfection of Colin Wolfe. And he wants to...

I'm having a hard time pushing thoughts of his offer out of my mind. He hasn't asked me about it. He's probably waiting for my lead. But I don't know how to bring it up—not that I've decided my answer yet. Fuck, actually I have. I want it. I want him. I know that's not really what he offered but maybe...

I'm too nervous to bring it up after the concert.

Or the next day.

We're traveling on the bus anyway. No privacy. I'll talk to him about it during our next hotel stay. Yes. That will be best. That's in two more days.

* * *

Colin and I set our bags down on the gray upholstered benches at the ends of the matching queen beds. There hadn't even been enough time to check-in to our room when we got in town. It was straight off the bus to get ready for the show, then immediately after the show to go eat. So even though it's not too late, we're exhausted.

I've been on the verge of hyperventilating all day.

Like, this is it. This is the time I told myself I would speak up.

Colin casually slings his guitar case on his bed, toes off his shoes, and rubs at his temple like he has a headache. If he has a headache, it probably isn't the best time to start this conversation.

"Gray?"

"What?"

"Can I ask you—" He pauses, chewing on his cheek for a second. "I don't know why I'm nervous." He walks over to me and my heart starts pounding. "Can I play the song for you? I think I finally have it all figured out."

Oh. "Of course." Damn.

He gets out his guitar, inspects the strings and dials quickly, then sits on his bed while I sit on mine, facing him. He settles the guitar in his lap, and I watch the tattoos on his arms and hands move as he strums. The guitar rhythm is simple but beautiful and I close my eyes to listen.

Colin starts to sing and I have to open them again to watch. Watching him sing may be my favorite thing on the planet. He makes it look so effortless, changing registers, adding a little vibrato or distortion to his voice to make it extra raspy and sexy. But mostly I love it because when he sings, I can feel all of his emotions, raw and real and deep. It's like when he sings, all of his emotions spill out of his body, overwhelming the senses, unable to be contained, and they flow right into my soul.

He starts into the chorus, and I haven't heard all of these parts yet.

> *So here is my heart*
> *Ugly and bruised*
> *Broken and abused*
> *But it pumps just for you*
> *If you want it to*
> *Only for you*
> *If you want me too*

He looks up from the guitar to me, and I realize I'm singing with him as he repeats the bridge and chorus again. Our eyes lock as we sing, "*Only for you, if you want me too.*"

He strums the last few lazy notes then sets the guitar down.

"I like hearing you sing," he says.

"Thanks." I play with the ends of my hair as the nervous energy from the last few days seeps back under my skin. *Now would be a good time to bring it up, right?* But I don't know.

He rolls his neck and yawns. "I'm exhausted. Never sleep that great on the bus. Think I'm going to get ready for bed. That okay with you?"

"Yeah, sure."

He lets me get ready first and I sit cross-legged on my bed in my white sleep tank and little pink cotton shorts while he's in the bathroom. I listen to him softly sing to himself while I fidget with my hands. They're cold, my head is hot, and my stomach is in knots.

If not now, then when?

Colin walks out wearing a thin, soft white cotton shirt and loose-fitting gray drawstring pants. He goes to his bed, throws back the thin duvet and then slides down his pants to reveal tight, black boxer briefs.

It's now or never.

He lets the pants fall to the floor and leans over the mattress, about to slide in.

"Col—"

He looks up. Shit, his eyes are so pretty.

"I, um. Can we talk?"

He waits expectedly for me to continue. Because, that's what's supposed to happen now. *How am I supposed to start?* He tilts his head and comes around to my bed with a furrowed brow.

"Everything okay?" He sits next to me on the bed, one leg bent, his knee touching mine, and the other foot on the floor.

"Yeah," is all I can manage. I'm still playing with the ends of my hair.

"You wanted to talk?"

I nod, trying to keep myself from looking away. We sit. Still not talking.

Colin breaks into the tiniest smirk. "You want to talk about the other night?"

I nod.

"You want to talk about what I said I wanted to do with you."

It's not a question and my face heats and I swallow hard as I nod again.

"Okay…" He waits.

My fingers are interlocked and twisting so hard it's starting to hurt. My pulse is so loud I hope he can't hear it.

"You're going to have to say actual words, Gray."

He's right. I know he is. Okay. Here goes. I am not timid. I can do this. I take a deep breath. "I want to try that with you." And now, I'd like to bury my face in my hands.

"I need you to be more specific than that." He's leaning in, lowering his voice even though we're alone.

"I"—*Fuck*—"want you to help me have my first"—Holy Mother of Jesus—"orgasm."

His smirk turns into a genuine smile, but it's gone again as soon as he starts talking. "I'd like that too. When do you want to do it?"

My stomach does a full turn. "Right now?"

His eyebrows shoot up.

"If that's okay," I add.

"Yeah. That's more than okay." He looks down to where my hands are fisted, down my bare legs and back up to me face. "First thing—you need to relax." He holds out his arms to me. "Come here."

I go to him and he envelops me in his arms. He holds me for what feels like several minutes, warm and firm, his cheek resting against my hair.

"I want you to know"—his voice is soothing and low—"that nothing we do will to leave this room. Also, I'm going to be telling you to do things, but you're the one in control. Always. You can say no or tell me to stop, okay?"

"Okay," I say in a breathy whisper.

"Good. Now, how about you lie down? Get comfortable."

I scoot up the mattress and he grabs another pillow for me from his bed then helps position it behind me. My heart goes wild whenever he's near, even when his arm barely brushes mine. The idea of Colin attending to me is too much.

He sits near my feet. "Take off your shorts."

I think I've stopped breathing.

"Leave your underwear on."

I hesitate and he puts his hands up.

"It's all you," he says.

I shimmy my shorts down and kick them to the other side of the bed and settle back down against the pillows.

"Now close your eyes."

I close my eyes and everything goes dark. Everything disappears but the soft pillows under me, the distant, vibrating hum of the air conditioning, and Colin's hand, lightly resting on my calf. Not in a sexual way, more of a calming way, so I know he's right here with me, anchoring me in place.

"How do you like to touch yourself?"

"I... I don't know." I put my hands on my stomach, not sure where to go from here.

"Do you like your breasts touched?"

"Yes." I slide my hands up my sides, over my shirt to cup my breasts. They're not large but they fill my hands.

"Has anyone else felt you up there before?"

"Yes." I rub over my breasts slowly.

"Over your shirt?"

"Yes."

"Over your bra?"

"Yes." I continue massaging my breasts a little more firmly.

"Under your bra?" His voice is thick and I continue touching myself.

"Yes."

"Does it feel nice?"

"Mm hmm."

"Do it a little harder," he orders.

I squeeze with more force, arching up into the touch, my breathing increasing in speed.

"How does that feel?"

"Good."

"Rub over your nipples."

My face heats at his words but I do it anyway. As I brush my fingers over the sensitive tips, they stiffen under my shirt. I'm sure he can see them and I try to cover my hard little peaks with my hands.

"You don't have to be embarrassed about anything in front of me. Especially your body's natural responses.

They're perfect. Now roll them between your fingers. Yeah, just like that. A little harder. Give a little pinch and tug. Do you like that?"

"Not as much," I say, almost out of breath.

"Okay, good. Rub down your stomach. Spread your legs."

Oh. My. God.

His thumb on my calf moves in the softest of circles. "Relax. Just like that."

I let my knees fall to the mattress, spread wide on the bed.

"Touch your pussy."

A jolt pulses between my legs.

"Over your panties, just like that. Just to get the blood flowing to the right places. How does it feel? Is it getting warmer?"

"Uh huh." My panties are silky under my fingers, warmth seeping through the fabric.

"You've done this before?"

"Yes."

"Do you want to slip a finger under your panties?"

"Mm hmm." My voice comes out almost a whimper. I slide a finger under the edge of my underwear to find myself already swollen, slick, and oversensitive there.

"Take them off."

My eyes shoot open at his words. He's sitting, almost hunched over, his gaze hungry on my body, his eyes almost black. He looks at me, taking shallow breaths.

"Here." He pulls back the covers so I can get under them. "I don't need to see anything. This about you, not me." He pulls the covers up to my stomach. "Now, take them off," he says again, in a gentle but firm tone.

I wiggle them down under the covers, careful to stay covered. It's weird, even though I'm under layers of bedding and he can't see anything, just knowing that he knows makes me sweat.

He sits back on his heels and his thick erection is clearly defined, bulging in his boxer briefs.

"Are you touching it?" he asks.

I slide my hand back down between my legs and nod. I rub over my mound as I watch Colin watch me. It's simultaneously hot and awkward. I don't really know what I'm doing. What if this doesn't work and then he's disappointed I didn't come?

"What's going on, Gray? Are you getting embarrassed again?"

I shake my head no. "I just don't know if this is going to work."

"You're thinking too much. Only think about sexy stuff. What turns you on?"

"Turns me on?"

"Yeah. What makes you horny?"

Luckily, I've been flushed this whole time so he probably doesn't notice this new wave of heat blooming in my cheeks.

"Tell me. It can be anything, as boring or as kinky you can think of. I won't repeat it or judge. I used to beat off to my mom's sewing pattern books."

"Really?" I try to stifle my giggle with little success.

Colin is unamused. "This is about you, remember? Tell me something."

"I don't know."

"There's got to be something."

My eyes flicker down to his boxers again. My mouth

opens in a little *oh* at the sight of his cock, even larger than before straining under the black fabric.

He notices my gaze. A coy smile touches his lips. "Do you like that I'm hard for you?"

Mayday! Mayday! My entire neck and face is going up in flames. I don't even know what to say.

"You know that it's for you, right?"

I look up at him, my heart beating wildly as he leans over me on his hands and knees.

"Does it turn you on, knowing that you turn me on?"

I turn him on? A surge of heat blooms between my legs at the thought.

"Yes." It's barely a whisper.

His smile grows at my response—it's devious and sexy. He pulls his shirt off and tosses it to the floor and the sight of him, stripped before me, is glorious.

"Get your fingers wet."

"Huh?"

"Lick them. It will feel better."

I take my hand out from the covers and bring them to my lips. They smell of the musk of my arousal and while I don't find it unpleasant, I don't really want to put them in my mouth either. Should I wipe them off first?

A tiny chuckle comes from Colin's chest. "You don't want to taste yourself?"

I shake my head and crinkle my nose.

"Okay, just try spitting on them. Unless…" He brings his fist up to his mouth and bites his knuckle.

"Unless what?"

He shakes his head. "I told myself this was going to be only about you. I wasn't going to touch you."

"Tell me what you were going to say. Unless what?"

He lets out a breath. "Unless you want me to lick them for you."

My whole body clenches at the thought. "Do you want to...lick them?"

His eyes are dark with want. "Yes. I do."

He wants to taste me? I hold my hand out toward him and he takes it gently. He slowly runs a flat tongue over the pads of my index and middle fingers. Then he takes the tips into his mouth and closes his eyes before sucking on them. It sends shivers down the length of my spine.

"Now touch yourself. Spread your legs all the way," he says, his breath hot on my moistened fingers.

I put my hand back under the covers. My warm, wet fingers slide through my folds, and it does feel better.

Colin lies down next to me on his side, propped up on an elbow. "Describe it to me."

I close my eyes. "Warm. Slippery."

"Start your fingers low, at your opening."

I do as instructed, telling him what I'm doing and how it feels. He tells me to dip in just enough to get my fingers extra slick and then rub up and down the sides, between each of my swollen lips and layers.

"Go higher," he whispers.

When my fingers reach the apex and touch the little nub, a surge of pleasure rolls through my core and I let out a little moan.

"Are you on your clit?"

"Uh huh."

"Keep rubbing it. Tell me how it feels."

"It's so sensitive. It almost tickles." I keep my fingers on it, rubbing in little circles. The sensation tingles all the way down my legs and pools behind my knees.

He tells me how to touch it. In slow, up and down strokes. Then faster, harder. On the sides, over the top, and then underneath.

"Oh." I gasp, electricity shooting through me when I touch it right there.

"Is it good?"

"Yeah."

"What do you like best? Slow, soft, or harder, faster?"

"I… I like it harder. Fast." I breathe.

"Then do that. Don't stop."

So I keep rubbing, touching, flicking over my clit faster and faster. My breathing is rough and I'm starting to moan. I close my eyes and tell him how it feels. How swollen and wet I feel, how my pussy feels wide open. How empty I feel.

"What?" he asks.

"I mean, I feel hollow. Like I need more pressure, like I want something inside me. To fill me up."

"Fuck." His breathing sounds shallow, pained. "Can you use your other hand? Put a finger or two inside yourself?"

I reach with my other hand, but I can't get in without sitting up and risking letting the blankets fall off me.

"Not from this angle." My voice is shaky.

"Hmm."

I keep stoking the heat between my legs but I grunt in frustration. I know feeling something inside me, hard and hot, would feel so good.

"I really want something inside. I think it would help me come."

"Fuck. Okay, we can get you a dildo or something for next time so you can fuck yourself with it while you play with your clit." He presses his wrist along the length of his erection, shifting his hips slightly on the bed.

I whimper.

"You like that idea?"

"God, yes."

"You're so fucking sexy. Are you playing with your clit right now?"

"Yes."

"Talk to me."

I tell him how it feels under my fingers, how sensitive it is, how it feels bigger and harder than when I started.

Colin's eyes roll back. "Do you know how crazy you're driving me? To know that you're touching yourself right now and I can't see?"

I start moaning in earnest now, dipping the tip of my finger into my opening and dragging the wetness back up to my clit to massage it. My pace intensifies as I feel Colin closer at my side.

"I can just imagine how hot, wet, and swollen your pussy is right now," he says into my ear. "I bet it's the prettiest pink. I can still taste it. You taste so good, Gray."

Oh fuck. My fingertips move furiously over the little bundle of nerves. Harder. Faster. A weird feeling is growing low in my belly, a pressure, like a coil is forming in my gut, tightening, building tension.

"Col, I think something's happening."

"Good girl. Keep going. Tonight, you're going to get yourself off, but if we do this again, I want to touch you next time. Can I?"

"Yes. Please, yes," I pant.

"I'm going to sink two fingers inside you while you play with your clit. I'll have you ride my fingers until you're writhing with need. I want your clit in my mouth when you come and my name on your lips, begging for my cock."

I've never had anyone say something so filthy to me. And it's Colin, I—

The tense coil inside me bursts, releasing all the pent up energy and a wave of intense pleasure throws my body into convulsions as I shout out.

Colin rolls to his back, a guttural grunt emanating from deep inside him. Then he sits up, hand on his groin, and gets up quickly, walking away from me toward the bathroom. He rips his boxers off and I catch a glimpse of his naked ass, smooth and taut. His crumpled up boxers are in his hand and it looks like he's finishing himself off and wiping himself up before he closes the bathroom door.

CHAPTER 16

It's not long before he turns the shower on, and I want to stay awake but my body is so tired and relaxed and sated. And my eyelids feel heavy and the mattress is warm and soft. I glance to the bedside clock and it's almost four in the morning. The sounds of rushing water through pipes and the ting it makes hitting tile and glass is soothing and sleep overtakes me.

"Hey."

The word barely registers in my haziness. I groan and roll over, away from the noise, and bury my face back between the pillows.

"Gray." Colin's voice comes through, quiet and soft, at the same time fingers lightly stroke along my arm.

Languidly, my eyes open and the blurry image of Colin's face comes into focus. Bright light is streaming through the sheer curtains, Colin and I having forgotten to close the heavier ones last night.

"What time is it? Is it time to leave?" I sit up, rubbing my eyes.

"It's almost ten. Check-out isn't until noon. You can go back to sleep. I'm sorry, I didn't want to wake you. I just wanted to let you know that I was leaving."

His hand is still brushing along my arm and I try to act like it's totally normal. I don't even notice it, actually. Totally unaffected. Thing is, it's a completely normal thing. He touches me like this all the time—just not in our hotel room. Not when we're alone.

"I've got a couple things to do before tonight. Then we have early rehearsal and a meet-and-greet with some radio station before the show. The bus will be here at noon to take you to the venue. You can just hang on the bus, or you can come find me—I mean, find us—anytime. If you want."

"Okay." I let out a huge yawn and blink at him.

He looks so good in a loose black tank top that shows off all of his incredible ink.

He leans over me. "Go back to sleep," he whispers with a little smile and then he kisses the top of my head before he turns to leave.

He kissed me. In our room. Not in a super intimate way, but still. He's never done that when no one's around to witness it. Obviously what we did last night blurred some already wobbly lines, but now I have no idea where the lines even are. Are there any lines anymore?

I'm not sure what's real and what's pretend. When we're out and he's holding my hand or wrapping an arm around me—is that just for show? Because not everyone in a relationship is so touchy all the time. So is he doing that just because he wants to?

And then what we did last night...

When he told me he wants to make me come with his fingers inside me and his mouth on my clit, was that true? Or did he just say it in the heat of the moment in order to help me come? Because it worked. It *really* worked for me.

***

I'm sitting on the bus in the parking lot behind the venue and have no idea what to do. I'm too anxious to write or nap—which is what I usually do when the guys are busy with band stuff. Colin did say I could go join them whenever. He'd wanted to say *me, you can come find me.* Does that mean he wants me to be there?

Ugh. I'm so confused about him.

This morning when he woke me up I was still half asleep and too groggy to comprehend how sweet he was being to me. He could have easily left me a note or a text letting me know he had to leave, but he woke me up like he just wanted to talk to me and kiss me goodbye.

I tried to go back to sleep after but got nothing more than some fitful tossing and turning accomplished.

I step off the bus and onto the hot pavement. We're just on the outskirts of downtown Denver and it's gorgeous out. The sun is shining over everything, not even a speckle of a cloud in the bright blue sky. Jagged mountains stand above the tops of buildings in the distance, their peaks dipped in brilliant white, even though it's nearing the end of June.

I've never been to Denver before, so I keep walking toward downtown. Right now, I seem to be in an area entirely made up of micro-breweries and tiny, hipster restaurants. I take out my phone.

Me: *Something might be happening with the singer*

Kyla: *The dark and serious looking one? OMG did you make out and then not immediately inform me?*

Me: *No, no making out*

Kyla: *Just a kiss then?*

Me: *No kissing*

Kyla: *So like what? Hand job over the jeans?*

Me: *omg no it's just the way he's been acting*

Kyla: *So nothing has actually happened yet?*

I don't know how to answer that without opening the huge can of worms that is our fake dating arrangement.

Kyla: *...*

Me: *Kinda, not really, but sort of*

Kyla: *WTF*

Me: *He basically offered to help me experiment with sexual stuff*

Kyla: *wut*

Kyla: *OMFG why did you not open with this information?*

I send her the anxious face emoji.

Kyla: *There's so much to unpack here I CAN'T EVEN. But mostly I'm just jealous your first time gets to be with someone who actually knows what he's doing and not two minutes with Darren Johnston in the back of his mom's minivan.*

Me: *I didn't say we were going to do it*

Kyla: *Why TF not? Seriously what does it matter who's your first v. your second or third? Virginity is a social construct that doesn't mean anything*

Me: *But how do I know if he actually likes me or just wants to get in my pants?*

Kyla: *We're talking about a summer fling here, not your future husband right?*

Me: *Right*

Kyla: *Then forget about all the feelings stuff and just let yourself enjoy the moment. If he's offering this opportunity then jump on it!*

Kyla: *Literally I mean jump on that dick*

Me: *Okay... how should I tell him I want to jump on it?*

Kyla: *One word: PEACOCK*

Kyla: *Put something on that you feel confident and sexy in then strut. You shouldn't have to do anything more than present yourself if he's into you he'll flock to you*

Me: *Flock? Way to keep to the bird theme*

Kyla: *I'm nothing if not committed*

Me: *Speaking of committed, how is Operation Get Wes's Attention going?*

Upon the last Wes update, things had been starting to progress and Kyla was quite optimistic that Wes was becoming susceptible to her specific brand of charm.

Kyla: *It's going well. I've recruited Eric to help me since you're absent.*

Me: *My brother Eric?*

Kyla: *Of course your brother Eric. Is there another Eric? He's my official wingman and he's doing a great job actually. You better be careful or he'll have replaced you as my new best friend by the time you get back.*

Me: *New best friend? I thought you two annoyed the shit out of each other*

Kyla: *We do, but idk, he's growing on me. I'll keep you updated*

Me: *Please*

I look up and realize I'm just about to pass an outdoor mall. Serendipitous, really.

Peacocking, huh? All right. I can do that.

* * *

I WEAVE MY WAY THROUGH THE DARK HALL, THE SECURITY GUY having barely let me through the door after scrutinizing my pass for several minutes. This venue is tiny and there are no dressing rooms, just a backstage lounge area not far from the stage which is also poorly lit. I turn the corner and stop just before going through the open doorway.

Currently, a local band is playing for the audience and all of my guys and the Donkey Lips guys are standing or sitting, chatting and drinking. There are also a few girls hanging around. Maybe they already procured a few groupies at the meet-and-greet earlier.

Colin is standing with Logan. My heart gives an abrupt thump at the sight of him. He's wearing the same black tank as earlier. It's low-cut on the sides and I can see the ripple of his abs when he turns in profile.

I'm overdressed. I should just go back to the bus and change into my cut-off shorts and Chucks like I normally wear to shows before he sees me and thinks I'm silly. I'm wearing a red romper I bought earlier today. It's little—the shorts barely cover my ass, but the top has a high neckline so I don't feel too exposed. Let's just forget that it's completely backless and I'm not wearing a bra. This peacocking idea was dumb.

Jace, one of the Boners—I honestly don't even care anymore—and a girl walk toward Colin and Logan. Jace is wearing a smug look, the brunette hanging on his arm, as he gets Logan's attention and cocks his chin, motioning down a hallway in the other direction.

"You guys are on in fifteen fucking minutes," Colin says.

"I'll make sure he's back in time." Logan hits Jace on the back as they start to walk away.

"You coming, babe?" Jace asks the girl.

"I'll wait here for you," she says, and then they disappear down the dark hallway. It's like this place can't afford lightbulbs.

The woman doesn't seem at all upset to lose her

companion. In fact, her face lights up as she stalks over to Colin and puts a hand on his shoulder to get his attention. I take a step backward, retreating farther into the dark. And then I recognize her pretty face, curly hair, and that perfect makeup application. It's Marnie, the groupie from Vegas.

"You know"—she lets her hand slide down his biceps—"I'm really happy to see you again. I still think about our kiss sometimes."

Colin looks down at her like he's suddenly noticed a fly buzzing around him, his face scrunched up. "Our what?" he asks, eyes squinted.

"Our kiss. Don't you remember? Spin the bottle."

"Oh. Right."

She steps closer in. "I wanted to let you know I'd be up for way more than kissing this go around."

Colin backs away. "Not interested. I have a girlfriend."

He looks past her to where Dean and Joey are sitting in the corner with a Boner and another random chick. He goes to sidestep her in their direction but she mirrors his step, blocking his path.

"I distinctly remember you being single when I asked in Vegas." She puts her hands on her hips.

He pinches the bridge of his nose and I'd feel bad for him if I didn't find this whole exchange rather amusing and strangely reassuring.

"It's fairly recent." He looks toward the corner like he's trying to send out a mental distress signal to his bandmates.

Marnie doesn't move. "Oh! Is it that little blonde that's traveling with you?"

Colin nods curtly, crossing his arms, muscles tensed.

"Hmm, she's really cute. I would totally be up for a

threesome with you guys."

The look he gives her so clearly says *what the fuck?* that I almost giggle.

"Yeah, no." He moves away from her again. But this time another girl comes up to them, smiling.

My chest involuntarily lurches forward. I should go rescue him.

Marnie positions herself at the perfect angle to arch her back and emphasis her rack. "Is your girlfriend not very adventurous? She did look pretty young. Does she even have any idea what to do with you?"

I step into the room, my sandals clacking on the floor just loud enough for them to turn my way. "I think I can figure it out," I say, striding toward them.

"Gray." The word is barely off his lips before the biggest, most beautiful smile overtakes Colin's face and if I thought he rivaled the sun when he smiled before, I was wrong. The way he's looking at me right now, with pure elation, his smile has the power of a thousand stars. A galaxy of them shining through his eyes.

He walks toward me and I pick up my speed. His arms are out and I wrap mine around his neck just as he scoops me up. My legs instinctively wrap around his waist as he spins me around.

Colin is spinning me.

And it's making me laugh and when we stop the smile on his face is still just as big. We're chest-to-chest, a little out of breath, heart pounding. His lips are parted—his beautiful, soft-looking lips and I want to put my hands on either side of his head and crush those lips to mine.

I'm sure he wouldn't stop me.

But if I kissed him, would he kiss me back?

And if he kissed me back, would it be real?

I look into his dark blue eyes—swirling with heat and emotion—like he might be having the exact same thought, his eyes searching mine for an answer to an unasked question.

I will him to hear my answer.

Yes. Kiss me. Please.

He tightens his arms around me and I squeeze my legs around his middle. Blood is rushing in my ears as our breath mingles in the inch between us. Then he buries his face into my shoulder, kissing my skin there instead, his scruff tickling against my neck before he sets me down.

* * *

I SING ALONG TO ALL THE SONGS, STANDING IN MY DARK LITTLE corner just offstage. I know the set by heart—the way Joey taps his sticks together four times before each song, the looks that pass between Logan and Dean as they play, and how focused Colin is as he sings. I love when Logan panders to the crowd as Colin sips water between songs, and when Colin does murmur a few words into the mic, they love him for it.

"I wanted to do something a little different tonight," Colin says into the mic after their last song. "Thought I'd perform a new song we've been working on for you."

The crowd goes wild and the stage is a blur for a minute as crewmembers carry out two stools, an extra mic stand, and Colin's acoustic guitar while the rest of the guys exit the stage. Joey gives me a freckled fist bump, Dean squeezes me on the shoulder, and Logan winks at me as they huddle around, watching the stage as Colin stands there alone, a single spotlight shining on him and his guitar.

"Someone very special is going to join me to sing this one, so give her some love." The audience starts clapping as Colin looks directly at me.

"That's you, Blondie," Dean whispers from behind.

"Go on." Logan gives my shoulder a nudge toward the stage.

I don't move. Just stand here, confused, but then Colin crooks a tattooed finger at me and smiles his same stupid fucking happy, beautiful smile, and I step out of the shadows and onto the stage.

The light from overhead is a bright white that softens to orange at the edges. When I look out to the crowd, the light is all I can see—a solid cone filled with the haze of the air and obscuring everything else. I can't even tell how big the room is or how many people are watching me. I've never been shy about performing but my heart is pounding.

The wood stage creaks under my foot. The black paint on it is worn down and chipping off more as I make it to the center of the stage. I keep my eyes on Colin and he starts to play as I sit across from him, our knees touching. The spotlight is warm on my skin.

The audience goes quiet.

There's no sound but the music he's making. And then he starts singing and it's only me and him. He's singing for me and I feel every note, every word.

I sing the words with him on the second verse, my voice feathery light to his low and gritty. The audience is still, quiet. But I can feel them. Energy sizzles through the room as the song builds. Colin's fingers move faster as he plays and I let go, belting out the chorus with him and I'm lost in it. In the words, and him, and the song, and how perfectly our voices can harmonize and mix one moment then contrast and stand apart on the next note. I keep singing before I realize he's stopped. He's playing and watching me with his dark eyes and a wicked little smile as he lets me sing the last verse before the final refrain.

I feel a shudder whisper through the crowd as he joins me on the last few lines. Soft. Slow. *If you want me, too.*

The song is over and he and I are quiet. I'm vaguely aware that the audience is clapping and cheering and lights are flashing and chairs are scraping against the floor. But I'm only looking at him. And he's only looking at me.

He's closer, his hand on my jaw, his thumb soft on my cheek. And he's leaning toward me. Everything is in slow motion.

His gaze lingers on my mouth and I don't even think I'm breathing. His lips are dark, moistened, his jaw line a sharp contrast against the black rose and skull tattoos on his neck, but I keep being pulled back to his eyes. They're asking the same question. Drawing me in. Closer.

Closer.

I put my hand on his knee to steady myself as his hand curves around the back of my neck, pulling me in, closing the last inch between us until our lips meet.

He kisses me soft. Too soft. Too gentle. His lips are warm, perfect, as he presses more firmly against me and the entire room spins.

He breaks the kiss too soon, our faces linger in place and I'm dizzy with him—the scent of him, the feel of his fingers on the nape of my neck. He presses a second quick kiss to my lips before pulling away.

CHAPTER 17

AFTER THE SHOW AND ALL THROUGH DINNER, I'M GOING crazy trying to figure out what happened on stage. He'd kissed me. I'd kissed him back, obviously. But *he'd* kissed *me*. Was it real? Or was it just for the show? It had been quick and there hadn't been any tongue or anything, so maybe it wasn't a big deal to him.

It's been two hours and I still can't stop thinking about it.

Colin is acting like he always does when we're around everybody—like he's my boyfriend, which doesn't help me out any. He held my hand the entire time until we sat down to eat and now he has his arm resting on the back of my chair around my shoulders as he talks with Dean and actively ignores Jace's attempts to get his attention.

"Hey, you guys going to play tonight?" Logan asks, his left eye twitching a little, already several shots into the night. "We're playing Truth or Dare."

Colin tilts his head toward me, asking a silent question. His blue eyes are bright, almost sparkling, as if he couldn't be happier to defer to me.

I don't blink or look away from him, just shake my head

slightly.

He gives me an almost imperceptible grin. "No," he says to Logan, "we're just going to head back to the bus."

My cheeks heat at the thought of going back alone with him. I want to talk to him about the kiss. I want to do it again.

But I'm also terrified he'll tell me it didn't mean anything and when he realizes I'm starting to catch feelings he will decide to end this—whatever this is. Whatever this is, I want it, even if it's fake. I'd rather have a fake Colin than no Colin.

Dean leans over to us. "You better take Joey with you. He's one drink away from challenging random people to an arm wrestling match."

Across the table, Joey's normally pale, freckled skin is as red as a tomato and starting to sweat. Our server, an older woman with a thick helmet of blonde hair, walks over to see if we'd like another round of drinks, and when Joey starts commenting on the size of her biceps and asking if she lifts, we know it's time to intervene.

"But I don't want to go back to the bus." Joey pouts, looking at his empty glass.

"What if...we get ice cream?" Colin says.

Joey looks up, eyes brightening. "Can I get a waffle cone?"

* * *

We emerge onto the street, triumphant with our ice cream cones in hand after an agonizingly long thirty minute wait in line. Joey got three giant scoops of some sort of peanut-butter-brownie fudge pecan brittle swirl that tower precariously above his chocolate-dipped and sprinkle-covered cone. He giddily goes for the top scoop, tongue out and waggling. He barely gets a taste before his overzealous tongue knocks the scoop right off and to the sidewalk with a thud. Ice cream is streaked down his arm and as he looks around, trying to figure out what happened, the entire cone slips out of his hand, crashing to the concrete and splitting down the center.

Joey looks up at us with wide eyes and then back to the ice cream shop, where customers are still lined up out the door, then back to the sad, broken waffle cone on the ground, ice cream already starting to melt and ooze out the cracks. He looks so helpless, his wide shoulders rounded in a slump and his mouth turned down. Even his bright neon yellow hair is giving him a sad clown vibe.

"Here." I offer him my single-scoop of mint chocolate chip.

"No, that's okay. I couldn't—" He looks like he might drunk cry.

"Really, I'm not even hungry. I just got it because you guys were. Please, take it." I hold it out to him.

"You sure?" But he's already reaching for it and I hand it to him gladly.

"That was really sweet of you." Colin leans over, whispering in my ear.

I shrug. "It's not a big deal."

"You can share mine, if you want."

"Thanks, but I'm okay." I wasn't lying about the not being hungry part, my stomach has been so twisted up all evening because of that kiss.

We walk down the sidewalk toward where the bus is parked. The sky is black with low-hanging, fluffy gray clouds covering most of the stars. There's a warm breeze but Colin's hand light on my back as we walk makes me shiver. It's not an unusual place for him to put his hand, but I don't typically wear backless things, and for some reason, his hand on my bare skin, gently caressing over my spine, feels like the most intimate touch I've ever experienced.

I look up at him as he eats, at the tattoos that contour under his jaw, at his soft lips—those lips were on mine earlier—and at his pink tongue as it peeks out from those lips to lick and lap up his quickly melting huckleberry ice cream. What I wouldn't give to have felt that tongue inside my mouth, mingling with mine...

He notices me ogling him and quirks his head toward me, raising an eyebrow. I probably have a crazed, desperate expression on my face.

"Want some after all?" He points his cone toward me.

He thinks I'm desperately looking at the ice cream. Right. I'm definitely hungry for the ice cream and not your mouth. Totally.

I nod to save face. We stop and he lowers it to me—Joey happily walking on with his cone, oblivious. I lift up to my tippy toes and swipe my tongue over the sweet and tart ice cream. I'm not trying to go slow or be particularly sexy about it, but when I look up and lock eyes with Colin, my tongue moving up his cone, I feel like I'm doing something naughty.

He watches me lick and bites his lower lip. At the same time, the hand on my back lightens, curling around the side of my ribs, his fingertips inching just inside the edge of my jumpsuit and I wonder if he isn't thinking the same thing I am.

After finishing our ice cream on the bus, I doggedly

ask Joey about all of his tattoos. His sleeves are all bright and colorful cartoon characters—mostly from nineties-era Nickelodeon. Some obscure, but some classics too. Some of them he drew himself and I'm amazed. I had no idea how talented of an artist he is.

Dean strides onto the bus around three in the morning, lamenting about how he went to three different clubs and didn't see even one bear.

"I mean, we're surrounded by mountains and forests and shit. I figured I'd be swarmed by bears."

"I think any bears around here would stay away from the city," I say, a little confused why he wants to see a bear anyway.

Dean presses his hand over his mouth and Colin gives my arm a little squeeze before running his fingertips down from my shoulder to elbow and back.

Joey gives a hearty chuckle and stands up. "I'm going to bed." His shoulders are still bouncing as he disappears to the back of the bus.

"What?" I'm missing something.

"When I say *bear*, I don't mean the lions, tigers, and bears kind. I mean the twinks, bears, and daddies kind," Dean says.

"Oh." Oh. I want to ask what classifies someone as a bear but I think I've already made an ass out of myself.

Luckily, as if reading my thoughts, Dean continues. "I like them big and burly and a little bit squishy, with a huge beard and as much body hair as possible." Dean looks off into the distance, as if he can perfectly see this beautiful, hairy man of his dreams. "Where are we heading next? Chicago?"

Colin nods, still lightly rubbing my arm. So light it tickles and gives me goosebumps.

"Fuck, there's got to be some bears there. I mean, the Chicago Bears! It's a thing, right?"

"It's a football team."

"I could get on board with a football player."

Dean says goodnight not much later and then it's just Colin and me.

Alone.

Colin unwraps his arm from around me and clasps his hands on top of the table. I already feel cold without his touch.

"So… Chicago…" Colin says after a few minutes of silence. "That's just a few hours from where you live."

"Yeah."

"I'm sure we'd be able to make the detour and take you back home. If you want."

His words are like a bucket of ice water. "Do you want me to leave?"

He looks at me soberly. "No."

Relief washes through me and I try to stifle the smile that's tugging on my lips. "Good, because I don't want to go back." Not yet, at least.

A tiny crease deepens between his brows. "Is everything okay at home? You never told me why you ran away." His concern is so sincere it makes my heart want to burst.

"No, no. It's nothing like that. Everything at home is fine. Wonderful. My family is great."

He keeps looking at me, his head slightly tilted, hoping I'll explain.

I huff out a breath and tell him the truth. About how I was supposed to be in a prestigious program this summer, but I lost my spot because I failed half my classes last semester and the ones I didn't outright fail, I either barely passed or took incompletes.

"Do your parents put a lot of pressure on you to do well in school? Are they super strict, harsh?"

"No. I just... I've never even gotten a C in school before, and I guess I was embarrassed. And I didn't want them to be disappointed in me." I look down so my hair falls over my face. "I also probably lost my spot in my program and my scholarship."

He flattens his hands on the table. "I don't know your parents, but from what you've said about them and knowing that you've never had problems with school before, I'd guess they'd be more concerned about you than your grades or money. Obviously something was wrong." He moves his hand closer to mine on the table, our pinkies almost touching.

I swallow the thickness in my throat. I hadn't thought much past my hurt pride. He's probably right.

"So, what happened? What was wrong?" Colin's voice is quiet as he slides his hand over just enough to hook his pinky with mine.

"I don't know. It started slow, I guess. I did okay first semester—mostly Bs—even though I had no social life and studied constantly. I probably took a few too many credits." Scratch that, I'd definitely taken too many credits.

He listens intently as I continue, but I can't look at him as I speak.

"The first day of second semester, I couldn't find one of my classrooms and I walked in late. The professor decided to make an example of me and point it out to the whole class. I was mortified."

He's still quiet and I focus on our intertwined pinkies. A

silent comfort. And I feel safe opening up.

"I dreaded going to that class every Monday, Wednesday, and Friday. I started becoming paranoid about oversleeping or being late. And then a month into the semester, I got the flu and missed a week of classes. I missed a test. Got a bad grade on a paper. Everything seemed to be spiraling further out of control. Some days, I'd wake up feeling so stressed about what might go wrong that day I would just stay in bed and do nothing at all. Missing more class only made things worse, which would make me more stressed, and then I'd feel guilty and angry for sabotaging myself."

He slides his hand so it covers mine. He holds it tight, giving it a warm squeeze and I finally look over to him.

He's regarding me with his pensive gaze—the one I'd felt when I first saw him across the dance floor, when he sang to me, the one that I swear can see into my soul. I know he sees me.

"It sounds like you put a lot of pressure on yourself to meet some high expectations."

I remember Kyla telling me I don't always need to be perfect. "Yeah. I guess so."

"It also seems like you were having some anxiety."

"I was just stressed." I shrug off the words.

"It's not anything to be ashamed about. It's a struggle for many people. It was probably made worse by the fact you didn't have any of your support system around. And it might help, before you go back to school, to talk to someone about it. Someone who knows a lot more than me and can give you strategies to cope with it in the future."

A month ago, I don't think I could have handled having a conversation like this, but something in the way Colin is holding my hand and looking into my eyes makes me feel safe. And cared for.

"Sorry. This whole thing probably sounds dumb."

He rubs his thumb over my knuckles. "No. I get anxious sometimes, too."

"Really?"

"Mostly when I have to fly. But also right before we go on tour."

"Do you not like touring? I would have guessed you loved it."

"I do. But there are a lot of triggers for me on tour—a lot of temptations and opportunities to fall off the wagon. When we're on tour, I have to stay vigilant and I always feel like I'm on edge. I can't just relax and have fun like the other guys. My career is at stake—my friends' careers, and my life."

I hold my breath, like if I move or make noise I'll scare him off, and I want him to keep talking. I want to know everything about him.

"I've never really had a problem with alcohol or pot. It was the harder stuff. On tour if I drink, I only have one beer. I don't go out partying and I don't participate in Logan's games."

"But you played Logan's games with us." I notice how close we're sitting. His thigh is rubbing up against my knee and he's angled toward me, looming over me close enough we could almost touch foreheads.

"I only played because you were there."

Oh yeah. The babysitting. But calling it that doesn't seem to fit anymore. "You wanted to watch over me." I warm at the thought.

He gives a small nod. "I've told you that I have this fierce need to protect you. But it's more than that."

"More?"

He licks his lips. "Definitely more."

He swoops down, his mouth capturing mine. I don't even have a chance to suck in a breath before he's swallowing me up, pulling my body tight to his. He parts my lips with his, immediately seeking entrance. His tongue sensual and strong as it glides inside. He still tastes like ice cream, sweet and tart.

I'm not sure if I'm breathing. But I don't want to come up for air—not if it means stopping. I'm being devoured, pulled under the water, happy to drown with him.

I don't know if I climbed onto his lap or he pulled me here but I'm consumed by the feel of him—his hands on me, his hips as I squeeze them between my knees, my fingers sunken into his hair as I hold him to me, determined to never let this kiss end.

"Whoa, sorry guys." Logan's words are a bit slurred from behind us.

Colin is breathing hard when we break the kiss and watch Logan stagger onto the bus. The sight of Colin's lips swollen from kissing, his eyes black with desire, his chest still rising and falling erratically makes my entire being contract with need.

The heat in Colin's eyes is quickly replaced with concern and he stands to lend Logan a steadying hand, but Logan shrugs him off.

"What are you on?" Colin whispers.

Logan replies loudly, "Nothing, just need to sleep it off." He goes on to collapse into his bunk.

Colin looks at me and I know we should go to bed too.

Reluctantly, we linger for a few more minutes, fingers interlocked, before he finally kisses my forehead and says goodnight.

CHAPTER 18

It was real.

I don't have to ask.

The way he yielded to each of my advances, welcoming them. The way he stroked his tongue along mine, tasting every kiss, desperate but slow, never rushed. The way he groaned when I bit his bottom lip and the way his fingers tangled in my hair.

None of that was for anyone but us. He didn't do it for any other reason than he wanted to. I wanted it too. And I want more.

I should go to sleep, but I keep fidgeting with the hem of my sleep tank and thinking about him. I can't turn off my mind. I keep thinking about how his lips feel.

I finally slide out of my bunk. The air is cool against my bare legs, the carpet is not plush, but soft underfoot, and the only noises are of the lulling sounds of the bus cruising down the highway and Joey's nose whistling while he sleeps.

Colin is in one of the top bunks and I climb up the side carefully, though my legs are trembling. I try to open his curtain as quietly as possible and stealthily sneak in but my foot catches on the last rung, my knee smacks the edge and I end up in a heap at Colin's feet, twisted in his bedsheets.

He shifts under me and lets out a deep grunt before propping himself up on his elbows. It's dark in the bunk but I can make out the exact moment the scowl on his sleep-fogged face softens when he recognizes me.

"What are you doing?" he asks with a little smirk.

"I don't know..." Seducing you?

His smile widens with a flash of teeth as he pulls back his covers. He's lying there, in nothing but black boxer briefs, as I take in all of his pale skin covered in tattoos, from the snake vised around a dagger on his right thigh to the eagle spread across his chest, the tips of its wings reaching from shoulder to shoulder.

"Come here," he says.

The bunk is so narrow there's no other option but to crawl over him. I hover over him in the dark, our noses touching. He lifts his face to mine just enough to press a quick kiss to my lips then pulls the covers over us, wrapping me in his arms and holding me tight to his body. His body, which is warm—and mostly naked. Don't forget mostly naked.

"I didn't want to stop," I whisper to him.

"Me neither."

And then his hands are in my hair and he's kissing me in earnest, rolling us over so he's on top, his weight pressing me firmly to the mattress. And I revel in the feel of him, running my hands up his smooth back as he greedily devours my mouth. He nips and licks and sucks at my lips, tastes my tongue, going back for more and more as I move my fingertips down his sides and then between us. His abs contract when I trace over them and he breaks our kiss for a second, panting hard when I tease my fingers along his waistband.

"What do you want?" he asks between kisses.

"What can I get?"

"Anything."

I smile as he kisses along my jaw and to my neck, sending a shiver down my side even though I'm so warm, wrapped up in him.

"I want—"

His large hand skims up my ribs to cup the side of my breast just before his thumb strokes slowly over my nipple through the thin fabric of my shirt, and I momentarily lose all thought.

"I want you to touch me this time, when I come."

"Fuck." His voice is raspy in my ear. "I want that too."

He moves his palm over my breast, taking it fully into his hand and massaging with just enough pressure that I push into it. He kisses down my collarbone, his hands sure and steady on my body, giving firm squeezes and gentle strokes. His lips brush over the swell of my breast and then he kisses the tip, making my nipple pebble beneath him. I let out the tiniest breath of a moan before he takes my whole nipple into his mouth, sucking on it through my shirt, making my back arch off the bed.

Every reaction my body gives, he takes, not hesitating to give me more. More touching, more kisses, more tongue, more heat, more of our bodies pressing against one another. Always following my lead. I grip onto his back, clinging to him, running fingertips over his shoulder blades and down to the dimples just above his ass.

He kisses me harder as he grips my hip then palms my butt before sliding his hand down my thigh. He hooks my knee and spreads my leg so that he can nestle his hips between my thighs. He ruts against me, the solid bulge in his shorts dragging all along my center. He keeps rolling his hips into me as our kissing grows more frantic. If we were naked, he'd be pushing into me and my body clenches at the thought, warming with desire, eager to welcome him in.

I'm writhing beneath him, my body screaming for more, more. Then his fingers are sliding up the inside of my thigh. Slowly. Slowly up past the hem of my tiny shorts and up higher to graze his knuckle over my panties, along my sex. The touch is light and deliberate and I'm surprised to feel the pleasure of it in the tips of my toes and a tingle of my lips. I'm keenly aware of how damp my panties are, and just days ago the thought would have embarrassed me. But right now, knowing that he can feel how wet I am for him only excites me.

But then his touch is gone as he slides his hand away from me.

My chest tightens and I can't catch my breath. In my lust-filled dizziness, I can only get out the word, "No."

He tenses over me, motionless. "No?"

I lick my lips and try to steady my head. "I mean, don't stop." I reach down between us and rub over the thin cotton of his boxers, up and down his long erection so he has no question of what I want.

At my touch, he momentarily closes his eyes and lets out a shaky breath. Then he brings his hand to his lips. "I wasn't about to stop," he says before licking two fingers.

And I remember him sucking my fingers into his mouth, wetting them before telling me how to touch myself with them.

He presses a kiss to my lips as his hand dives down the

front of my shorts and under my panties. Heat floods in my body, all rushing to the spot where his two fingers are parting my folds and rubbing slick through my core.

"You feel good," he murmurs against my mouth.

"Mmm," is all I can manage as he works his fingers expertly between my legs.

He strokes me long and slow at first, teasing. Then he quickens. His fingertips flutter over my clit, sending a jolt of electricity through my bones and I gasp into his mouth. But he doesn't stop kissing me or let up with his hand. The touching feels amazing but the fact that it's Colin giving me this pleasure—touching me, teasing me, kissing me, enjoying my body—heightens everything.

He builds my pleasure quickly, the tightness forms, swirling under the surface, and just as I recognize what is happening, he slows his pace. My clit is throbbing for him and he knows just how to touch it, where to touch it to elicit the perfect responses—like he's playing an instrument and knows exactly the notes to hit.

"Do you like this? How I'm touching you?" he asks against my lips.

"Yes," I whimper.

He dips a finger down and rims my entrance before gliding back up to stimulate my clitoris, harder, faster. The tension is coiling again, my muscles tighten and the familiar ache inside me is longing for more.

As if reading my mind, the blunt tip of his finger goes down again, sinking slowly into me.

"Is this okay?" Colin breathes heavily.

"Yes. More."

He answers by sinking the finger in fully to his knuckle.

"Oh." I clutch him tight around the neck.

"Good *oh*?"

I nod enthusiastically against his cheek, feeling his eyelashes flutter against my skin.

"Good." He rocks his finger in and out of me, the heel of his hand maintaining pressure on my oversensitive clit, barely satiating its need. "I didn't think we'd be doing this on the bus," he says quietly. "There's not enough room to spread you out how I'd like."

I tilt my hips to meet his thrusts. "You seem to be managing," I say breathily.

He speaks against my lips. "But I want to taste you. All of you. I want your legs wide enough to bury my face between them."

My skin tingles at his words.

He's still penetrating me slowly, rhythmically, as he nips along the seam of my lips. I part them to allow entry and he licks in my mouth, along my tongue, sucking on my lips, and then he's kissing me hard, long. As he plunges his finger in me faster and faster, he does the same with his tongue and I imagine he's fucking my mouth as if it were my pussy, like he's showing me what he wishes he were doing.

Then he pulls his hand away, leaving me empty and wriggling with need below him. He licks and sucks on his two fingers and his thumb, closing his eyes and humming while getting them nice and wet.

"Ready?"

All I can do is moan with anticipation.

This time, two fingers split my entrance and when they fill me, it feels different. Like being stretched, like it's too much, but also like feeding a craving I didn't know I had.

"Okay?" he asks.

"Yes."

His moistened thumb presses against my clit and starts to rub in circles as he pumps his fingers and coaxes the fluttery contractions to start low in my stomach. He goes faster, his thumb furious, and when he crooks his fingers inside me, hitting a spot that sends waves of intoxicating heat through my body, I know I'm on the brink.

I fumble with my hands as our kissing becomes frantic, making my way down to his boxers, wanting to feel him, touch him like he's touching me. I slip my hand into his underwear. His hard cock is hot in my hands. He hisses. I grasp it tentatively, sliding my fingers up and down his length.

"Harder," he pants between kisses.

I grip him more firmly but keep getting distracted by his thumb and how maddeningly it's driving me to the edge.

He doesn't let up as he whispers in my ear, "Can you feel how tight your pussy is around my fingers? That's how tight I want your hand around my cock."

Oh. Oh god.

I squeeze him hard, trying to keep my fist tight around him.

"Shit. Yeah, just like that." His words come out strangled. He closes his eyes and whimpers when I start to move my hand. Even under him, I feel the power I have over him and I remember the words he said last night.

You have all the control.

Emboldened, I explore him with my hand, from his thick base to the slit at the tip of him. He moves against my hand in the same rhythm his fingers thrust inside me and we're lost in each other.

And then I'm breaking beneath him. His mouth muffles my cries as my climax erupts and waves crash all around me, lapping at my skin so my entire body is aflame and tingling at the edges.

He hums against my lips as I regain awareness, and I can feel his smile. "So perfect."

He's still huge and hard in my hand and I jack my fist up and down him again.

"Christ," he whispers, "you need to slow down. I'm close to coming."

I go faster. I want him to come. I want to see his expression. I want to hear what comes out of his lips when he finally releases. And I want to know that I gave it to him.

"Gray, please, there's nowhere..." He's panting heavily and I can feel the tension in his muscles as his abs contract. "I don't want to come in my underwear again like I'm fucking sixteen."

"I've got you," I say against his neck. "Just tell me when." I kiss and nibble along his neck and collarbone.

"Fuck—I'm—now."

There's no room to bend and I can barely see in the dark but somehow I get down fast enough to wrap my lips around the head of his cock just as he starts to pulse, shooting warm liquid into my mouth. It happens so quickly I don't have time to second-guess or think too much on it. I just swallow it down and continue to suck until he's entirely spent.

I slide back up his body where he cups my face in both hands. He presses a sweet kiss to my lips, then a second one, and lets out a contented sigh.

I feel equally as content. And also like I just ran a marathon on two hours of sleep. The weight of the exhaustion falls on me in one giant heap.

"I should go back to my bunk so we can sleep."

"Fuck no. I want to cuddle."

"There's not really enough room for two."

"I think we can make it work." Colin hugs me to his chest and pulls the blanket over us, nestling me into the dip of his shoulder.

I love the feel of being pressed up against his body. I like that he's holding me here, that he wants me this close. I close my eyes and sink into him, into the darkness of sleep. But before I fall away, I feel his fingers stroking through my hair and hear his quiet words as he sings the sweetest lullaby.

CHAPTER 19

"Hey! Hoo boy—" Logan's voice is too loud, too happy, and way too close.

I open my eyes to the light shining in from where Logan has pulled back the curtain just enough to stick his head in. He's sporting his signature big smile, which highlights his chin dimple, and his chocolate brown eyes are bright and lively—way too chipper for how shitty he looked last night, if you ask me. But he also has the decency to look a little bashful, having caught us in Colin's tiny bed together.

Colin grunts and covers me with his arm—even though I'm completely dressed—as he rolls me over and turns his back to Logan. "Go away."

"Are you guys going to stay in bed all day?"

"Maybe." Colin squeezes me tighter, nuzzling his face into my neck.

Being wrapped up with him, under his weight, his intoxicating scent surrounding me, feels perfect.

"We're going to be stopping pretty soon to eat. Just wanted to let you know." Logan shuts the curtain and we're alone again.

I don't think I'd mind spending the whole day in bed with

him. His breath tickles along my neck and I involuntarily scrunch up my shoulder and let out a quiet giggle. He tightens his arms around my waist and then his lips are brushing against my skin. Before I know it, his lips are on mine and then I'm tasting his tongue. His hands are on my sides—my ribs, my hips, fingers gripping into my ass holding me against him. Against his erection. I rock against him, teasing along his length and I'm so achy for him, pulsing hot between my legs. And he's so hard. Hard for me. He wants me. And I want him. I've never wanted anybody like I want Colin—all of him.

And then a loud gurgle sound churns from my stomach.

Colin breaks our kiss to chuckle softly against my lips. "Hungry?"

"Yeah, I guess." Hungry for *something*.

He touches a quick kiss to my nose. "Let's feed you, then."

* * *

I TAP ON THE TABLE, STARING AT THE PAGE—ERRANT SCRIBBLES and thoughts, words crossed out and rewritten as I try to wrap my head around the nebulous idea forming in my brain.

I look over to where Colin is lying on the little couch on the bus. He's propped up on his elbow, one leg bent, looking intently in his notebook. He's actually writing. His fingers move deftly across the page, his black pen scratching in a frenzy of inspiration. He stops every few minutes, parting his lips to hold the pen between his teeth as he reads. His eyes flick back and forth over the words he's written before he starts at it again.

TO BE YOUR LAST

I could watch him all day.

But the other guys will be back soon and I know Colin likes to write when it's quiet. They had wanted to run to the liquor store after we ate lunch. Or was it dinner? It's late afternoon. I don't know—this sleeping half the day and being up all night is really throwing me off. Everything about this summer so far has been kind of crazy—I guess that's what I wanted.

I glance back to Colin, watching the pen between his lips. His lips... He looks at me just at that moment and my cheeks heat at being caught staring.

He gives me a lopsided smile. "Hey."

"Hey."

He runs his teeth across his lower lip as his gaze lingers on me for a moment before he goes back to writing. Just that one look, one word, one smile, and I'm done for.

Something clicks in my mind and I pick up my pen.

I leapt into the depths
Telling myself I wouldn't drown
But as the water filled my lungs
It burned like a fire
And now a new danger takes me down
As flames consume me from the inside

Happy with those words, I'm about to close my notebook, but something stops me. I flip the pages instead. I turn to the page with my Fuck-It List—my let's-be-crazy-and-wild-screw-expectations list. My heart quickens as I look at the bottom of the page, at the place where I want to add another thing. I start writing the words before my brain has even processed the idea. I don't know why I'm compelled to write them, but there they are in all caps. *LOSE MY VIRGINITY.*

There. I wrote it down, the thing that creeps into my brain every time Colin kisses me. I want him to be my first. I guess I've been holding on to the romantic idea that I should be in love with the person I lose my virginity to, but why? Maybe Kyla is right and it's really not that big of a deal. Isn't it enough that we like each other, that we want each other, and that I trust him?

Even as I'm thinking this, a small but insistent voice in the back of my head is saying *but it is a big deal and what if you're already in love with him?*

The door to the bus swings open. Logan, Dean, and Joey stomp up the steps, laughing, back-slapping and yelling about something while hauling their paper bags of loot.

I slam my notebook shut.

"You fuckers are so loud." Colin sets his notebook down and slides in next to me, hoisting me into his lap as the rest of the guys pile into the seats around us. Joey is to my right, lining up mini liquor bottles along with an assortment of salted nuts, and the twins are across from us, popping the caps off a couple of beers.

"Hey, we need to start announcing our presence. Don't want to interrupt you two again," Logan says with a wink.

"Speak for yourself. I'd be into it." Dean shrugs.

Colin tightens his arms around my waist.

"I don't think I'm hairy enough for you," I say.

Logan lets out a hard laugh right as Joey chokes on the handful of spicy peanuts he had just shoved in his mouth. His coughs turn into laughter as I pat him on the back. Dean tips his bottle to me with a smile and takes a big drink.

TO BE YOUR LAST

"What were you doing?" Logan asks.

"Writing," Colin answers.

"Boring." Logan rolls his eyes then leans in toward me. He makes a big show of covering one side of his mouth with his hand even though Colin can see him just as well as I can, then he whispers loudly across the table, "If you ever need to be rescued from Mr. Grumpypants"—he gestures not-so-subtly toward Colin—"give me the special signal and I'll take you to go have some actual fun."

"And what kind of fun would we go have?" I ask.

He sits back and runs his index finger across his lips. "Hmm..." And then his eyes widen and he grabs my notebook before I realize what's happening.

I try to snatch it back but he has it, open in his hands.

"Let's consult the Fuck-It list," he says enthusiastically.

Shit.

"Can I have that back—"

But he's already flipped to the page, his eyes scanning down the list. "Most of the list is crossed off. This is awesome—" Then he goes quiet right at the time he must get to the bottom of the list.

I want to bury my face.

Logan clears his throat and his expression returns to normal as he looks up. "How about getting a piercing? That's on the list and we have all day free in Chicago tomorrow before our show the next day."

"Um, maybe," I say, trying to sound normal, relieved he isn't saying anything about that last line.

"Cool."

Logan and Dean then start discussing what kind of piercing I should get. Joey chimes in with the horror story of his first attempted piercing—at home with a sewing needle—and how it has ruined him for life.

I just stare at my book, still sitting open to that page. Maybe if I just don't call attention to it...

Why did I write it?

Colin must feel my tension, or maybe I'm just sitting weirdly stiff on him, because he runs an open hand across my back and whispers in my ear, "What's wrong?"

"Nothing. I just don't like people looking through my notebook." That's true, even though Logan isn't really looking through it.

Colin just grunts, snaking his long arm quickly to retrieve the book for me. He hands it to me, still open to that stupid list. And I know the second he sees it.

And dammit, why did I have to write it in HUGE FUCKING CAPS?

His eyes flash to me. He tilts his head, his stare pensive, while Dean tells Logan why nipple piercings would be the "worst fucking idea" for me.

I avoid the silent question in his eyes while feigning excitement in the idea of sticking metal through some part of my body.

It's quite easy, actually, to avoid eye contact with Colin throughout the evening, since I'm sitting on his lap. As long as I look straight ahead, I can ignore the embarrassment.

After a while, I tell the boys I'm tired and am going to bed early.

Joey stands so I can slide out of the booth and Colin follows, grabbing my hand so I have to turn and face him.

"Do you want to talk for a little bit?" he says, touching his forehead to mine.

Heat rises in my chest. I'm not prepared for this conversation yet. "No. I'm just exhausted and I want to go lie down."

"Okay." He tips my chin up with one finger and presses two quick kisses to my lips.

* * *

A TATTOOED ARM LIES HEAVY OVER MY SIDE, HIS FINGERS entwined with mine. His front is curled around my back, his breathing steady.

I twist and turn to see his face. A crease forms between his brows and he frowns in his sleep as he tugs me back to him, practically smothering me. I giggle softly against his collarbone until he stirs and a low grunt vibrates in his chest.

"Hey," I say, watching his dark eyes blink open.

"Hey." His voice is thick with sleep.

"You came in here and didn't wake me up?"

"I wanted to let you sleep since our late night activities left you so tired yesterday."

I can hear the cocky smile in his words. And I can feel his erection stiffening against my hip. The air is thick, and even though our bodies are pressed firmly together, there's a huge elephant between us. A sex elephant. I should just address it. Or we could just make out. I'd be totally down for making out.

"Gray."

I look up from staring at his lips. "Yeah?"

"I saw what you wrote on your list."

Okay, here we go, I guess.

"And I just want you to know that I don't expect that from you." His voice is quiet and low and I swear I can feel his heart pounding through his chest at the same rhythm as mine.

This is it, time to be Bold Gracie. Fearless Gracie.

"And if I've been moving too fast I want you to tell—"

"No." I put my fingers to his mouth then whisper against them. "It hasn't been too fast. I want it, and I want it to be with you."

I feel more than hear his breath hitch. "There's no rush. When do you have to go back to school?"

Ugh. My chest deflates. "I don't even know if I'm welcome back at school at this point. And even if I am, if I've lost my scholarship, I won't have a choice." And I'm almost certain I've lost my scholarship.

He hugs me tighter, tucking my head under his chin. "I didn't mean to stress you out about school. I just wanted to know how long I have you for."

My stomach tightens and a horrible ache pulses through me. We lay quietly for several minutes while Colin runs his fingertips up and down my back and I do the same, tracing little circles over his bare skin.

After a while, he whispers, "You don't have to go right back to school, you know. Taking a break—a semester or a year—to get to know yourself a little better might be a good thing. Maybe you'll decide on a different major altogether. Or maybe not. But there's nothing that says you have to get it right on the first try or that you can't take your time in figuring it out." His tone is gentle, just like his touch.

"And what will I do if I take time off?"

"You could run away with me."

CHAPTER 20

I don't know what to say and my throat is too constricted to form words anyway. I take his face in both my hands and crash my lips to his. I pull him toward me and he comes easily, laying over me, caging me with his arms, his hips nestle perfectly into where my legs are spread for him. I hook my ankles around him and our bodies undulate together of their own accord as we kiss.

Everything about this feels just right—the way his mouth greedily devours mine, the weight of him on top of me, the friction just where I want it.

I break the kiss, panting. "I don't want to wait."

"Mm." He kisses me harder, pressing his erection against my center and sending a pulse of pleasure through my blood. "You sure?"

I squeeze my legs, grinding against his pelvis and I'm throbbing and aching for him now. "Yes. Do you have condoms?"

"No. Wait, you mean right now?" He sits up to maybe look at me better but hits his elbow and head in the confined area of the bunk. "Ow, shit."

I bite my lip to keep from smiling too big. He rubs his

head then lays back down over me. He brushes hair out of my face with his fingertips, his dark eyes on mine the whole time.

"Hotel, then?" I say.

"Yeah." His tone is low.

Mine is barely a whisper when I say, "Tonight."

* * *

My senses are heightened all day. My skin heats every time Colin looks at me. Every little touch sends my heart racing. Every glance. Every kiss. My heart pounds, a fire igniting just under the surface.

I can hardly concentrate on my crossword puzzle as I sit on his lap. He massages my lower back, my hips, my thighs. I'm hot and needy. I try not to squirm against his crotch but the pulsating deep in my core is so insistent I can't help it. I can feel how much he wants me too.

I give up on the puzzle altogether when he starts laying sweet kisses to the side of my neck. I lie back against him, tilting my head to give him better access. He presses a few more chaste kisses down to my shoulder before resting his cheek against mine. I revel in the feel of being in his arms. But I want more.

Tonight.

Tonight.

When we go up to the room to set down our bags, we stand there—looking at the bed. The single, king size bed. He turns his gaze to me. We don't say anything.

Tonight.

His eyes are eating me alive and he bites his lower lip so hard that it's turned red when he lets it go. I swallow hard as he comes closer. I have to look up to keep eye contact. The air is electric. I can hear it crackling. Feel it vibrating. Taste it.

Not until tonight.

I lift my mouth to his just as he wraps his hand around the back of my neck. The kiss is gentle, long, sensual. He presses against the length of my body, deepening the kiss, his tongue strokes along mine—a promise of what's to come.

Tonight.

Everything in my body is haywire. My skin is buzzing. I can't think straight. I've forgotten how to breathe. I'm not even sure if I'm standing or he's holding me up.

There's a loud knock on the door.

"Let's go!" Logan yells through the door and there's muffled laughter outside the room.

There's another *rap-tap-tap* on the wall and it kind of sounds like they're skipping down the hall.

Colin breaks the kiss. He smiles against my lips as he twists a few strands of my hair with his fingertips. He kisses me one more time on the nose before we leave to follow the guys. He always seems to want to kiss me one more time.

Tonight. It's happening tonight.

I'm thankful the Donkey Lips guys are off doing their own thing. The five of us get giant hot dogs and walk along the Riverwalk. I clean a bit of mustard off the corner of Colin's lip with my thumb and he nips at it before catching my hand and kissing my knuckles. My stomach is all fluttery.

Tonight.

We stop to watch a street musician play the hell out of a harmonica. When Logan notices the guy has a banjo, he asks if he can jam with him—because, of course that's what Logan would do. Colin holds my hand as we listen and watch as Logan plays the banjo with exuberance, Joey stomps out a beat, and a crowd starts to gather.

We manage to get a selfie at The Bean in Millennium Park just before it starts to get dark. I look at the picture on Colin's phone. Our figures are distorted in the metallic sculpture behind us, but it's clear that Colin's arm is wrapped around my back. I'm pressed to his side as Logan, Dean and Joey swarm us from the outside. Joey's eyes are half closed, a goofy grin, his cheek against Colin's arm, barely reaching his shoulder. Dean and Logan are crushed against me, Dean grabbing Logan's face, which is smashed up in a half-grin, half-grimace as Dean plants an aggressive kiss on his cheek.

And Colin is smiling. His big, brighter-than-the-sun smile.

It's the best picture.

We stay downtown to eat a late dinner. Conversation and beer is flowing, but Colin doesn't drink anything and neither do I. I don't want anything to distort tonight. I want to remember it all with crystal clarity.

He runs fingertips up and down my arm and I can't help but stare at him.

Tonight. Tonight, he's mine.

"So what are you thinking?" Logan's voice cuts into my thoughts.

I rip my eyes off Colin and snap my neck toward Logan across from me. "Huh?"

"What did you decide, about tonight?" He points to my plate. "Are you going to eat that?"

"Uh, go for it. What are we talking about?"

He snatches the last bacon-wrapped asparagus from my plate and takes a big bite. "What are you going to get pierced? Damn this is really good."

Oh. Yeah. "I—um. I don't know."

Logan starts talking about the cool shop he found and how he already called ahead. I flash my eyes toward Colin. I'm giving him my most panicked crazy eyes but his demeanor is that of his usual stoicism.

"Logan," I begin, "I don't think, uh—"

"We're going to stay in tonight." Colin finishes for me, calm and sure.

Logan looks between us, his mouth downturned. "Really? You're bailing?" Disappointment flashes in his big, puppy-dog brown eyes. And sadness—an emotion I've never seen in them. He turns to Dean. "What about you?"

"I wasn't planning on getting anything, so if Gracie's not going, I think I'm going to go Bear hunting."

Logan huffs out a breath and stands up, dropping the uneaten half of the asparagus on his plate. "Fine." He runs his hands through his hair, making it look wild. "Can you spot me tonight?" he asks Dean, gesturing to the table.

"Sure." Dean quirks a brow as Logan turns to leave.

"Can we go tomorrow?" I spit out. "After the show?"

"Sure." He gives me a tight-lipped smile before walking away.

* * *

My guilt is replaced by anxious excitement as Colin and I walk hand-in-hand to our room.

While Colin is in the bathroom, I stand at the foot of the bed, staring at the little black condom packet he left on the nightstand.

This is happening. Now.

Should I take my clothes off? Or will he want to undress me? Jeans are awkward to take off someone else, right? So I shimmy out of my jeans but now I'm standing in my shirt and underwear and this feels weird too. I hastily change into my thin sleep tank and cotton pajama shorts and sit on the bed.

I look up from where my hands are knotted on my lap when he comes out.

He's in nothing but black boxer briefs. He locks on me immediately and he's so beautiful.

He tilts his head. "Something wrong?"

"No. I just... I know this isn't a big deal for you, but—"

"Of course it is." He comes to me.

"Yeah?" I meet his eyes. My chest feels too tight to contain my beating heart.

"Yes. Being your first is a big deal." He sits next to me and rubs his hand along my arm. "Even if that wasn't the case, it would still be important to me. I haven't had sex in almost a year."

"Really?"

He nods. "That's the last time I had a girlfriend." He drags his lips softly against my cheek. "And I've told you I don't sleep with women unless I'm in an exclusive relationship with them."

He kisses me gently on the mouth as both of his arms wrap around my back, holding me close to his chest.

I deepen the kiss, tasting fresh mint on his tongue. He lets out a soft little growl and I break the kiss.

"So..." I pause to catch my breath, my pulse racing. "Does that mean we're in an exclusive relationship?"

He bites my bottom lip, tugging on it with his teeth. "Aren't we, though?"

My breath catches, my heart stops.

"Are you fucking around with other guys?" he asks, a teasing grin on his face.

I shake my head, heat growing in my cheeks.

"Good." He pulls me into his lap and brushes my hair behind my ear. "Because I can't even see anyone but you."

And then he kisses me. I tighten my arms around his neck to press flush against him. He digs into my hips, stroking his thumbs up my stomach as he slides further under my shirt. I pull away from him, panting, and lift my arms. Without skipping a beat, he pulls my shirt up over my head and throws it aside.

He glances down at my bare breasts. His lips are red and swollen from kissing. He swallows and licks his lips before he speaks.

"You know I would be perfectly happy climbing under the covers with you and just cuddling all night. Naked cuddling preferred."

I bite back a smile.

"I swear we don't have to do anything more than that, if you want." He glances down at my body again, his eyes dark, pupils dilated. His chest rises faster and I can see him physically restraining his desire.

I move closer, emboldened by my effect on him, loving the feel of my breasts against his bare chest. "I told you what I want. I haven't changed my mind."

He trails his fingertips lightly up my back as he looks into my eyes. "You know I'm going to take care of you, right?"

I nod.

He lays me down on the bed, covering me with his broad shoulders. He takes his time, planting kisses all over, from my lips down my neck to the soft skin between the swells of my breasts. My stomach flutters as he kisses the underside of one breast while his hand gently massages the other. I let out a quivering breath when he takes one of my pink tips into his mouth, sucking harder than I expected while tugging my other nipple between his fingers. It feels so good it almost hurts.

"Too much?" he asks.

"No."

I cradle his head to my chest as he continues kissing and sucking. I rake my fingernails over his scalp and dig my fingers into the back of his neck with every spark of pleasure, my body undulating under him of its own accord.

Then he kisses down to my belly button and over to my hip. He nips at my hip bone just above the hem of my shorts and it makes me buck with a squeal.

"Oh yeah, I forgot how ticklish you are."

"No, I'm really not—"

But he nips at me again while tickling my other side and I'm laughing too hard to protest. My abs ache when he stops but I hardly have a second to notice because then he hooks his fingers into my waistband.

I lift my hips and he slides my shorts and panties down in one smooth motion.

And just like that, I'm completely naked, lying outstretched in front of Colin Wolfe. I prop myself up and watch him as he devours me with his blue eyes.

"You too," I say.

He stands and peels his boxers down, letting them fall to the floor. I can't help but stare at his cock jutting between his legs and how it bobs as he crawls back onto the bed. I don't have much to compare it to but it's long and smooth and I like it.

And it's going to be... He's going to put it...

My breath comes shallow as a wave washes through me, a mixture of nerves and dread and excitement.

Then his lips are on my ankle, my calf. He kisses up my leg to the inside of my knee, barely nudging them apart. I spread my legs a little wider for him and he kisses up another inch.

"Will you spread all the way for me?" His breath is warm on the sensitive skin of my inner thigh as he smiles up at me.

My stomach quivers as I whimper and spread my legs completely. I close my eyes and focus on the feel of him massaging my legs as his lips move higher and higher. I know where he's going, what he's going to do, he told me as much. But no one has ever put their face in my pussy, kissed or licked me there. I don't know what to expect.

I don't expect him to use his thumbs to spread my folds and stare unabashedly at my open pussy. Then he murmurs about how pretty and pink and glistening it is before he drags a flat tongue all along it.

I gasp at the new sensation. His tongue is warm and wet and strong and when he flicks the tip of it over my clit, it sends tingles through my body and to the arches of my feet. I keep my eyes closed and try to hold still. I think if I accidentally make eye contact with him while he is down there I could die of embarrassment. I know I shouldn't be embarrassed, especially since he is clearly enjoying himself. He's devouring me and I can't tell if the noises he's making are him humming a song or groaning in pleasure.

He licks me in long, torturous strokes and then quick, harder lashings. My skin is too sensitive and I'm squirming beneath him so much he has to hold me down by the hips. It feels too good. I can't catch my breath. It feels like electricity is coursing through me, just under my hot flesh. And when he closes his mouth around my aching clit and sucks, heat floods to my pussy, making me impossibly wetter. I cry out but he just keeps lapping me up, building the tension, enticing my pleasure over the crest.

"You like that?" he asks.

"Ughummph."

His mouth is quickly back around my clit, licking and flicking and sucking. But this time he slips a thick finger inside me.

"Oh. God. Yes." I press my hands to my face, physically trying to stifle my groans as the spasm starts low in my stomach.

"That's it," he says. "Let go."

And I come. My slickness coats my thighs and his hand and I can hear the wet sounds as he slides a second finger in and I ride them through the last waves of my orgasm.

I'm left trembling, my lips prickling with numbness as he crawls over me and then I feel his gentle kiss.

"Open your eyes."

I look at him, my vision a little blurry and my mind still dizzy. He's on his elbows, his face just inches above mine and when he comes into focus his eyes are dark, hooded, lust-filled. His lips are parted, dark and swollen and I can't ignore the fact that his cock is pressed between us, hard against my stomach.

"Are you good?" he asks.

I nod and try to say yes, but it comes out more as a

breathy gurgling noise.

He smiles. A small smile, just enough to show the edges of his teeth and to soften the hard lines of his face. He sweeps a few strands of hair off my forehead and kisses me again.

"You still want this?" He reaches for the condom on the bedside table.

I swallow and take a deep breath and nod.

"Need you to say it."

"Yes," I choke out. "I want it. I want you."

He sits back on his heels, his cock even longer and thicker than earlier, the head dark red and shiny, and I watch as he rolls the condom on.

Quickly, he's back over me, his chest brushing against the tips of my erect nipples as he takes my mouth. He kisses me hard and long, again and again. He kisses me until my heart is racing. He kisses me until I forget his erection is sheathed and ready to fuck me. He kisses me until my whole body is writhing beneath him, desperate for more.

He leans up on one elbow, his lips hot on my cheek and moves his other hand down between us.

"Tell me to stop—if it hurts." He grips his cock, guiding it to my entrance.

I nod.

There's no way I'm going to tell him to stop.

I'm so wet and swollen down there I'm pulsing and aching to be filled, but when I feel the blunt tip of him drag through my folds and nudge at my opening, a wave of emotions hit me at once. A strange mixture of nerves and fear, but also exhilaration and lust. Is it going to hurt? Maybe. But I still want it.

"I'm going to go slow," he whispers as he covers my

body with his.

The weight of him, the heat of his skin on mine is wonderful. He and I are all that exist in the entire world and I feel safe as he surrounds me, interlocks his fingers with mine and kisses me slowly. Almost as slowly as he starts sinking into me.

I'm sure I'm not breathing.

The head breaches my entrance and he stills for a moment, just the tip of him inside, stretching me. So much thicker than his fingers.

He squeezes my hands as he slides in another inch. And then another.

The intrusion feels foreign, but it doesn't hurt. It's so different than anything I've felt before, than I could have imagined.

He lets out a soft grunt against my lips as he pushes further in until his hips hit my thighs.

"Oh," I let out a shaky breath, hoping it doesn't betray me.

"Okay?"

"Mmhmm." I try to steady my breathing but my chest is heaving under him. I'm so full. Colin is filling me. He's inside of me. It doesn't seem real. "Is it... Are you all the way in?"

"Not quite."

My eyes go wide and he smiles.

He kisses my neck and behind my ear while I try to adjust to the feel of him—around me, on me, in me.

"You feel so good. God, Gray... I need"—his voice is almost hoarse, thick with desire—"to move."

I give his hand a squeeze, not sure I can speak, and he starts to withdraw, almost as slowly as he entered. The sensation is new, breathtaking. And this time, when he pushes back in, he does it in one fluid motion and a little moan escapes my lips. That felt good. New and weird and good.

He rocks in and out of me a few more times, his skin hot as it slides along mine. Everything is on fire and yet I want more. When I thrust my hips up to meet him, he hisses.

"Fuck." He stills over me, his breath coming in shallow pants.

And then he pulls out of me. All the way out.

I sit up. "Wha—"

But before I can protest, he buries his head between my legs again, fucking me with his tongue. I fall back to the pillow, back arching, eyes rolling to the back of my head. His eating is crazed, frantic. His tongue is hard, fast on my throbbing clit and then he is plunging fingers inside me as he kisses and sucks on it.

"Oh, god. Colin… yes."

Contractions start in my stomach as I clench around his fingers.

"There it is." He slides his fingers out and circles them on my clit.

It's enough to push my orgasm over the edge as he shoves back inside me just in time for me to pulsate around his dick. He lifts my leg and then he's thrusting into me deeper, harder as I ride out the last rushes of pleasure. This one is longer, more intense. My head is swimming, heart pounding, mind lost.

He keeps pushing into me, his rhythm steady but increasing and I like how he isn't being careful with me anymore. Like he just can't help it—the need is too great.

I'm just as overcome by him.

And then there's a deafening pounding on the hotel room door.

"Colin!"

It sounds like Joey.

Colin pauses inside me, squeezing his eyes shut as he gnashes his teeth. "Go away."

"We need you—"

"FUCK OFF." He's hovering over me, muscles tensed, barely in control.

"It's Logan. He might be dead."

CHAPTER 21

Colin is out of me before I even comprehend Joey's words, ripping the sheet off the bed and then wrapping it around his waist. He bolts to the door, snaps the metal lock and throws the door open, letting it bang against the wall.

I grab a pillow and hug it tight, covering my body, even though the bed is not visible from the doorway. I sit there, naked, unable to move, unable to think, unable to do anything. Apparently I'm not the deer that bounds off gracefully into the trees—I'm the one that freezes in front of the headlights and gets hit.

Joey's words are frantic, jumbled. Dean found him. Bathroom floor. Drugs. Vomit. Not breathing. Called 911.

Then Colin's back in the room, sheet gone, and he's hastily putting on pants. That's what I should be doing. I get up and look around for where my clothes landed on the floor.

"You stay here," he says.

I look up at him. "What? No, I'm coming with you."

"You don't need to see this." His tone is harsh but his eyes are pleading.

I shake my head. "He's my friend too and I'm coming."

He drags his hand over his scalp, jaw tightening.

Sirens wail outside. High-pitched and getting louder. We both frantically find our clothes and shove them on.

No one's allowed in the room so we wait in the hall as paramedics rush in.

Dean comes out of the room, hysterical. He'd been administering CPR until help arrived as directed by the 911 operator. He drops his phone to the carpet, face contorted in agony as Joey lays a hand on his back and then he's hunched over, crying onto Joey's shoulder. Joey's barely keeping it together himself, but he stands unwaveringly while Dean leans on him.

Colin wastes no time calling us a ride to the hospital. I'm amazed at how steady and normal he sounds when he's talking on the phone. When he ends the call, he leans against the wall, head in his hands, eyes closed.

I want to go to him, but I'm still frozen. Rooted to this spot in the middle of the hall. Still shocked. Waiting for the truck to hit.

Time stops. It's probably only been minutes since they went in, but it also could have been a lifetime. The paramedics finally come out of the room, hauling Logan on a gurney. I only glimpse him for a second before they're racing down the hall. He's unconscious, face slack, pale. He looks lifeless.

Then it hits me. Hard. It's a blow to the chest that's both sharp and blunt. A pain that's burning hot and ice cold. A sob echoes in the hall, heart shattering, otherworldly. It's coming from me. And then the tears come, hot on my cheeks just as strong arms wrap around me. I bury my face into Colin's chest. He's warm and solid and silent. I take deep breaths, inhaling his scent and slowing my frantic pulse.

He kisses my forehead and then he's ushering me down the hall after Joey and Dean.

I reach for Dean's hand and he looks over at me with eyes so big and sad and brown and so much like Logan's it's disarming. He squeezes my hand tight and I don't let go.

The ride to the hospital is short.

When we get there, everything is a blur, trying to figure out where he is and what is happening. It takes a while for the confusion to settle and someone with information to let us know what's going on.

They performed life-saving measures. He's alive. Barely. They're going to pump his stomach.

That's all we know for a while.

Dean paces up and down the length of the room, his hands visibly shaking. Joey is sitting in the chair across from me, his eyes closed, lips moving slightly—I think he's praying.

Colin is away from everyone, talking on the phone. He already called Logan's parents because Dean said he couldn't handle it. Now he's having a conversation with their band manager. He hasn't glanced my way at all.

He hangs up the phone but he stays where he is, standing in the corner in his black jeans and plain white T-shirt. The pallid fluorescent lighting overhead casts shadows on his face.

I want him to come sit with me, but maybe he needs space right now.

That's probably it. Everyone deals with stress differently.

So I continue to sit. Dean continues to pace. Joey continues to pray, and Colin just stands alone in the corner. I find myself staring at him, so confused by his distance.

Finally, he looks up and our eyes meet. I motion for him to come over. After a moment he reluctantly pushes off from the wall and takes the seat next to me. But it's strange to be sitting next to him without his arm around me.

I reach over to hold the hand he's resting on his knee but he moves it away before I touch him to rub the back of his neck. My chest feels hollow.

A doctor finally comes out and we all stand as he talks. Logan is being moved to a different floor. His condition is still critical but he's breathing on his own so that's encouraging. We won't know if he's suffered brain damage or other side effects until he wakes up.

"I need a fucking smoke," Dean says, letting out a shaky breath before he leaves down the corridor.

Joey goes in search of coffee and then it's just Colin and me, alone.

"We need to talk," he says in a low voice.

I nod and follow him over to a secluded grouping of club chairs near a window.

I can't read him. I want to try and take his hand again but I don't dare. His energy is dark. His eyes hard.

"I didn't know something like this would happen, I'm sorry," he finally says.

"Don't apologize." I scoot closer to him, resisting the urge to touch him, comfort him. "You couldn't have known."

"But I should have. I know better than anyone how easily this can happen. This was our big shot. Maybe our last one."

"Blaming yourself won't help anyone."

I know my words aren't getting through by the look in his eyes. He's torturing himself in his head. I've been trying to convince myself of the same thing these last couple hours. But I know if we had gone with him tonight, this wouldn't have happened.

"So...what are we going to do now?" I want to take his hand so badly.

He shakes his head, swallowing. "I'm going to do what I should have been doing this whole time. I'm going to be here for the guys and look out for them. And I'm going to look out for you."

I warm at his words until his gaze meets mine. His blue eyes are cold, his expression blank.

"You need to go home."

I'm slack-jawed. What the hell is he talking about? "But—I don't want to go home."

"Gray, it's over. The tour is over. We are over."

"Are you kidding me? You were inside of me a few hours ago and now we're done? Just like that, you're pushing me away?"

"Sounds about right."

"No. It doesn't. This isn't going to work because I know you. I know tonight meant something to you. I know I mean something to you. Don't end it like this."

He looks at me, face hard, unmoving, jaw clenched. "I should have seen Logan was spiraling but I didn't. I've been so distracted and wrapped up in you—"

"So you're saying this is my fault?"

"No. I just—I can't handle having you around right now. You don't need to be exposed to this shit anyway." He drops his head to his hand, pinching the bridge of his nose. "You should have never come in the first place." He shakes his head and exhales. "You don't belong here."

His words are a slap to the face and all I can do is sit, open-mouthed, staring at him in shock. I wait. I wait for him to take the words back, to say they came out wrong, he didn't mean them. To say sorry. To say anything.

But he doesn't. He doesn't even look at me.

After several minutes, he finally lifts his face toward me. His eyes look tired. "I'll pay for your ride home."

"That's it? That's all you have to say to me?"

"Yup." He doesn't look at me when he says it.

Venom boils in my gut.

"Go fuck yourself."

I sprint outside, refusing to slow down, turn around, or look back.

When I get outside, I search around for Dean to see if he's still out smoking, but I don't see him. I didn't get to say goodbye to him or Joey. Or Logan.

Cars whoosh by on the street. In the distance, a horn goes off. All of the city lights keep the sky a hazy charcoal gray instead of inky-black and studded with stars like back home. There are millions of people in the city around me and I have never felt so alone.

I just want to go home.

It's more than a three hour drive, and I can't even imagine how expensive a ride that long would be. So I get out my phone.

My fingers feel boneless as I dial Kyla's number. It's almost three in the morning and I'm sure she's asleep but I'm praying the ring will wake her.

It rings.

And rings.

And keeps ringing.

Then it goes to voicemail.

I leave a message, begging her to call me back as soon as she can, that I need her.

I wait.
Five minutes.
Ten minutes.
Fifteen minutes.
I call again.
It's the same.

I could call my sister, Court. I know she'd come get me, and maybe she wouldn't even ask too many questions. No, she'll definitely ask all the questions, but I know she won't judge my answers. I hover my thumb over her contact about to hit call when I remember Court is on her honeymoon right now—they left for Belize last week.

My stomach drops as the realization of what I have to do sinks in. I'm wobbly. A cold sweat breaks out across my skin as I make the call.

"Gracie? Are you okay?" My dad's voice is deep and gravelly from sleep but the concern in it is clear.

His genuine panic guts me.

My throat is tight and it's hard to push words out. "I'm fine. Can you come get me? I'm at Mercy Hospital in Chicago."

"What?" I can hear him shuffling around, probably getting dressed. "Are you hurt? Why didn't the school call us?"

"No, I'm not a patient. A friend of mine is. I just—" My voice breaks and I try to swallow a sob. "I just need to come home."

There's a short silence. "I'll be there as fast as I can."

I'm grateful he doesn't ask me any other questions, but now all I have to do is wait.

I can't go back upstairs. What would I do? What would I say? I don't want to see him. I can't.

So I sit on a bench that's a little bit away from the front doors, nestled near some shrubs and a tree. I need to focus on something—anything else.

I take my notebook out of my purse and open to a blank page. I stare at it until it becomes blurry. My eyes can't focus through the welling tears. I blink rapidly and shake them away. I won't cry. I will not.

I lift my chin up, feeling the breeze, cool against my face, drying my unshed tears. Leaves rustle soothingly overhead.

I turn several pages until I come to the list. I let out a hard, curt laugh when I read *LOSE MY VIRGINITY* at the bottom. I cross it off.

Then I write *Fall in love*.

Under that, I write *Have heart broken*.

And I cross those off too.

CHAPTER 22

Today

The two empty glasses clink together as I pick them up from the bar and wipe up the spilled droplets of beer and tequila until the wood surface is shiny and clean.

"Two more of the stout." A man with a large white mustache sets a twenty dollar bill on the counter in front of me.

I stick the abrasive towel into the side of my waist apron and take the twenty with a smile. "Sure thing."

"Keep the change," he says with a wink as his gaze drifts down my body.

I'm not dressed scantily—though I'd probably make better tips if I was. I'm wearing a black tank top that barely shows any cleavage and black pants. That's really the only requirement when I'm working the bar, wear black. And after almost two years here, I know how to spot a skeevy guy and one who enjoys flirting. This guy is innocent enough, if a little obvious after a few beers. The trick is to flirt back just enough to gain a rapport but not enough that they think you actually want to go home with them.

I take the bill and set the two large glasses of dark, frothy liquid down in its place. He takes them away to a table where another man with salt and pepper hair is sitting. Most of the tables are still full of people chatting boisterously, ordering another round of drinks even though their meals have long since been eaten. A couple of coeds who look to be on their first date are playing shuffleboard in the corner and a large group of young professional guys are playing darts in the back, their ties loosened and suit shirtsleeves rolled up.

Out the large front windows, the sky is newly black. Red lights streak past as the rest of the city lies in the background—tall buildings with their windows lit up like checkerboards. The green glow of the nearby intersection reflects on the pavement as people walk by.

"Hey." My coworker, Mila, leans on the bar carrying a tray of empty dishes. "The dinner rush is dying down. If you still want to get off early, this is probably your best chance."

"Oh yeah. You're right."

She sets down the tray, brushing her long black ponytail back to reveal the thin line flower tattoo on her delicate shoulder, surrounded by filigree and strings of beads that drip down her slim arm. "Did you forget Ethan was coming back tonight or something? I thought you'd be jumping up and down to get out of here. Two weeks is a long time for your boyfriend to be gone." She raises one dark, defined brow suggestively.

"I didn't forget," I say in a bright voice.

Two weeks is a long time, longer than his usual trips. Though we haven't actually had sex in over a month.

Thirty-four days.

TO BE YOUR LAST

But who's counting?

"He's gone for work almost as much as he's here. I guess after a year together, I'm just used to it."

"I don't think I could do it." Mila shakes her head as she picks the tray back up and heads toward the kitchen.

I am excited to see him, though. And hey, maybe tonight our dry spell will finally end. That would be nice.

Yeah, if my sex life with Ethan were described in one word, that would be it.

Nice.

Terry, the owner, bumbles out of the back a few minutes later wearing a Grateful Dead T-shirt that is probably old enough to have grandchildren. His silvery-blond hair is long but thinning on top. Tonight, it's secured in a loose ponytail at the nape of his neck.

He looks at me with his light gray eyes as I approach.

"It's about nine and the dinner rush is over, so do you think I'd be able to leave early tonight like we discussed last week?"

"What now?"

"Remember, my boyfriend is coming home from his trip tonight?"

"Oh. Right, right." He looks around the dining room and at the people playing games near the stage in the back. If it were karaoke or open mic night, there's no way I'd be out the door before midnight. Terry sighs and adjusts the little glasses on his short nose. "Better hurry. If the bar starts picking up like it usually does around ten, you'll never get out."

I hurry through my cleaning and refilling the salt and pepper shakers. Ethan texts me that he's landed at O'Hare at nine-thirty, and by nine forty-five, several new patrons have sat around the bar. Seeing my imminent panic, Terry quickly settles my tips before disappearing back into his office.

Mila leans over the counter. "How'd you do?"

I count the bills twice. Not bad for a Thursday night. Actually, pretty good. Hopefully this weekend will be even better now that the weather is warming up, school is letting out, and summer is almost upon us.

I let out a breath. "Maybe I'll actually be able to pay for classes this term without picking up extra shifts."

"I thought moving in with Ethan was making paying for school easier. You're still doing the online courses, right?"

"Yes, it has helped." I don't tell her that finances were the biggest factor in my decision to move in with Ethan so quickly. "But I was hoping to be able to take more classes at a time to finish sooner."

She smiles wide just as a few more people walk through the door. "Save yourself."

* * *

Ethan walks through the front door of our apartment only a few minutes after me.

"Hi, babe," he says, an easy smile lighting up his face as he rolls his suitcase in behind him. He's wearing a navy sweater, the collar of his white undershirt showing just enough to be in bright contrast to his tan skin. His thick, blond hair has grown just enough these last two weeks that the ends are starting to curl. He'll probably want to get it cut immediately.

"Hey, E." I go to him and wrap my arms around his neck. He hugs me with his free arm. "I missed you."

TO BE YOUR LAST

"I missed you too. Do you want to hang out? Watch a movie or someth—"

"I'd love to, but I'm all gross from the plane and exhausted from traveling. I'm just going to go take a shower and go to bed."

He kisses me on the cheek and I smile up at him. "Yeah, of course."

He disappears into the bedroom. I stand in the living room for a few minutes. Our window is small and the view consists of a white concrete building, but I guess it goes with the white walls and beige sofa.

But even though I can't see the city, when I close my eyes, I can hear it. Cars on the street, a whistle, a horn in the distance, and if I concentrate I know I'll be able to hear the 'L' train go by soon. All of these things that had seemed new and exciting when I'd moved to Chicago two years ago are now so familiar.

That old feeling creeps up again. The wanting more, something different, a new adventure.

There's nothing to do, so I turn off the lights and go to our room to get ready for bed. The sound of running water rattles in the walls as I change into my sleep tank and shorts and slide under the cream-colored covers. I sit and wait for the water to shut off and then Ethan comes out from the bathroom, all clean and naked.

I perk up, letting the sheet fall to reveal my white tank top, which is almost see-through. I think my boobs look pretty nice and perky in it, but he's already turned around, fishing a pair of athletic shorts out of his drawer so I only have a view of his pale backside.

"You can forget the shorts…if you want." I try to lower my voice so it comes out all sexy, but it sounds more like I have a dry throat.

He glances over his shoulder as he steps into his shorts. He gives me a lopsided grin as his eyes briefly drop to my breasts. "I have to go into the office early tomorrow. I really just need to go to sleep, babe." He turns off the light and climbs in next to me. "But I promise we'll do something this weekend, okay?"

I nod but I'm not sure if he can see it in the dark. He gives me a quick kiss then rolls over to his side of the bed.

* * *

The room is dark. Still. Everything is quiet except for the low, deep breaths coming from an otherwise motionless Ethan beside me.

He's been asleep for hours.

I'm not surprised to still be awake. I'm usually just getting home from the bar around now. But this is more than sleeplessness. A feeling of unease hangs over me. It's heavy enough to be undeniable, but too thick for me to understand it. I'm exhausted and my mind is foggy, and my body is restless, and the longer I lay here, the more uncomfortable I become.

I finally slip out of bed, grab my phone, and tiptoe to the living room.

I shouldn't do it.

It's been a long time since I've allowed myself to do it. Months.

Though, if I'm honest, I think about doing it almost every day.

I curl up on the couch under a blanket and take out my phone. I pull the blanket up, huddling under it as my screen lights up and I type in the search bar. It pops up immediately.

The video.

It's titled *Wicked Road's Colin Wolfe sings with Mystery Girl*.

It went viral only a few weeks after it all ended. Interest in the video combined with Logan's overdose, near death, and harrowing recovery equaled internet gold. The video exploded. The band exploded.

I click on the video, the screen shaking slightly as it starts to play.

It starts with Colin sitting on the little stage with his guitar. The air around him is hazy, the lights bright on his face. He's talking to the crowd but the noise from the audience around the person recording is too loud to hear what he's saying. But I know what he's saying.

And then I walk out. In that stupid bright red jumpsuit.

The voices in the crowd raise and then they quiet as the music starts. Colin strums the guitar, his eyes locked on me as he starts to sing the words.

The video quality isn't the best and it was shot from the side of the room so that Colin's face is in full view but only the back of my head is visible, except for a few glances of my profile. Hence why I have remained Mystery Girl.

It was the secret everyone wanted to uncover. It was the topic of more than one entertainment news show segment. There were rumors, conspiracies. But the guys never revealed my identity. They refuse to answer questions about the Mystery Girl. I even saw a video of Colin storming out of an interview when the interviewer asked about me.

That was before I banned myself from following them. From watching them. From listening to them. From having my heart torn apart over and over every time I read his name or saw his face or heard him sing.

It hasn't been too hard. I rarely listen to the radio and if I do, I keep it on top forty pop stations. If I'm with Ethan, we listen to country.

So I don't let myself have anything to do with them.

Except for nights like this.

I watch as Colin sings and then I join in. My voice in the video is quiet at first. Then it gets higher as we harmonize through the chorus. Our voices complement each other well, one moment blending together and the next standing apart, letting each one shine. Perfect.

That summer feels like a lifetime ago, but also like it was yesterday. Sometimes I think it was a dream, but when I watch this video, I know it was real.

For me, anyway, it was real.

The song ends, and this is where I always stop the video. I never let myself watch the next part.

But I don't turn it off tonight.

I watch as Colin reaches for me, a quirk of a smile on his lips as he leans in and kisses me. I can almost remember how his lips felt.

The crowd goes crazy with hoots and screams and unintelligible yelling. But I just stare at Colin, mesmerized by how tightly his eyes are closed when his face is pressed to mine, and then by the big, gorgeous smile that brightens his face afterward.

It certainly looks like it was real for him, but I know his feelings were never as strong as mine were. Not after he pushed me away so quickly, so easily, so completely.

I blink and tears fall down my cheeks unexpectedly.

And this is why I don't let myself watch it. The hurt. The

pain is blunt and brutal, and burning and sharp at the same time. It feels like no time has passed. Just as fresh as that night almost two years ago. I turn it off.

Ethan hasn't moved when I climb back into bed. I close my eyes but I can't get the image of that kiss out of my head. The memory of how dizzy and alive I felt in that moment is overwhelming and devastating.

I listen to Ethan's restful sounds as I lie awake. He worked really hard when we first met to get my attention. I think he asked me out four times before I agreed. He made me feel treasured and...happy. He was the first person to make me forget about Colin.

At least for a while.

Ethan is stable. Comfortable. Safe. And maybe that was exactly what I needed a year ago. But I don't think it's what I want anymore.

With this realization, the dark cloud of unease brewing overhead finally breaks.

* * *

"You're up early," Ethan says as he walks into the kitchen.

"I didn't get much sleep." I stare down at the mug between my hands, half-filled with lukewarm coffee.

"Sorry, babe." Ethan moves around the kitchen in his khaki-colored slacks and a light blue dress shirt, starting the coffeemaker and grabbing a bright green apple off the counter.

He takes a bite of the apple and reads the news on his phone as coffee starts to drip into his thermos. It's just another early morning for him. He's completely unburdened.

"This isn't working for me anymore."

He looks up from his phone in mid-bite. "What was that? Do you need fresh coffee?"

"No. I was talking about us. We aren't working. I think we should break up."

He sets down the apple, his mouth open for a second before he regains composure.

"I know we haven't gotten to spend much time together lately, and I'm sorry about that. Work should slow down in a few weeks—maybe we can take some time off together?" He smiles at his suggestion and looks at his watch. "Let's talk about it tonight, yeah?"

"I'm working tonight, and there's nothing to talk about. I want to break up."

"Grace, I'm about to be running late for work. We'll discuss this when I have more time later, okay?" He nods enthusiastically as he grabs his thermos and leaves out the door.

I sit, staring at the closed door for a while. I can't decide if he's just in complete denial, doesn't believe me, or didn't actually hear a word I said.

Maybe after a year of dating I do owe him a long conversation, but it's not going to change my mind. The problem isn't how much we're apart—the problem is when we're together. The problem is just the memory of my first kiss with Colin stirs more emotion and passion in me than the entirety of the last year with Ethan.

I can't stay.

I spend the next few hours packing up my things and deciding what I'll leave behind, considering I only have two suitcases and a couple boxes I found in the closet. Luckily, I don't have many personal items and almost everything in the apartment is Ethan's, since it was his place when I moved in six months ago. Moving in together so quickly was probably a mistake, but at the time I was convinced it made the most sense.

When I'm done, I leave my key on the counter and, after taking one last look around, lock the door behind me.

* * *

Leaving wasn't as hard as I thought it would be. The scariest part of all this is the fact that I now have no place to live, very little money, and no idea what I'm going to do next.

I sit in my car after loading it with the remaining contents of my life, trying to decide where to go. I end up just driving around for a while and thinking. I haven't driven much since moving to the city and it's sort of relaxing.

My sister, Court, gave me her Jeep Wrangler last year. It's old—the battery is on its last leg, the white paint is chipped, and there's a dent in the hood. It was my older brother Charlie's before her. But it's small and easy to maneuver around and park in tight spaces, perfect for me— not so much for a growing family. It would also probably be uncomfortable to sleep in, but that would be a last resort. I could go to a hotel for a few days but most of the money I have saved up I need to pay for school.

I could go home. I know I can always go home, but...

I park around the back of the bar. It's only just opened, but the lunch crowd will be showing up soon.

Mila greets me as soon as I enter and immediately knows something is up. I don't know if it's my overall grumpy demeanor or the fact that I'm at work when I'm not scheduled to be here.

"What's going on?" she asks, tilting her head.

I lean in and whisper, "I broke up with Ethan."

"Really? I thought things were good between you two."

"I mean, sure. Things were fine. Good even, for the most part. But I want more than good. I want—" Colin's face flashes through my mind. His fingers interlaced with mine, his arms holding me close, his lips soft on my skin. His smile. The stomach-flipping butterflies that stirred from just one look. The heart-ripping misery I felt when it ended. "I don't know what I want. But Ethan's just not it."

"I'm sorry, hun. Do you need a drink?"

I smile for the first time today. "Maybe."

"I'll make it a double."

I don't drink much but this drink is going down mighty easily. I sigh and rub the side of my face after finishing the last of it.

"It's never easy," Mila says with a small smile.

"The worst part is that I'm now essentially homeless and if I don't find a place fast that's really cheap, I'll have to withdraw from classes next term."

"We're not going to let that happen. You can stay with me."

"What? Oh my gosh, Mila are you sure? I won't stay long, I promise." I've been to Mila's place a few times and it's small. Like, extremely small, and I know I'll only have the apartment-sized sofa, but it's better than my car.

"I insist. And you can stay as long as you need." She bends down, digging something out from under the bar. "Here." Mila slides a little gold key over to me on the counter. "I have to work a double today, but go and drop off your things. Relax. Take a shower or whatever before your shift."

"Wow, thank you. I don't even know what to say. You're the best." I stand and practically climb up onto the bar to reach over and hug her hard.

The dining area is getting louder and tables are starting to fill up. Mila grimaces then heads out to her section with her notepad in hand and her little black apron low on her hips.

Terry pops out of the back room just at that moment. His long golden-white hair is loose today. He squints a gray eye at me. "Are you working right now? I didn't think you were on the schedule."

"No, I'm not working, but I will be later tonight."

"Ah. Mic night. Are you going to perform too?"

I sometimes read my poetry on open mic nights, but I haven't written anything new recently. "Maybe."

He gives a noncommittal grunt and retreats back to his office.

I feel slightly buzzed already and realize I probably ought to hang out for a bit before driving to Mila's place. Maybe have some lunch. Definitely some water.

I turn the key in my hand, feeling the cool metal on my skin. It's amazing how quickly everything can change.

"Gracie?"

The masculine voice behind me is a ghost from my past. Goosebumps rise on my arms as I turn around to see him.

"Logan?"

CHAPTER 23

Logan is standing near the front door, backlit by the bright afternoon sunlight streaming in from the expansive windows. His face lights with the same charming smile I remember. His hair is shorter but still curly and wild, his eyes the warmest brown.

I'm crossing the room without conscious thought. Toward Logan, who's coming at me with his arms outstretched and before I know it I'm entangled in a tight hug and being swung from side to side.

Logan pulls back and holds me by the shoulders. "Gracie, wow. It's amazing to see you again. You look great. I love this." He points to my nose.

I touch the tiny stud in my nose. "Oh yeah. Well, I had to finish off the list."

He nods, eyes wide and glittery, mouth open and we just stare at each other, struck silent in shock.

After a beat, he shakes the blank look off his face. "Hey, want to have lunch with me?"

"Yeah, I'd love that."

We sit over in a quiet corner away from other tables.

"It's so crazy that you're here, I mean—what a

coincidence. I was supposed to meet Dean here for lunch, but then he bailed on me."

"Dean's in town too?"

"Yeah. We're all here. We've been prepping for our world tour for months and this is our last break before it starts next week. We're doing a little work in the recording studio on the next album right now." Logan's eyes get wide and he starts slapping the table. "Oh my god, come to the studio with me! This is perfect, running into you like this. It was meant to be. You need to record the song with us!"

"Song? What song?" I know exactly what song he's talking about.

"*The* song. The one from the video. You know about the video, right?"

I nod then take an awkwardly long drink of my water.

"Man, Rick would probably have a heart attack if we told him we were going to record that song. The label has been on our asses wanting us to record it. They bring it up at every meeting, I swear, but Colin refuses. He always says that he won't do it without you."

My throat constricts at the mention of his name but Logan goes on and on.

"It would be so cool, and obviously you would get paid plus royalties, plus a co-writing credit—"

"That all sounds great, but I'm not interested, Logan."

"Oh, okay. That's cool too. You should still totally come with me though. All the guys will be so excited to see you and hang out."

He's here. In the same city as me. He could be close, around the corner. The idea makes my heart race and a surge of cold rush through my veins.

I keep my head up and smile at Logan but I feel it

wavering. "I don't think that's a good idea."

He holds my gaze with his big, dark brown eyes, his smile fading to a soft line. "He wants to see you, Gracie. I know he does."

I shake my head. "The way we ended was so abrupt, I don't think—"

"I know why it ended. The situation was shitty, and the only way he thought to protect you from it was to get you as far away from it as he could. And I'm the one who made it shitty."

"What happened between Colin and me was not your fault—"

"But it was, and I'm sorry."

"No. If anyone should be apologizing here, it's me. I've always felt terrible for leaving when you were in the hospital. I should have stayed until you woke up, until we knew that you were going to be okay. I was a horrible friend."

"Pshh. I never thought that for a second." His chair screeches against the floor as he stands and scoops me up in another hug.

He sits back down just as our food arrives. We dig in, and Logan asks if he can have a bite of my club sandwich almost immediately then offers to share his roast beef French dip.

As he's finishing up both of our fries, he says, "Maybe you're right. Maybe you coming to the studio isn't a good idea. I didn't think about it being hard for you guys, I just know it would make him happy. He's never gotten over it. God, if you thought he was broody before, it's ten times worse now. Makes for writing good songs though. I guess that's the only upside to being heartbroken."

I almost spit out my water. "Heartbroken? No one's

heart got broken." Except mine.

He looks at me incredulously, his face all twisted up in bewilderment.

"It wasn't even real."

And then I tell him about how Colin and I faked everything. We were never actually together. We were never in love. I say it with conviction. It's the same way I've convinced myself over the last two years.

"Pretend, huh? Sure didn't seem that way."

Yeah, to you and me both. "It's true."

Logan just looks at me for a while, head cocked, a thoughtful look in his eyes, while chewing on the inside of his cheek.

"Have you listened to any of our last two albums?"

"No." I can't.

"I think you should."

* * *

I HAVE NO IDEA WHERE TO PUT ANY OF MY STUFF IN MILA'S apartment. The closet by the front door has several colorful scarves tied to the handle along with a few purses hanging from it. I open it carefully to see it is bursting with coats and sweaters and sparkly dresses and shoes. So many shoes.

So I just leave my suitcases by the bright red couch and sit, glad I left the boxes in the car—I think they're going to stay there.

Mila's entire place could probably fit in Ethan's living room. There is no dining area, just the kitchen with dark wood cabinets in a U shape, so small that the oven and refrigerator cannot be opened at the same time and you definitely could not fit more than one and a half people into it at once. Said refrigerator is covered in magnets and photographs.

There's a teeny tiny window over the sink—which is full of dishes—where herbs sit in the sunshine, potted in a random assortment of different plastic cups and containers.

The walls are a cheerful yellow color, except for one spot that has been faded by the sun. It's directly across from the large sliding glass door off the living room that leads to a deck that is large enough for exactly one chair.

My eyelids are heavy with the weight of not sleeping last night. Vivid teal drapes frame the slider and I decide to pull them shut. I sink back onto the couch—it's soft and velvety as I lie down, grabbing a leopard print throw pillow to rest on.

I close my eyes.

But I can't sleep.

Logan's words keep nagging at my mind.

I shouldn't do it.

I think you should.

I fumble for my phone and for the second time in two days, I search Wicked Road. They've put out two studio albums in the last two years since their big record deal. Before I can change my mind I hit download. And in the darkened room, I listen.

I listen to several songs. They're all new to me but I recognize Joey's heavy drum beats and Logan's skilled guitar-playing. But everything comes back to his vocals. The voice that I can never forget, that sends shivers down my spine. I try to focus on the lyrics and I recognize many of them from when he let me read his notebook. I can see the slanted words written hastily in black ink covering the lined pages. I fall into the music, nodding my head to

TO BE YOUR LAST

the rhythms, a smile threatening to tug at my lips even as something deep inside of me aches.

And then I get to a song where I don't recognize any of the lyrics. It's slower. Colin's voice is deep and it breaks as he starts into the chorus.

You were my stars
Bright in the dark
A shot of life to my heart
Torn apart by the storm

The song is called "Gray Skies". Is it—is it about me? The title is probably just a coincidence. I listen to the rest of the songs on the first album but when I go to click on the second one, I see what it's called and I don't think it's a coincidence anymore.

It's called The *Gray Album*.

I scan the list of titles. The first song is called "Haunted". Then there's "Hate Me". My heart sinks when I read the next one: "The Wolf Who Loved the Lamb".

My heart is beating rapidly as I hit play and I don't think I'm breathing. I listen through in a haze, lost in the music, feeling that invisible connection to him again. I try to focus on the lyrics. The lines speak to me and I know. I know they're all for me.

You can't hate me
More than I hate myself

Oh but I lied
I lied
I fucking lied

And we died
We died

The last song is just titled, "Gray."

Everything is gray since you've been gone
I was wrong
I was wrong

I lie silent and still after it's over. I realize my cheeks are wet.

There are so many thoughts and emotions swirling and twisting in my mind. Tugging in all directions, forceful, angry, sad, hurt, yearning. I can't handle them.

So I get up and fish out my notebook and pour every thought out on the page instead.

* * *

"Did you get settled okay?" Mila asks as I hand her back the key. "Sorry I only have the couch for you, and I'll have a spare key made tomorrow. I should probably have one anyway, right?"

I nod, making sure to hold my smile as wide as I can. "It's really great, Mila. Thank you again for letting me stay with you."

"Psht. It's not even a thing." She waves a hand.

It is, though. Mila is my coworker. Yeah we're friends, but we're not that close, and for her to offer her home to me so freely is definitely a thing. So much has happened today that my emotions are close to the surface, and just this little realization has my smile cracking and tears starting to well up.

Mila gives me a small smile, her dark eyes full of understanding.

"You'll get through this. I know you will."

I nod again, unable to speak. She thinks this is all about the breakup, but she doesn't even know the half of it.

Terry pops around the corner just at this moment. I think he might actually live here. He's wearing a tie-dyed shirt covered in yellow swirls that bleed into green then blue, faded after many washes.

"Gracie, just the person I was looking for. Remind me, did you say you were going to perform tonight?"

I glance at the notebook in my purse. I'd filled three pages with words in a frenzy this afternoon and then spent some time composing a new poem from them—the first poem I've written in months. But I don't usually read a poem without having practiced and memorized it.

"I don't know," I say.

He clicks his tongue. "Ah, okay. Well, I guess you've got some time to decide."

The bar and restaurant fill up as the evening goes on, a typical Friday night. Half the patrons are sitting at the tables eating, chatting quietly and clapping as performers start to take the stage. Some people sing, some speak their poetry quietly and others spit it out like a fierce rap battle. The other half of the bar is rowdily throwing darts and taking shots and betting rounds of beer.

I'm so distracted I can barely remember simple drink orders and I've almost broken three glasses already.

My phone vibrates in my back pocket and I pull it out, hoping Terry doesn't choose this moment to pop out.

Ethan: *Did you pack up your stuff and leave?*

Me: *Yes, we broke up this morning or do you not remember?*
Ethan: *I thought we agreed we were going to talk tonight*
Me: *I didn't agree to anything. I can't talk about this right now, I'm at work.*
Ethan: *Fine. I'll call you later.*

I don't want to talk later. I want to scream.

I clench my fists and shove the phone in my purse just as Terry wanders out from the back. He looks around for a minute then gives a nod and pushes up his thin glasses when he sees me. "Are you going on?"

The stage is empty and it's getting late. I can't scream, but I can do this.

"Yes."

I walk up to the stage, the familiar butterflies stirring in my stomach as I step up to the microphone. I introduce myself, trying not to think too much about how many eyes are on me right now.

"I wrote this earlier today, so I'm just going to read it for you. It's called *Deep*."

I open my notebook, grateful to be holding a tangible thing. And I read.

I am a bird. A flame.
Delicate but strong.
I can fly far and for however long,
but I still hear your song.
You're a witch. A Siren.
Calling me back. Calling me down.
I can't get too close, I think.
But, maybe just one drink.
It's cool and sweet
but then you pull me in deep

and I sink.
I sink.
Overtaken by the black and the ink.
The water's like oil, slick on my feathers
and I know I'll never be free of your tethers.
It fills my lungs, in through my throat.
No more breathing or sighing.
Or fighting. Or flying.
And I'm not even trying,
because the truth is I love the dying.

My fingers shake slightly as I lift my head to gentle applause and murmurs, the wave of adrenaline giving way to the feeling of excitement and accomplishment. I smile out to the crowd and thank them.

But just as I turn to exit the stage, I see them. Piercing dark eyes from across the room.

He's sitting in shadows, a black cap pulled low, his head resting against his hand, two fingers at his temple. I'd recognize the angle of his jaw, the lines of his nose—but those eyes.

I'll always know the intensity of Colin Wolfe's stare.

CHAPTER 24

My heart is thumping wildly, the sound reverberating through my bones. Heat blooms under my skin and I think I'm about to break out into a cold sweat. I can't look away from him. I don't even blink.

But then I stumble, not realizing I'm at the edge of the steps, and barely catch myself before I fall. When I look back, people are getting out of their seats and so many of them are crossing in front of me to go to the bar or the bathroom that his spot in the back corner is obscured. And when I get closer, he's not there.

I hide in the back. There's twenty minutes left of my lunch break before I have to go back out there, but the thought of eating makes my stomach turn. I sit, doubled over, until my heart steadies itself and I no longer feel shaky.

Of course Logan would tell him about me. I shouldn't have been surprised to see him. But I was—even more so by my body's visceral response to him.

Is he going to talk to me? What am I supposed to say? We're not friends, but we're more than acquaintances. We know each other intimately, but we're also strangers. He's literally famous—a millionaire—and I'm no one. But I'm

TO BE YOUR LAST

Mystery Girl. I'm Gray.

We have this weird little history, a time together that was so brief it shouldn't even matter. But it did. It does. It changed the trajectory of my entire life.

And he's here.

When my break is up, I take a few deep breaths and go back out to the bar. Mila smiles and nods from the other end of the bar as she fills up a line of blowjob shots for a group of giggling women. Rory, the other bartender working tonight, leaves for his break and I look around the bar.

I don't see him.

I look farther out around the restaurant, to the same corner he was sitting in before. But he's not there.

Maybe I just imagined him. Maybe my long, crazy day with absolutely no sleep has finally caught up with me and I'm straight up hallucinating now.

Or maybe it was him, but he just came to see me to fulfill some sort of morbid curiosity and now he's gone.

Luckily, the bar is so busy on Friday nights I don't have too much time to dwell on him and whether or not the sighting was a figment of my imagination.

But when I get back to Mila's place and collapse onto the couch at three in the morning, I can't sleep even though I'm completely exhausted. After an hour of restlessness, I put in my earbuds, put on The Gray Album, and fall asleep to Colin's voice.

I sleep all day, well past when I should reasonably get up and do things before work. I also wake up to two missed calls and four text messages from Ethan.

Ethan: *I know we haven't had much time together lately but I know we can make this work*

Ethan: *Just come home and talk to me*

Ethan: *Please call me*
Ethan: *You're overreacting. Come home.*
Nope. Can't deal with this right now.
What I really need to be doing right now is looking for a new place to live. I already feel like I'm intruding, but Mila doesn't seem perturbed that I bummed on her couch all day as we go in together for the Saturday night shift. It should be even busier than last night and I'm hoping for lots of tips and lots of distraction.

The restaurant is packed. It's standing room only at the bar and with every group that migrates away after a round or two of drinks, two new waves take their place. I'm barely able to get away for my break, telling Mila I'll only take fifteen instead of the usual thirty.

Two more missed calls and texts.
Ethan: *Are you seriously ignoring me?*
Ethan: *This is ridiculous*
I need this to stop, so I call him and try to calmly explain again that I don't want to be in a relationship. I don't want talk it out or try to make it better, I just want out.

"You're being really immature about this, Grace. You're not usually this emotional. Is it your time of the month or something?"

I hang up on him, almost in tears.
But I don't let them fall. I steady myself and go back out to the bar, back to work, back to busy, back to distracted.

An hour later, I'm rimming glasses with salt and pouring tequila shots. Mixing up a gin and tonic then a Long Island iced tea. I'm humming to the music playing overhead and muddling some basil and mint for a mojito.

"Gray."
Everything stops. I'm motionless. He's the only one

who calls me that.

I slowly look over my shoulder, the blood thumping in my ears is deafening.

And there he is. I knew it was him but seeing him here, right in front of me, has me paralyzed and unable to speak. He somehow looks better than I remember. More beautiful, more intense. I've only seen him through a screen and the real thing is so much more. I forgot about his gravitational pull, his aura.

I'm walking to his spot at the bar before I've consciously made the decision to do so. And now I'm face to face with those eyes again. He's in a long-sleeved black shirt, only the tattoos on his hands and neck visible. His black hair is longer on top now—it's thick with textured pieces that sit in every direction.

He's really here. He's real.

My throat is completely closed up and I can't form words. I don't even know if I'm breathing.

"Hi," he says low. His voice is a caress.

I can't stop staring at his mouth. His lips, slightly parted, are full and soft and I want to taste them. Bite them. Lick them. Kiss them. I also sort of want to slap him. How dare he still make me want him after he threw me away? How dare he come here and add extra chaos to the storm that is my life right now?

"What are you doing here?" I manage to choke out.

His gaze holds mine. "I wanted to see you."

I swallow.

And then someone shouts from my left about ordering another round and a girl in a tube top is waving frantically behind Colin's shoulder for my attention. So I get them drinks, trying not to make eye contact with Colin every time I pass him. But when I do, he's always watching.

He doesn't break eye contact as I walk back over to him. I don't know what I'm doing.

"You're busy. When do you get off? I'll wait for you."

Wait for me? "What? Why?"

He runs a hand through his hair, his jaw muscles clenching. "I haven't had the chance to talk to you in two years. I want to. I need—" He lets out a sigh. "You know, things were kind of crazy after everything happened with Logan and the record deal. But we all tried to contact you."

They did?

"Did you block us or get a new number?" he asks, not quite able to keep his voice steady.

"New number." New everything, really.

People start to crowd the bar again. A tall woman shakes a fifty dollar bill at me.

"Can I have it?"

I look back at Colin. "Have what?"

"Your number."

Right. I can't—I'm having a hard time reconciling what's going on right now. Too many emotions are swirling around in my head and I feel the tears I held at bay earlier threatening to rise back up. Faces are everywhere. Everyone wants my attention. I'm overwhelmed. It's too much. Everything right now is too much. Ethan. Colin.

"Gray?" He's looking at me expectantly.

"I can't do this right now. I've had a hard couple days, Colin. I need you to leave."

Something in his face dims.

"Okay." He stands to leave but he stops, his fingertips skimming the edge of the bar. "I loved your poem last night."

And then he moves away and is swallowed up in the

crowd and gone before I can respond.

I turn my back for a second to catch my breath but Mila is standing in front of me. Staring and open-mouthed.

"That was Colin-fucking-Wolfe," she says.

"I know."

* * *

"No effing way. I cannot believe you know the lead singer of Wicked Road and you didn't tell me!" Mila bombards me as soon as we enter her apartment. She is, apparently, a big fan, and now I'm in for it.

"I don't really know him." *I just lost my virginity to him.* Whatever.

"Don't lie to me, G. Whatever conversation you two were having was legit intense. Tell me everything—wait, I need to go make popcorn."

So she goes to the kitchen and starts making popcorn, and because the kitchen is literally two steps away, I just turn and watch her and keep talking.

"There isn't much to tell. He's friends with the guy who was the best man at my sister's wedding, so they ended up playing at the reception—"

"Hold up. You know all of them? The whole band?"

I nod weakly.

"So you only met that once, at the wedding?"

Sheesh, she should be an investigative journalist or something.

"We hung out a little after that, but that was two summers ago. I haven't seen them since."

Mila studies me for a moment and then she freezes. Her eyes go wide. The kernels are popping in the microwave behind her, little explosions to punctuate her stunned silence.

"Holy. Shit. You're the Mystery Girl!"

"What?" I shake my head but I can feel my cheeks immediately heat. "That's crazy, I'm—"

"Yes, yes you are. I can't even right now. This is crazy." The microwave beeps but she ignores it. Then she gasps. "Hold the fucking phone. You've kissed Colin Wolfe?"

If I thought I was blushing as hard as I could, I was wrong. I'm ten times hotter and probably ten times redder than before. I can't really deny it at this point.

Mila cackles with glee.

"We were seeing each other, sort of, for just a really short time. But it ended abruptly. He said I couldn't handle being in his world—and that was before they got crazy famous."

He was probably right. I probably couldn't handle it.

But then the lines of that last song play in my head.

I was wrong

I was wrong

"Hold on." Mila's hands are balled up in little fists of excitement by her face before she finally turns and retrieves the bowl of popcorn. She sits, grabs a handful and says, "I'm ready. Start from the beginning."

* * *

I HAVE THE NEXT TWO DAYS OFF WORK AND I SPEND THEM trying to find an affordable place to live. All of the one-bedroom and even studio apartments I see available are too expensive unless I work double my current hours.

So I peruse the listings of people looking for roommates.

TO BE YOUR LAST

I find a couple in my price range, but in one I would be the fifth roommate—is that even legal?—and the other one is already taken by the time I call.

Ethan has called and texted more but I ignore them. Ignoring my problems has never worked in the past, but I don't know how to tell him any more clearly that I just want to move on.

Even worse, every time my phone buzzes, a feeling of excitement fills me. A silly, unfounded hope that it's Colin. Even though I know he doesn't have my number.

Moving on. I'm moving on with my grown-up, adult-ass life. Starting now.

That includes making adult-ass decisions, like whether or not to stay enrolled in next term's classes. They start in a few weeks and Monday is the last day to withdraw.

I don't withdraw.

I don't know where or how I'll land, but I guess that's why they call it a leap of faith. I've been doing things that scare me ever since—ever since I got in that van and left with the band. I've been betting on myself and that's what I'll continue to do.

* * *

Tuesday's shift is uneventful, slower than normal even. It's just me and Rory working and a few regulars sitting at the bar as we near close.

So I go in the back to get a head start on the closing checklist and make sure everything is stocked for the early shift tomorrow.

"G—" Rory's voice calls from the hallway. "There's a guy asking for you."

I step out of the stock room, straightening my black top and wiping my hands on my skinny jeans. And before I even have the chance to think about Rory's words, I look up and Colin's there. Sitting at the bar again in the same spot as before.

My chest constricts at the sight of him and I'm reminded of what an emotional mess I was last time we talked. I'm immediately putty before him and I hate it. I'm in control of my thoughts and feelings and I won't let him swoop in and stir me up just to break my spirit all over again.

I straighten my spine and walk over to him.

"Hi."

He looks up from under his thick dark lashes, the tiniest of smiles flashes across his face before it's gone again.

"Can I get you something to drink?" I say coolly, even though everything inside me is bouncing and on fire.

He shakes his head. "I'm fine with this." He gestures to the glass of ice water in front of him.

"If you don't want a drink, why are you at a bar?"

He leans on his forearms, a glint in his eyes as he lowers his voice. "Well, you wouldn't give me your number."

"And you, apparently, can't take a hint."

He sits back, the smirk staying on his lips this time. "We're leaving Saturday to go on tour. I was hoping you and I could get something to eat before then. Talk. Catch up."

I'm already slipping. I want to say yes. Yes to anything. Everything. Being near him is like experiencing a high I've never been able to get anywhere else. He's dangerous.

"Why? What do you want to talk about?"

"I want to apologize. Grovel. Whatever you'll let me."

Needles prick the back of my eyes. Two years ago, I would have died to hear this. But I guess he was right two years ago when he decided I was too inexperienced and naïve. I know twenty one is still young, but I'm neither of those things anymore.

"No need to apologize," I say, holding my chin up while I fill a new glass with ice. "That was two years ago. Am I supposed to still be pining and heartbroken just because you were my first?"

I don't look at him as I fill the glass with water. He doesn't need to know that I've listened to every song on *The Gray Album* on repeat before going to sleep the last three nights. He doesn't need to know that every time Ethan touched or kissed me, a little voice in the back of my mind would say *it's nowhere near as good as it was with Colin*.

It was never going to be.

But when I slide the drink in front of him and my eyes meet his, dark blue and swirling with emotions, I see them clearly—the pining and the heartbreak. It steals my breath away for a moment. But just as fast as the emotions were there, they're gone. His expression, once again, unreadable. His eyes, blank.

"Miss?" Someone at the other end of the bar is holding up an empty glass, rattling the ice at the bottom.

"Excuse me," I say to Colin and then go to help the customer.

And when I look back, his seat is empty.

Completely empty.

I take his glass from the bar. The little white napkin is sticking to the condensation on the bottom of it, and when I pull off the napkin to toss it, I see the writing.

The black ink has bled into a dark blue where it was covered by the wet ring of the glass but I know the handwriting.

RAE KENNEDY

I was your first
But all I want
Is to be your last.

CHAPTER 25

Wednesday night is busier at the bar. It's already ten minutes away from last call. And he hasn't come in.

I keep glancing at the seat where he sat, subconsciously thinking he'll be there this time. Hoping. The napkin from last night is tucked safely in my front pocket, all thirteen words memorized and on repeat in my mind. I knew he wanted to talk. He said he wanted to apologize. But the little note on the napkin says he wants more than that.

Much more.

Why didn't I just give him my stupid number?

"He's not coming, is he?"

I jump at Mila's words as she comes to stand at my side. "I don't know."

And he doesn't.

I'm still in denial as we lock the doors and turn off the lights. Maybe he'll come running up to the door and bang on the glass, out in the rain, until I run out and he throws me in his arms and kisses me hard while proclaiming his undying love for me.

I know that scene won't happen—partially because it's not actually raining—but none of the rest of it happens either.

Mila and I climb into my Jeep and I drive back to her apartment. But when we park and she gets out, I can't.

"I think I'm going to drive around for a bit, clear my head."

"You sure?"

I nod and turn the ignition.

And I drive.

I drive through downtown and out to the suburbs and before I know it, I'm on the little two-lane highway that leads to my hometown.

It's almost five-thirty in the morning and still dark when I pull onto my parents' long gravel driveway. I drive past the rows of poplar trees and parked pickup trucks and to the two-story farmhouse.

Everything is a shade of blue, lit only by the moon. Flat plains of grass and gently rolling hills sprawl out in all directions, the view uninterrupted by buildings or lights or roads or people. The air is cool and quiet as I step out.

A warm light glows from inside the house and through the wrap-around porch—the only sign of life.

I head toward the door, toward the faint orange light against the blue. But before I reach it, the hinges of the storm door screech and sigh as my dad and Eric exit the house in their thick flannel shirts and work boots.

"Gracie Lou!" Dad spots me first and has me smothered in his arms faster than I knew he could move. "I didn't know you were comin'."

"Neither did I. I just have a day off, so I decided to come for a visit."

"Is everything all right, pumpkin?" he asks quietly, studying me, his bushy eyebrows knitted.

"Yeah, Dad. I'm fine."

"Okay, then. There's still some breakfast inside. Go fix yourself a plate while it's good."

"I will."

Then Eric wrangles his arm around my neck, pulling my face to his chest.

"Hey," I say into his shirt as I turn my head to breathe.

"We miss you around here." He finally loosens his arm a bit. "Especially Kyla. Does she know you're here?"

"No, I didn't tell anyone."

"Well, you better tell her before everyone else finds out. She'll freak if she finds out she was the last to know."

"You're right."

"Of course I am."

I roll my eyes and give him a half-hearted slug to the shoulder as I pass.

Mom practically faints when she sees me, shouting and screeching in indecipherable syllables as she hugs me, pets my hair, and then promptly slides a plate full of food in front of me.

She's already making plans to have the whole family over for dinner by the time I finish eating and excuse myself to my room. I collapse onto the bed. Exhaustion catches up to me and I want nothing more than to sleep after the realization that I haven't slept in a bed in almost a week. But before I shut my eyes, I make sure to text Mila where I am so she doesn't worry and Kyla so she doesn't strangle me.

* * *

KYLA DOESN'T STRANGLE ME, JUST JUMPS ON MY BED ON ALL

fours while squealing with excitement that she just couldn't wait to see me any longer.

She did wait until almost two in the afternoon, so I have to give her credit.

"Spill it. What's going on? Why are you here on a random-ass Thursday?"

"I had some stuff on my mind so I went for a drive to think. I just sort of started heading in this direction and decided to keep going, since I haven't been back in a while."

"Oh, I'm well aware of exactly how long it has been since you've visited. Fifty-eight days. I can give you the hours too if you'd like. Now. What are we thinking about?"

"Where do I start?" I sit up, blinking until she's in focus. "I guess from the beginning. First, Ethan and I broke up."

Kyla's eyes widen with unrestrained excitement and her hand goes to her chest. "Did you break up with him, or did he break up with you? And don't even think about telling me it was a mutual decision because that is the lamest thing ever."

"I broke up with him."

"Oh, thank sweet baby Jesus. I won't say anything bad about him. Just that he owns way too many pairs of boring-ass khakis, he always took you for granted instead of treating you like the goddess you are, and he needs to learn a new way to style his hair because the side part is not his look."

"Wow. I thought you weren't going to say anything bad about him?"

"I didn't say bad things. Those were purely unbiased facts and I stand by them."

I can't help but smile. She is unapologetically accurate.

"What else happened?"

"What?" I say, thrown off.

"You said that was first. What's second?"

"Oh, I...well after... nothing. Never mind."

"What—what was that, what were you just about to say? You were about to say something. Tell me, tell me, tell me!"

I blow out a breath. "It happened after I broke up with Ethan, but I saw Colin."

Kyla presses her hands flat to the mattress. "Shut. Up. How soon after was this?"

"Well, I actually ran into Logan first, who told Colin where I work. It was later the same day. A really weird coincidence."

"That's not a coincidence. That is what we call kismet."

Kyla has an unhealthy obsession with the idea of fate.

"I think he wants to get back together." I don't know why I'm whispering. "I guess, that's assuming we were ever really together in the first place."

"O M F G. Of course you two were together. Anyone who's seen that video can tell you were both cuckoo for cocoa puffs about each other, and of course he wants to get back with you. You're fucking delightful. The question is, do you want to be with him?"

Being with Colin... being his and him being mine, for real... That's the dream I never allow myself to have.

"I don't know. I mean, yes, I want to be with him, but he kind of messed me up last time. I don't know if I'll be able to really trust him—trust us—again. And that's not even considering how he's suddenly uber famous and leaving on tour in two days. I checked the dates. This tour is nine months long. I don't know if it's worth opening this wound just to have him turn around and leave again."

Kyla looks at me for a minute with pursed lips. "Well, if you're asking my opinion, which I think you are—like, that's what we're doing here, right?—I would say stop thinking about it so hard. If it works out, great. But if it doesn't, life will still go on."

I nod. "I'll think about it."

She narrows her eyes at me. "Didn't I just explicitly say to stop thinking about it? At least bone him one more time before he leaves. You deserve a proper fucking because I know Khaki Pants wasn't doing that for you."

"Ky, oh my god." I'm trying not to smile but I can't suppress it.

"Am I wrong?"

"You're so bad, but I love you."

Kyla springs forward and hugs me tight around the middle. "I love you, too. But I have to warn you, this only seeing each other every couple of months is not doing it for me, and your position as my favorite Gallagher sibling is precarious at best. If we don't step it up, Eric is going to ascend to the top spot and you know how that will only further inflate his ego."

I let out a soft chuckle. "Noted."

* * *

DINNER IS CHAOTIC AND LOUD AND FUN AND DELICIOUS. Court and Tuck are here along with my older brothers, Jack and Charlie, with their wives and children. Then, of course, my parents and Eric and Kyla. And we somehow all squeeze in around my parents' old table, which isn't meant for more than eight.

Mom serves up roasted chicken with new potatoes and

carrots, cinnamon apples and buttered rolls. My nephew, Forrest, is showing everyone the hole in his smile where he's just lost his third tooth. My three-year-old niece, Rosie, is charming everyone with her bouncy blonde curls and big blue eyes as she sneaks bites off their plates and stuffs fistfuls of smashed rolls into her pockets. Tuck can't keep his hand off of Court's belly, rounded with their first child, as they beam at each other and revel in their shared glow.

They all seem so happy and content in their lives, their careers, their relationships. And as all of these conversations are going on around me, in my childhood home, surrounded by family, I can't help but think that I don't quite fit here anymore. Whatever I'm looking for, it isn't here. Something is missing. Someone is missing.

* * *

I MAKE IT BACK INTO THE CITY FRIDAY AFTERNOON JUST IN time for my double shift at the bar.

He's leaving tomorrow. This is it. The last chance.

Is he going to show up tonight?

I'm on edge, fidgety and frazzled all afternoon, constantly playing with the hem of my little black dress.

Until I turn around and I see them.

Logan barges over the counter to squeeze my shoulders and I run around to greet them, only to be immediately squished in a Dean and Joey sandwich. Dean has a couple new piercings in his face and Joey has grown out a fluffy red beard. I let them know how happy I am to see them, but I can't help but look around, over their shoulders and toward the door.

"He's not with us," Dean says.

"We don't know where he is," Joey adds.

"But we fly out in the morning and we wanted to see you before we left," Logan says.

And so they stay. By some miracle, the Friday evening rush starts hours later than usual and Logan takes every opportunity to regale Mila with stories about that summer. Jumping a fence to go skinny-dipping, running from the cops, getting me my first tattoo, playing strip poker. Mila is doing a good job of hiding how high-key freaking out she is about them right now. At one point, I even see her running a hand up Joey's arm as he tells her about some of his artwork.

After a couple of hours, Dean corners me over by the register and slips me a card. It appears to be a business card for a recording studio.

"What's this?"

"His number."

I turn it over and on the back is a handwritten phone number.

"Call him."

"You think I should?"

"You should have seen his face last week when Logan told him he ran into you. I haven't seen him that happy since—since before Logan's overdose. Since the last time he was with you."

A few minutes later, Joey pulls me aside. "So, uh, does your friend Mila... Is she single?"

I nod with a smile. "Yep."

"Okay. Cool. Cool cool cool cool." Then he leans in a little closer and lowers his voice. "We're all rooting for you, you know. Not just for you and Colin, but you."

"Thanks, Joey."

I give him a hug and the pink in his cheeks deepens as he goes back to the table.

Later, as I'm standing between Logan and Dean as they argue over who's going to pay the tab, I see Mila and Joey canoodling in the corner, her fingers fully immersed in his beard.

Logan and Dean finally decide to split it but then start bickering over how much to leave for a tip. They leave me way too much, but instead of arguing, I decide to accept the gift and split it with Mila.

It's getting later in the evening and as the bar starts to really fill up, the guys head out, giving me hugs on their way. Logan slips something into my hand as we embrace.

I glance at it. It's a hotel room keycard. I raise my eyebrow at him.

"That's his room."

"You think I'm just going to barge into his hotel room?"

Joey smiles sheepishly. "He wouldn't be disappointed if you did."

The thought of being alone with Colin in a hotel room again sends a jolt of excitement through me and my skin starts to heat and simmer as I remember Kyla's words. *At least bone him one more time before he leaves.* I know Logan sees me blushing.

He runs his fingers through his wavy hair. "Hey, who knows where we'd all be if I hadn't fucked up two years ago? If this is another shot for you two, I want to help you take it."

"Thanks," I say.

It's open mic night and one of the first truly warm weekends of the year and the restaurant and bar are packed. I'm keenly aware of both of the cards in my pocket—their weight, their size and shape—every time I move. My heart thumps wildly knowing that I could have him on the other end of a phone or the other side of a door.

Every spare second I get, I stare at my phone. I put his number in and have the text screen open. But I don't know how to start. What am I supposed to say?

I wish he were here.

Maybe I can start with that. I'm watching the blinking cursor when Mila starts jabbing me in the side with her elbow.

"Gracie, ohmygod."

"What?" I look at her in confusion.

But her eyes are locked forward. "Gracie, look."

I follow her gaze to the stage where the next performer is sitting down with his guitar. He's in black jeans and a black T-shirt that shows off his sleeves and I watch the tattooed fingers as he places them along the strings. His face is lowered but I can just make out the slope of his nose. And when he lifts his face to the light to speak into the mic, I lose my breath.

"I'm going to play a few songs tonight, if you'll let me," Colin says to the crowd, most of whom aren't paying that close of attention. He quirks a little smile to himself, like he's amused at being ignored.

But then he starts in with some chords and the second he starts to sing, something lurches inside of me, urging me forward, the pull, the connection. He sings the last song on *The Gray Album*. The one just called "Gray". The whole song is an apology. His apology to me. And while I already know the lyrics, hearing him sing them, stripped down to just vocals and a guitar, in front of me raw and vulnerable, moves me to tears.

As he continues, people start to take notice. They're watching. They're recognizing. They're whispering amongst themselves. They're moving closer to the stage and taking out their phones. They clap when he finishes and he looks up, his eyes alive with the rush of performing.

"I don't do a lot of covers but this one has a special place in my heart, if you'll indulge me."

The whispering grows to murmuring and more people start to file in, joining friends already watching, gathering around the stage, filling in the gaps.

And then he starts to play and sing "Time After Time." His gaze instantly zeros in on me, as if he knew my exact position this whole time. I guess he has. I haven't moved and I can't possibly move now, our eyes focused on one another, him singing only for me, just like the first time I saw him.

It takes me seconds to blink, to breathe again when the song is over.

He leans forward to address the crowd again. "I'm going to play a very special song for you tonight. I haven't sung it in a long time, but I think you might know it."

With the first strum I know he's playing the song. *The* song. A hush sweeps through the room as he starts to sing.

I untie my apron, letting it fall to the floor. "I'm taking my break."

I don't wait for Mila's response. I just walk out from behind the bar, toward him.

CHAPTER 26

His eyes follow me as I weave through the crowd. He keeps playing, keeps singing, keeps watching as I get closer. I duck behind a tight pack of guys and when I emerge near the side of the stage, Colin is scanning the crowd, having lost sight of me.

I step up to the stage just as he's about to sing the first chorus. And then he sees me and he smiles. His real, big, beautiful, earth-shattering, sun-stealing smile. I join in on the chorus, our voices harmonizing effortlessly like always.

I'm vaguely aware of a shift in the crowd. They get louder, their energy heightening. Someone shouts, "It's her!"

But I'm focusing on only him. He stands as I meet him center stage and we sing louder, our eyes locked. We're so close. My body hums with excitement. And he looks at me with more intensity than I can describe as he sings the lyrics.

So here is my heart
Ugly and bruised
Broken and abused

But it pumps just for you
If you want it to
Only for you
If you want me too

I nod, breathing heavily. He looks at my lips and we continue singing. He steps closer and I can barely hold the last note.

As soon as he finishes playing the last chord, he swings the guitar behind his back. We each take a step and then his hand is cupping my face.

"I'm sorry. I'm so sorry," he whispers.

I can barely make out the words as the audience erupts in noise standing from their seats.

I lift my face just as he bends toward me and our lips crash together.

It's not soft or gentle—the kiss is explosive. It's needy, barely-bridled desire. He pulls my body flush with his and I wrap my arms around his neck.

We separate to catch our breath, our foreheads pressed together. I register the hoots and whistles coming from all around.

"Come on," I say breathily.

I grab Colin's hand and pull him off the stage. Our fingers are intertwined and I can feel the heat of his body at my back. I lead him through the "Employees Only" door.

He pushes me up against the other side of the door instantly as our mouths meet again. Lips and tongues devouring, sucking, licking, stroking, thrusting.

My fingers are in his hair, holding his face to mine. I can barely breathe or think as my hands roam down his back and around his stomach, up to his chest. Having him this close, touching his body, feeling his warmth, breathing in his scent—I didn't think I'd experience any of it again and it's intoxicating.

He's gripping my hips, my thighs, squeezing my butt and pulling me close. His thigh is between my legs, in just the right spot, pressing against where I'm aching with need. He grinds his pelvis against my hip, his erection painfully conspicuous.

"This way," I pant between kisses. I lead him down the dark corridor, around a corner to where it's pitch black and away from everyone else. This is where we load shipments from the alley on Mondays and Thursdays. No one will be coming back here.

We stumble in the dark but don't stop kissing or groping or grinding and I'm up against the wall again. I reach down and rub the length of him over his jeans.

"Gray. Fuck." He sucks in a breath. "Come home with me," he begs between kisses.

"I—"

He starts kissing and sucking my neck and, oh god, that feels good.

"I still have to... Oh... Ah... I have to finish my shift."

His hand slides up the outside of my thigh and under the fabric of my dress. "I want you. I want you so fucking bad. Tell me you want this too."

Warm fingers knead at the apex of my thigh and hip, playing with the strap of my thong.

I moan as he kisses me again. "Yes. Yes yes yes yes. I want you."

His voice is hoarse. "When are you off?"

I shake my head. "I don't want to wait." I grip his cock through his jeans and pull at the snap.

He puts his hand over mine as I feel for his zipper. "Here? Are you sure?"

I yank the zipper down. "Yes. I need you. Please. Right now."

Colin bites his lip in an effort to hide the guttural groan that escapes. He drops to his knees in front of me, roughly hiking my skirt up to my hips and burying his face between my thighs.

His mouth is hot against my mound, kissing and sucking through my panties. He lifts my leg, spreading me wider and resting my knee over his shoulder. He slides my soaked panties over and licks me in earnest. Wet. Warm. Swirling and licking and sucking and fucking me with his tongue.

"Shit. Holy fuck. Colin—" I brace myself with one hand against the wall while the other is on top of his head, fisting his hair. I love that it's long enough to hold on to. Just the sight of Colin's head between my legs is enough to do me in but he's eating me out. So. Good.

I'm going to come soon. Pleasure pulsates through my body and coils low in my abdomen. My clit throbs with heat, growing more sensitive with every lick. And then he stays on it, licking hard and sucking in pulses.

I bite my lips to stay quiet. My knees weaken as my orgasm starts to unravel.

He groans with his own enjoyment.

"I'm…oh god…I'm—" My legs almost give out as it hits.

Colin holds me up as I come, still buried in my pussy as I rock shamelessly against his face.

Once I stop shuddering, he stands. His lips are dark, swollen and wet with my arousal. His pupils are completely dilated, eyes black. He kisses me hard, pinning me to the wall as I reach between us. I put my hand down his boxers to grip his cock, finding it huge and hard and ready for me. I pull it out and stroke it as I suck on his tongue at the same time.

He breaks our kiss, out of breath, our chests heaving in rhythm.

"I don't have a condom."

"I'm on the pill." I squeeze him harder and his eyes roll back. "I want you inside me now. Please, Colin."

He hooks my leg in his elbow, my other foot on tiptoes and with my panties still pushed to the side, he runs the blunt head of his dick through my wet folds and enters me in one quick thrust. I let out a gasp as I cling to his neck.

He fills me up and I'm consumed with relief. Relief with how good it feels, how right it feels. Relief that this is exactly what I need and exactly who I want.

"Christ, Gray. You feel so fucking good," he breathes shakily in my ear. He moves slowly out and presses back in. "Is this what you want?"

I shake my head. "No. Harder. And don't stop."

He grits his teeth and his fingers dig into my ass as he plunges into me hard and fast, fucking me up against the wall. He's relentless as he fucks and fucks and fucks. I dig my fingernails into his back.

"Is this what you need?" he rasps in my ear.

"Yes."

I try not to make any noise but the wet sounds and slapping skin echoes around the walls with every thrust.

It's quick and primal and I clench around him hard. He grunts, tensing and jolting as he comes too.

CHAPTER 27

We don't move for several moments. Panting. Satiated. He holds me up against the wall, my legs wrapped tightly around his waist.

He's still inside me.

He brushes strands of hair off my face with fingers that are...trembling? And then touches his nose to mine.

"Does this mean I can have your number now?"

I laugh, nodding. "Yes."

A broad smile plays across his face and then he leans in to kiss me softly. He shifts us so I'm on my feet then pulls out of me.

I whimper at the loss of him, unable to hold it back.

"Are you okay? Was I too rough?"

"No. It wasn't too rough."

"Good." He adjusts himself back Into his pants and fastens his jeans before looking back to me. "I missed you."

"I missed you too." I blink away the tears I feel welling up as it hits me just how much I've missed him. And he's leaving again. Tomorrow.

Warm liquid is starting to drip down my inner thighs and I grimace a little.

"I need to get cleaned up and go back to work."

"Oh shit. I'm sorry, I shouldn't have—"

"It's okay. I wanted you to."

We exchange a look and he runs his hand through his hair.

"I guess I should go too." He glances down the hall the way we came. "Is there a back exit somewhere?"

"Yeah." I point out the door that leads out to the alley.

"Right, okay." He looks back and forth between me and the door a couple of times before striding back over, pressing a hand to my back and kissing me again. He applies gentle pressure, lingering. I rise to my toes to kiss him back, fervently, desperately.

Is he leaving now? Am I going to see him again?

He ends the kiss and levels his face with mine. "Can I come back? When you get off, can I meet you here? We can go to your place or you can come with me. I don't care. I just want to be with you."

I swallow hard and nod enthusiastically, temporarily unable to speak. "I'm between places right now. I'm sleeping on a friend's couch, so..."

"You'll come with me then?"

"Yes."

He does his quick two-kiss goodbye and I watch him go out the door before I retreat down the dark hall to the bathroom.

After I clean up, I catch sight of my reflection. I'm still flushed pink, my lips are dark and puffy, my hair is disheveled. I finger-comb my hair and smooth it down, straighten my dress, and splash cold water on my face in an effort to not look like I just had sex. But the way Mila looks at me with her jaw dropped and one hand on her hip when I get behind the bar tells me the attempt was futile.

"Did you two just do what I think you just did?"

I blink, not sure what to say. The silence is enough answer for her. I'm still too much in my I-just-got-fucked-up-against-a-wall-in-the-back-of-a-bar-by-the-sexiest-man-alive fog to even be embarrassed.

I try to go about working as if it's a totally normal night and I'm a totally normal person, but it's not long until people start giving me sidelong looks.

Guys seem to be flirting harder. Extra winking. More boob ogling. Bigger tips.

Someone asks me outright if I'm Mystery Girl

A group of tipsy girls start asking questions rapid-fire style. *Are you two, like, together? Is he still here? Can we get a selfie? Is he a good kisser?*

Trying to deflect all of the questions is overwhelming. Finally, after giving the girls a round of free blowjob shots, Mila pulls me away.

"Rory and I think you should go home."

"You do?"

"G, you're basically being harassed and half the people swarming the bar aren't even ordering anything."

"Are you sure that would be okay?"

"We can handle it. And we'll tell Terry you were really sick if he asks."

"Okay."

My insides are twirling and dancing with excitement as I grab my things. My heartbeat quickens. I climb in my Jeep with the hotel room key card gripped tightly in my hand.

* * *

The hotel is in a high-rise building downtown. Its lobby is all polished marble floors and rustic wood wall treatments and elegant black light fixtures. I walk briskly past the reception desk, trying to hold the short skirt of my dress down while the tanned man with the perfect coif of black hair follows me with scrutinizing eyes.

I stand in front of the bank of elevators, watching the little down arrow light up and listening to my heart thump.

I'm alone in the elevator. There's no music. Just me and the digital number above the door going up and up. I pass floor four, five…eight, nine…fourteen, fifteen, then finally it stops on the sixteenth floor with a bright ding and the shiny doors part.

I step into the hall and look down at the keycard where 16-A is written in scrolly script. Suite A is just to the left and then I'm face-to-face with a solid wood door. The *Do Not Disturb* sign hangs on the handle.

Should I knock? Should I have called first? I was too excited when I left the bar. I just wanted to see him.

That's all I want still. So I slide in the key and push it open.

The space is large and dimly lit. There's a kitchen space just off the entrance and a sitting area beyond with white couches and a plush rug. And there he is. Sitting in a side chair, silhouetted by the sparkling lights of the city that shine from the expansive floor-to-ceiling windows that make up the entire west wall of the suite.

He whips his head toward me, standing quickly as if startled.

"Hi." My voice cracks.

His long legs close the distance between us.

"I'm sorry, I—" I hold up the key card. "Logan—"

He cups my face in his hands. "I'm glad you're here."

I tip my face up at the same time he crashes his down to mine, our lips meeting hard and then the kiss turns surprisingly soft, warm.

He breaks away, still holding my face. "That you're here at all, like this, I—" His throat bobs. "I swear I went there tonight in hopes you'd agree to talk with me. I wasn't planning on laying you out against a wall."

"I'm not complaining."

He bites his lip to hold back a smile while his eyes go dark, hooded.

My breathing gets heavier too.

"I wasn't prepared," he says.

"I know." My face heats as I remember telling him to go in me bare. "I'm on the pill. I promise I never forget it."

"I trust you."

"And I'm...clean. I renewed my prescription last month and they always run the tests."

He nods, rubbing up and down my arms. "I'm good too. I haven't been tested in a long time, but I... I've only been with one person in the last three years."

It takes me a second to process his words.

"Wow, you haven't?"

"No."

"Oh. Um, I have—"

He shakes his head. "I don't need to know. I don't care. I just want you. I want to be near you. Listen to your voice. Touch you, hug you, kiss you." He nuzzles his nose into my hair. "Be inside you again. If you want."

I want. I want so bad.

"I could use a shower," I say.

"Okay." His fingers fall along my sides, skimming my

thighs and then grasping at the hem of my dress. "Can I?"

I raise my arms in answer and he lifts it over my head, and to the floor. He steps back and admires my body for a moment before reaching for me and pulling himself close again.

He kisses the corner of my mouth, my jaw, and down my neck while his hands apply just enough pressure to dull the ache in my breasts. He hooks his thumbs into the lacy cups, brushing over my sensitive skin before pulling them down to expose my pert nipples. Then he dips his head to kiss and suck on each one as his fingers delicately maneuver the clasps in the back until my bra falls away.

"Beautiful," he murmurs against my skin.

I gasp as he sucks harder, a sharp bolt of pleasure surging through my body. I feel tingly, my insides going to goo, warm and pliable. I pull away and he looks up at me with confusion, his eyes still hooded with lust. I give him a coy smile before turning my back to him and wiggling my hips to shimmy off my underwear, arching my back and bending just enough so he gets a good view.

"I was going to take those off," he snarls behind me, "with my teeth."

I glance over my shoulder. "Oops." And start walking toward the bedroom area where I presume the bathroom is. The unmistakable sound of clothing hitting the floor thuds behind me.

The shower is all glass and white marble and the water heats almost instantly. I know he's watching me from the doorway as I step in. I close my eyes and let the hot water rain down over my hair and face.

And then he's behind me. His body warm and firm, pressed against my back. I lean into him, laying my head back on his shoulder as the water pelts my front.

The scent of coconut fills the steamy shower as Colin lathers what appears to be the entire contents of a mini bottle of body wash between his hands. I'm about to giggle and ask him how dirty he thinks I am but then his warm hands are on my body. Washing me.

He starts with my shoulders and down my arms. My shoulder blades and down my back, around my hips and over my ass, his fingertips grazing just inside the cleft of my cheeks. And then he presses my back to his chest again so he can wash my front.

His hands glide easily over my skin, slippery with soap. Over the swells of my breasts, down the center of my stomach, the curve of my hips. Over my pelvis. And then he cups his hand between my legs, his fingers eagerly rubbing and slipping all over my most sensitive flesh. I whimper when he finally starts circling my clit, coaxing instant pleasure and sending waves of achy need through my body down to the arches of my feet.

"Do you like that?" he asks in my ear.

"Yes."

His cock is hard and upright, nestled perfectly against my ass, and I rock back against him. He holds me tighter to him and presses kisses to my open neck.

"That feels good," he says.

"Uh-huh," is all I can muster as I throw my head back, his fingers bringing me closer to the brink, the hot water and steam encapsulating us.

But then his hands move back to my breasts and the build-up starts to slip away. I'm about to protest when his cock slips between my legs, rubbing along my folds and then to my clit. When he pulls back, the ridges of the head of his cock drag perfectly over my too-sensitive clit, which is now buzzing and throbbing with anticipation.

Water streams in rivulets down my body, washing the bubbles away, and I watch as the pink head of his cock pokes in and out from between my legs as he ruts behind me. He's rubbing my breasts, teasing my nipples as he continues to kiss my neck. The friction of his erection thrusting against my pussy is almost too much and my stomach tightens as the tension builds again.

"I could come like this," I say huskily.

"Me too. But I'd rather be inside you."

I'm about to bend forward and let him press into me when he reaches for the lever and turns the water off.

He wraps me in a white, fluffy towel and I dry myself as Colin towels off in front of me. He finishes first then proceeds to grab my towel and help me dry off, mussing my hair with a big grin while he stands before me, completely naked.

His body is long and lean, his beautiful skin covered in ink. He's gotten more tattoos, mostly on his legs and his upper thighs...and now I'm definitely just staring at his cock. It's still mostly hard, pointing outward and bobbing with his movements as he dries me. I'm not even going to pretend I'm not staring at it. I like it. It's beautiful. And sexy as hell. And in this moment, even if it's just for tonight, it's mine.

An unexpected squeal leaves my lips as he swoops down and lifts me in the air and carries me, naked, to the bed.

He pulls the covers away and lays me down before crawling behind me. He rolls me to my side and presses to my back, tucking his knees up against my legs and wrapping his arms tightly around me. I clasp my hands over his, holding them to my chest.

"What are we doing?" I ask.

"This is called spooning. It's one of the best forms of cuddling."

Colin Wolfe fucking loves cuddling.

"I'm aware. But aren't we supposed to cuddle after sex, not before?"

"Nope. We can cuddle before, during, and after."

"During?"

"Mm hmm."

He grazes my earlobe with his teeth as he trails his fingers down my arm, leaving goosebumps in their wake. Then he rubs down my side and massages my hip, his thumb working in deep circles on my rear. I let out all of the soft sounds of desire I held back when he was pleasuring me at the bar.

He's kneading my ass and my upper thighs and his fingers keep almost skimming my sex. I'm quivering for him, undulating against him.

"Are you still wet for me?"

"Uh huh."

And then he sinks two fingers inside me from behind, quick and smooth.

"Shit, you are so wet." He pushes them in and out. In and out. Nice and slow.

I sigh, writhing, wanting more. Needing it.

His fingers slip out and the wide head of his cock presses lightly at my slick entrance.

"Is this okay?" he asks, lips at my ear.

"Yes." I lift my bottom and arch back to nudge him in already.

He brings his hand to my lips. "Suck." And I take the two fingers that were just in my pussy into my mouth at the same time he eases his cock inside me.

I moan around his fingers, sucking them, tasting myself on them. While I'm sucking, he's working his cock in and out of me at a tortuously languid pace. He slides out slowly and every time he surges back in, it's deeper than before.

He slides his fingers out of my mouth and reaches around to rub the wet tips over my clit as he keeps grinding into me. Rocking in and out like he has all the time in the world.

"Oh, god. Colin. I love your cock."

He chuckles behind me.

"And your hands. And—"

He's building up the tension in my body again. Everywhere his skin touches mine is hot and liquid and my body is coiled, ready.

"And I need—" I let out more gasps as he circles my clit harder.

"What do you need?"

"I need to come," I cry.

"Kiss me."

I twist my head around and he leans forward to capture my mouth with his. The kiss is passionate, deep. His tongue hard and then soft. His breathing is labored. He's holding me close with one arm tight around my chest, stimulating my clit with his other hand while thrusting harder into my pussy.

I'm at the edge. About to burst.

He keeps kissing me, keeps pounding into me, and then I explode. I break the kiss to cry out.

Waves wrack my body and I bear down around his cock.

"Yes, just like that." Colin is fucking me harder, faster. His hand, over-slick with my juices, is still focused on my clit, drawing out my pleasure as I continue to contract around him. "So fucking good."

And then he's kissing me again, grunting, his movements becoming erratic and then he's pulsating inside of me as he releases.

His heartbeat is rapid against my back as we lie here, neither of us making a move, his body still wrapped around mine. We stay like this, cuddled, for a long time.

I don't realize I'm nodding off until Colin's words startle me awake.

"I'm sorry." He brushes my hair away from my face, tucking it behind my ear.

"Hmm. For what?" I roll over to face him

"For how I acted after Logan's overdose. I was an asshole." He caresses down my arms to my hands and back up.

"You were. But that's in the past. We can leave it there."

He continues running his hand over my skin and shivers work down my spine. He pulls the covers up over our naked bodies and I snuggle in close to his warmth.

"Do you ever regret that summer? Being with me?"

"No. I've never regretted it. I was angry with you for a while, but mostly I was just hurt at how easy it was for you to push me away."

He turns me to face him, hands on both sides of my face. "It wasn't easy. I watched you. I watched you sit outside the hospital on that bench for three hours until your dad picked you up. I wanted to go out there and hug you and bring you back in with me every second. And every second I didn't do it I was dying inside."

I hold his face too, surprised to see a tear shedding in the corner of his eye. I wipe it away and kiss his cheeks, his nose.

"I was okay," I say. "In some ways, it was good for me. I had to go home and tell my parents the truth about where I'd been and school. Then I made the decision to take a break from school and move to Chicago all by myself. And I did it. I got a job, a place, and saved enough to start taking online creative writing classes. I don't know if I ever would have pursued writing if it wasn't for you."

He kisses me sweetly on the forehead and asks me about my classes. I tell him about what kind of writing I've been doing and when I started reading my poetry. I tell him about my job at the bar and Mila. I don't tell him about Ethan because I'm sure he doesn't want to hear about him—at least not right now.

His fingers skim over the words tattooed on my rib. "Ever regret this?" he asks.

"Nope. I've never regretted getting that either. I can still remember exactly how I felt when I got it."

"How did you feel?"

"Lost. Confused. I had no fucking idea what I was going to do with my life and I was scared."

He lays two soft kisses to my tattoo, his nose brushing the underside of my breast as he does.

"And how do you feel about your life now?" he asks.

"Hmm. Well, I still have no fucking clue what I'm doing. But I'm not scared anymore."

He gives me a sleepy smile. "Good."

I look into his eyes, asking the question I don't want to voice. Pleading for him to answer. *What are we doing here? Is this just tonight? Are we together? Am I just going to be a booty call when you're in town? What are we?*

But he doesn't say anything and neither do I.

CHAPTER 28

COLIN IS STILL WRAPPED AROUND ME WHEN I WAKE UP, HIS limbs heavy, holding me close. The room is quiet. The light from the windows is hazy.

I listen to him softly intake breath for several minutes before wiggling around in his arms so I can turn and look at him. He looks peaceful when he's asleep. Younger. His skin is smooth. His lips are barely parted, full and soft. I want to kiss them, bite them, lick them, kiss them again.

I lean in to him to kiss those pretty lips, at the same time I feel his morning wood press into my stomach. I rub against it as I kiss him, finally sneaking my hand between our bodies to grasp it fully. I stroke him and he grows harder in my hand. He groans quietly in his sleep, his hips rocking, his cock rutting into my hand instinctively.

Then his fingers wrap around the base of my neck, tangling in my hair, and he's kissing me back.

"Morning," he whispers against my lips.

"Morning," I say, squeezing his erection, tugging it harder.

He opens his eyes and watches as I move, kissing down his chest. His stomach flexes as I kiss farther down, and he's at full mast when I take his cock full in my mouth.

"Fuck." he says through gritted teeth.

He combs his fingers through my hair as I bob up and down on him. I lock my eyes with his as he starts pumping into my mouth.

"Do you… Do you want me to come like this?" he asks in a husky voice.

I shake my head no. I take two more long, cheek-hollowing pulls before letting it fall out of my mouth and crawling back up his body.

"I could wake up like this every morning," he says with a smile before kissing my lips.

"Oh, yeah?" I smile but it falls quickly. We don't have every morning to do this. Just this one.

"What's the matter?" He touches my cheek, rubbing it with his thumb.

"When do you have to leave?"

His face softens. "I already missed my flight."

"What!" I glance at the clock. It's a little after nine already. "I wasn't trying to—"

"Shh. Gray, I made the decision to turn off my alarm last night. I wanted more time with you."

"But—aren't you going to be in trouble?"

He shrugs. "I'll get a later flight. I'm going to miss some press stuff and Rick is probably going to kill me, but I don't care right now."

"So…we have a little more time?"

"A little? We have all the time."

I lean into his touch. "But you still have to leave. Your first show's tomorrow night."

He pulls my face down to his and kisses the tip of my nose. "I booked a flight for later tonight. I got a second ticket, too. Just in case."

"In case?"

"In case you want to come with me."

My eyes shoot open. "On tour?"

He nods. "I want you with me. You said you don't have a place to live right now and your classes are all online. You'll have plenty of downtime for schoolwork."

My heart pounds wildly at the thought. *Go with him.* "You're serious?"

"Yes. Come with me."

Go with him.

"I'd need a reliable internet connection for school."

"Done."

"And my sister is due in August. I need to go home when the baby comes."

"We can make that happen."

Go with him. He's your new adventure.

I feel the urge to say yes, but something is holding me back.

"Um." This is all happening so fast. "Can I think about it? It's kind of a big decision. It'd mean quitting my job and uprooting my life. I mean, this tour is the better part of a year."

"You're right. Of course you can think about it. Take as long as you need. I'll buy you a ticket to whatever city we're in."

"Okay."

He takes my hand, interlacing his fingers with mine. "I still have to leave tonight, though." He kisses my knuckles. "I was kind of hoping you'd be there to hold my hand. Thought it might make the flight more tolerable."

We spend the rest of the morning and afternoon before

I have to go to work in the fancy bathrobes. We order room service and eat in bed. We make love. He lays his head in my lap as he reads my poems and sings me new songs as I stroke his hair. And we do everything we can to not think about saying goodbye.

* * *

"What are you doing here?" I hiss as I walk around the bar so I can keep my voice low and usher him to a corner.

Ethan crosses his arms. "You were ignoring all my calls and texts so this is apparently what I have to do to talk to you."

"Ethan, I don't have anything more to say to you, we're over. And I definitely don't want to do this here. I'm at work."

He takes both my hands in his, leaning in, his eyes pleading. "Will you just come home and talk to me after you get off?"

I'm sad for him. Sad that he just doesn't get it. Sad that I didn't end this much, much earlier.

I stare at him, unblinking. "Why would I want to talk to you when you obviously aren't listening to anything I say?" I huff in exasperation and that's when I see him over Ethan's shoulder.

Colin is standing by the front doors with his hat pulled low, shading his face, long sleeves covering his arms. Our eyes meet.

Shit.

I yank my hands away from Ethan—because that doesn't look suspicious at all—and Colin walks slowly toward us.

"What's going on here?" Colin asks, his expression eerily calm.

"Leave us alone, dude. I'm having a private discussion with my girlfriend."

Colin's eyebrows shoot up and he looks at me, his eyes asking a silent question.

I snap at Ethan, "Ex-girlfriend." I look back to Colin, my voice quiet but steady. "Ex-girlfriend."

Colin's expression stays the same yet, inexplicably, I can sense the change. Something about his eyes. He comes to my side and wraps his arm around my waist, holding me securely against him.

"What the fuck, Grace?" Ethan looks at me, his face scrunched up, nostrils flaring. "Who the hell is *this*?"

Colin doesn't miss a beat. "I'm with her."

"Are you kidding me right now? We've been apart for a week and you're already hooking up with someone else? How long has this been going on? We're you sneaking around with him behind my back while we were together?"

Colin curls his hand around my hip with a reassuring squeeze.

"Goodbye, Ethan."

He glares at me, face flushed, jaw clenched. Colin pulls me in tighter. Finally, with white fists at his sides, Ethan turns and leaves without another word.

Watching him walk out the door, I feel an overwhelming sense of relief, like a weight has been lifted off my chest and I can finally close this chapter of my life.

I turn to look up at Colin. "Hey."

"Hey." He quirks a lopsided grin at me.

I don't think I'll ever get tired of Colin Wolfe smiling at me.

"Shouldn't you be on your way to the airport?"

"Yeah." He wraps his other arm around me and leans in

closer.

I glance toward the back, hoping Terry doesn't choose this moment to walk out.

"I needed to see you again. I don't know how I'll be able to leave without knowing when we'll be together next."

"I know. I wish I had an answer for you. But it's not an easy decision for me. The last time I ran away with you, it was a rushed decision. And...you broke my heart."

He looks down at me, his emotions—his own heartbreak—pouring out of his eyes. "That's the last thing I wanted to do."

"I just have to think it through. It's like, fool me once, shame on you, but fool me twice, shame on me, you know?"

He furrows his brow. "Fool you?"

"I don't think you were trying to fool me, but you were good at pretending. I still don't really know when the pretending stopped and the feelings began. It makes it hard to trust our relationship or know exactly where we stand when I don't know what parts were real and what was fake."

"Pretend? Gray—" He comes even closer, cupping my face. "I've never pretended with you. Ever. Not two days ago, not two years ago. Every moment between us, every touch, every kiss—"

He lightly brushes my arm and I melt at his words while staring helplessly at his parted lips.

"I only ever did those things because I wanted to. Because I wanted you. Desperately. Because I'm so fucking in love with you. I've been in love with you for two years. You were in my head every day."

"You're in love with me?"

"Of course I am."

My heart is thumping so loudly in my ears it overwhelms

my senses.

He's in love with me? He's in love. With me.

"So everything between us, it was real for you too?"

"All of it. Always."

It's like the air has been sucked from my lungs. I have no breath. No voice. And even if I did, I have no words. I stare at him dumbly, unable to put together any coherent thoughts. I'm not even sure if I've fully comprehended what he's saying.

"I have to go." His words pull me out of my stupor.

"Right. The airport."

"Yeah." He lets out a shaky breath and rubs the back of his neck and I notice a slight tremor in his hand.

"Anxious?"

He nods. "The usual flying nerves." He gives me a weak smile and all I want to do is hug him, comfort him.

I throw my arms around him and he tugs me in tight. Tighter. The embrace is all-encompassing. Desperate. I turn my head upward and his lips find mine. He kisses me hard and it feels like I haven't kissed him in years instead of hours. I savor this moment. His arms wrapped around me. His soft lips pressing against me. His sweet scent. How I can feel his heart beating in pace with mine.

When he breaks the kiss, he looks as frantic as I feel. "I really have to go now."

I nod and try to smile through the ache in my chest. "Bye."

He touches my cheek, wiping a tear away with his thumb before I even realize it had fallen. "Bye, Gray."

He presses one last kiss to my forehead then walks away.

And he's gone.

It feels like some part of me has splintered and is now being torn and ripped from my body. Another tear falls and I wipe it away quickly. As I turn around patrons are trickling in faster. Soon the dining room will be filled with the dinner rush.

When I look to the bar, Mila is there. Her eyes are wide and locked on me.

"Girl. Why are you still standing here? Go!"

CHAPTER 29

I knock on Terry's ajar office door.

"Come in." He looks up from some papers as I walk in. "How can I help you, Gracie?"

I'm not sure what to say. I've never quit a job before. Should I just rip it off like a Band-Aid? Do I thank him for giving me a job two years ago when I had no experience? Do I just start crying? So many options.

"Um. I need to talk to you."

"Okay." He waits for me, his gray eyes patient.

"Have you ever done something crazy? Something that's maybe a little reckless but you just felt like you had to do it?"

He tilts his head. "Something crazy...like?"

"Like running away to follow a band on tour?" I laugh nervously.

Terry takes his glasses off, sets them on the desk and sits back in his chair. A wistful little smile crosses his face. "Iron Maiden. Nineteen eighty-three. The World Piece Tour."

We share a look. A moment of understanding.

"There's a plane I need to catch. Like, right now. And I

don't know if I'll be back."

"Sounds like you better get going then."

* * *

"No, no, no!" I slap the steering wheel as I frantically turn the key in the ignition again. The engine whines and stutters but doesn't roll over. "Not now. Not now, please."

I throw my head back against the seat and take a deep breath. I glance at my phone. The flight leaves in two hours. I still have enough time. Maybe. Hopefully.

By this point, my fingers are wobbly as I try to start the stupid Jeep one more time. It sputters again, then cranks louder, then finally, blissfully, the engine roars to life and I scream.

I pull into traffic, my heart beating wildly.

I'm immediately stopped at a red light. *Come on.* I just need to get to him.

One hour fifty-five minutes.

I'm at another red light that turns green right away but there are still pedestrians in the street. And they're just walking all nonchalantly, not even trying to hustle. I want to yell at them. I honk.

One hour thirty-seven minutes.

I finally get onto I-90. The truck in front of me is going so slow. Almost ten under the speed limit and I can't get over because the lane next to me is packed.

I throw on my blinker and hope for the best. I'm white-knuckling it down the interstate and it still takes forever to get to the exit for O'Hare.

One hour twelve minutes.

There's nowhere to park. I go to the next lot. I park so

fucking far away I have to take a shuttle to get to departures.

Fifty-three minutes.

There are lines everywhere. People everywhere.

I have to stand in line at one of the kiosks to print off my boarding pass. Luckily, an older woman notices me fidgeting—I also might be mumbling to myself aloud—and she lets me go ahead of her.

Thirty-nine minutes.

I jog toward security, fumbling to get out my ID. My only saving grace is that I have no luggage. I literally have nothing besides the clothes on my back—the same little black dress I've worn to work the last two days, my phone, and my purse. Not even a toothbrush.

The heavy-set TSA agent whistles when he checks my ticket. "Did you bring your running shoes?"

I try to muster up a laugh but it comes out as more of a high-pitched whimper.

I am coming out of my skin as I wait in line. My entire body is vibrating with adrenaline. At each agonizingly small step forward, I check the time.

Twenty-eight minutes.

They've already started boarding the plane by now. Our tickets are first-class—because, of course they are—so he's probably already on the plane. He's already on the plane.

There are so many people in front of me.

I finally make it to the metal detectors.

Fourteen minutes.

I throw my purse and shoes into the bin. My skin is buzzing as I go through the detector and I literally hop from foot to foot as I wait for my stuff to come through the other side.

For some reason, my hands won't fucking work and it

takes three tries to get my left shoe back on.

Eleven minutes.

I sprint through the terminal toward the concourse.

Seven minutes.

As I look around for my gate, a pleasant feminine voice comes over the speakers announcing the final boarding call for my flight, direct from Chicago to Los Angeles.

I run to the gate, flailing my arms just as one of the agents is starting to close the door.

"Wait! I'm here." I'm completely out of breath.

The agent with his hand on the door handle pauses and looks at me as though he's contemplating whether or not to just shut the door anyway but the other agent sticks out her hand. I give her my pass with a hurried, "Thanks," and then I'm walking through the tunnel to the plane.

I can't believe I made it.

Two flight attendants wave me on and shut the door behind me as soon as I'm through and onto the plane.

CHAPTER 30

Our seats are in the second row and as I step forward, he's there. He's sitting by the window with his head leaned to the side, one tattooed hand over his eyes while the other is resting on his knee, which is bouncing rapidly up and down.

I go silently to him and wrap my hand around the hand on his knee. He startles and jerks his hand away as he sits up. And then we're face-to-face and everything is right again.

"Gray. You're here."

"I'm here."

He smiles and I smile and I might also be crying again, I can't tell anymore.

"I love you," I say.

"God, I love you so much." He pulls me in, his fingers in my hair, and kisses me passionately. Our tongues mingle and taste and his happy sighs sound like he's humming a beautiful song.

I'm about to shamelessly climb onto his lap when a throat clears behind us.

I turn toward the flight attendant who, in an

exceptionally cheerful voice, tells us the fasten seatbelts sign is on. Then she stands there with a saccharine smile on her face and doesn't move on until we are both seated and seatbelts latched.

Colin squeezes my hand and I squeeze his right back. I don't let go of his hand the entire four-and-half-hour flight.

* * *

We are all over each other as we stumble into Colin's hotel room. We only break our kiss when he takes his shirt off. Then his lips are back on mine as he pulls down the straps of my dress, exposing my breasts and ripping a side seam in the process. I'm going to need to buy some clothes tomorrow. I blindly grasp for his jeans and fumble with his belt before yanking his zipper open.

We giggle as we trip over the clothes bunched around our ankles and kick them off before falling to the bed.

Colin pulls back, poised over me and gazing at me with hooded eyes. His dark hair is going all directions, ravaged by my hands, and his face is mostly in shadow.

"I love your pink lips," he pants.

He presses a chaste kiss to them.

"I love your pink-tipped breasts."

He kisses down the curve of one breast to lick and kiss a peaked nipple before sucking on the other and drawing a pained moan from me. He hums with desire.

"And I really love your pretty pink pussy."

He continues kissing down my quivering belly, worshipping my body. Every touch of his lips leaves a path of tingling fire in its wake. His kisses are different this time because he doesn't just want me. He loves me. And I can feel that love in each tender, reverent caress.

His stubbled jaw brushes lightly along the sensitive flesh of my inner thigh and then he kisses me there. Tentatively at first. Teasing.

Warmth blooms under my skin, the ache, the need deep inside me growing until I spread my legs as wide as they will go, urging him further.

And then his mouth is there, wet and hot, licking my throbbing center with fervor.

I'm completely open for him and I let go, lost in the sensations. When my climax comes, it's strong and fast and unexpected and I scream out. "Oh fuck...Colin...yes."

I'm still coming down off my orgasm when he crawls over me and slides inside my wet pussy, his hard cock filling me so perfectly that when he's fully seated I let out an "oomph."

He moans too.

"Fuck. You feel so good. So tight."

He pushes in and out of me harder.

I rock my hips up to meet each of his thrusts, and he tells me how sexy I am and how amazing each clench of my pussy feels around him. He tells me how much he loves me and how I'm his.

"God, Gray, you're going to make me come so fast."

Then he comes hard, groaning my name, tensing and shaking with his release.

Our bodies are slick with sweat when it's done, and we hold each other while our heartbeats steady themselves.

I kiss his salty skin along his collarbone and over the tattoos on his neck to his jaw.

"I want you inside me every night," I breathe.

"I think I can make that happen," he says with an impish

grin on his lips.

And then he rocks back into me. His hips rolling in a slow, methodical rhythm.

"Colin you're—oh fuck—you're still hard."

"Mm hmm."

He kisses me long and deep as we make love slowly this time, savoring the feel of our bodies uniting along with our spirits. If there's a heaven, I don't need to experience it because nothing could be better than this.

* * *

WE'RE PULLED OUT OF OUR DOZING BY A QUIET BUZZING. Colin untangles his naked limbs from mine to fish his phone out of his pants, which ended up somewhere on the floor between the bed and desk. The screen lights up his face as he reads and smiles to himself.

"What is it?"

He hands me his phone and I read through several missed texts.

Joey: *Just checking in, did Gracie decide yet?*

Dean: *Is Gracie coming? Don't mess this up Col, we just got her back*

Logan: *We know your plane landed. Is Gracie with you?*

Almost an hour later, there's another text from Logan.

Logan: *Never mind. My suite is right next to yours and I can hear both of you. Loudly.*

I'm blushing even as I fail to contain my laughter. Colin smiles too. His big, beautiful smile.

I close out of the texts and then I see the picture he has as his phone's wallpaper. It's the picture of all five of us in front of the bean sculpture at the end of our blissful day in

Chicago two years ago.

"I love this picture," I say.

"Me too." Colin takes the phone and looks at our faces for a minute. "This was the best day of my life. Until the end when it became my worst. A lot has changed since this picture. Everything, really."

He looks to me, his expression serious. "It won't be easy being with me. I don't come with a quiet, peaceful life."

I take his hands in mine. "I don't need a quiet life."

"Okay." He lies back and pulls me to his chest. He kisses my head and whispers into my hair. "I would understand if you change your mind."

"I'm not going to change my mind about you."

He strokes through my hair as I listen to the steady rhythm of his heart.

"What I'm trying to say is, I won't let anything to come between us again. I'd quit the band tomorrow if that's what it took."

I prop myself up on my elbow to look at him.

"What?" I'm stunned by the conviction in his voice. "I don't want you to do that. The band is your dream. You've worked so hard for it."

"It was my dream. I dreamt about it for half my life. And once I got it—made it big, the fans, the fame, the fortune—all I thought about was you. Honestly, never at one point in the last two years have I been as happy as I was in that picture."

The confession has my throat tightening. "Really?"

He grins at me lopsided as he combs his fingers through my hair. "Yes."

"Well, I'll never make you choose. We can have both."

"What about you? Do you have something you want

to do?"

I haven't thought too much about my future. I've been mostly taking everything as it comes. One class at a time, one bill at a time.

"I don't know. I have thought about putting a poetry collection together and trying to get it published, but it didn't seem like a very practical career path."

"Fuck practical. That sounds so cool."

He kisses me hard and we settle under the covers, wrapped in each other's arms.

Ever since graduating high school, I've felt like I was floating through life, not really sure where I was going or what I should do. After my original plan failed spectacularly, I felt out of control. I've been trying to regain that control these last two years but never have I felt like this. Like I'm in exactly the right place, my feet firmly on the ground.

And it's him. He's my anchor, my comfort. And I know no matter how high I fly, he'll be there. I don't have to be in control and I don't have to be afraid of trying or failing or falling, because with him I am safe.

I am loved.

I am home.

* * *

Adrenaline-fueled butterflies flutter in my stomach as I stand behind the huge scaffolding and look out beyond to the outdoor amphitheater where thousands of people are gathered on the grass and crowding around the stage. I wipe my palms on the front of my cut-off shorts.

The sun is low in the hazy turquoise sky, glowing around Colin. He's standing front and center, making all of his edges fuzzy. He finishes the song and glances back to me before speaking into the mic. His voice is deep and clear and exuberant.

"I'm going to bring out a very special guest. You've probably heard rumors about her, theories. I'm generally pretty private but I want to finally introduce her to all of you."

The crowd goes wild as I walk out. Colin breaks into the biggest, most gorgeous smile. The sun. He is the sun and the moon and I feel the gravity anchoring myself to him and nothing has ever felt so right as when I cross the stage to his open arms.

And though he's addressing the crowd, he doesn't take his eyes off me. "This is Gray. She's my home, my heart, my everything."

He leans in and kisses me. A slow kiss that deepens and intensifies and takes my breath away. I fist my hands in his shirt, holding on with everything I have as the crowd erupts behind us.

I'm hardly aware as the other members of the band shuffle around us with their instruments and start to play the first notes of our song.

ABOUT THE AUTHOR

Rae has always been a creator. She has degrees in Architecture and Interior Design but also loves to draw, paint, bake, and, of course, write. A hopeless romantic, she's been married to her high school sweetheart for eleven years. Together they have three children and live in the Pacific Northwest.

For more info and a complete list of books, visit www.raekennedyauthor.com

TO BE YOUR ONLY

CHAPTER 1

I LICK MY FORK CLEAN OF THE DECADENT CHOCOLATE FROSTING and drop it to my plate next to the remnants of my second slice of cake. Yeah, I had two pieces of cake, no one is at the cake table tallying how many each person has. There is no cake gatekeeper. Besides, there were two different kinds of cake—the bride's cake and the groom's cake, I can't be expected to pick, well actually, I did pick, I chose both. And I'm the type of girl who likes to have my cake and eat it too. And right now, the piece of cake that I want is Wes.

"I'm going to go talk to him," I say as I stand from the table.

Gracie—the Bonnie to my Clyde, the Thelma to my Louise, the Syd to my Nancy—fuck, do they all die at the end? I can't remember but I think they all die at the end. Anyway, Gracie—my best friend, who doesn't die at the end—gives me a little squeal and a thumbs up.

"Good luck!"

I strut through the grass toward him. Strut would be a loose term here, because, can one really strut while wearing heels in grass when your left heel sinks into the earth on every third step? Well, I'm making it work. Remember your training. Shoulders back, suck in the tummy. Oomph. Definitely ate to much potato salad.

Wes is standing near the dancefloor talking with Gracie's older brother, Eric. Neither of them brought a date to the wedding, thank God, because if I had to spend the evening watching Wes dance with someone else I'd probably tear my hair out. I already had to watch him date Gracie's older sister, Court, for four years. Four fucking years—much to the chagrin of my tender, pre-teen heart.

And now, on Court's wedding day, it is finally going to be my turn. I mean, they broke up five years ago and now she is married, he can't possibly pine over her any longer. Right? I've hoped and wished and dreamed these last few years as I became a woman that Wes would finally forget her and notice me, but he hasn't. He sees Gracie as a kid sister and I am just Gracie's friend, sidekick, the weird girl who always tags along and never shuts up. But not tonight.

Tonight is my night. Tonight, he is going to notice the shit out of me.

"Hi," I say as I stand in front of them, directing my smile to Wes and trying to resist the urge to tell him how nice he looks in his suit.

Because he looks fucking fantastic in this suit. It's navy and the pants cling to his muscular thighs, the jacket makes his shoulders look even more broad. He isn't wearing a tie, just a light blue dress shirt with the top two buttons undone revealing a hint of his toned, tan chest. But if I tell him about how I like his suit I will probably start spewing about how his shirt is the exact same shade as his eyes. His gorgeous, beautiful, perfect eyes.

"Rosenbaum," Eric says.

I glace to him, narrowing my eyes. "Gallagher," I return

flatly before gazing back to Wes.

"Hey Kyla." Wes flashes me his bright white smile and my uterus flutters. It definitely does, that's a real thing.

"You look real nice tonight." Wes glances down at my dress briefly before returning to my face. He's too gentlemanly to blatantly ogle me. Even though my boobs are right here—like, they look amazing in this dress, not going to lie.

"What are these?" Eric flicks my earring.

I reflexively smack his hand away and glare at him. "They're peacock feathers."

"I luh." He looks at my earrings then down to my dress, definitely lingering on my legs and boobs. He shrugs. "They match your dress. It's a good color on you."

Wrong. This dress is the perfect color on me. It's a deep emerald green that compliments my dark auburn hair and fair skin to perfection. Anyone who has picked out as many dresses as me or been through the pageant circuit knows their colors. I look best in a Fall color palette, particularly jewel tones.

"Thanks," I say, keeping my voice even, then turn back to Wes.

Ah, Wes. He makes the smile return to my face. "I noticed you haven't danced all night and neither have I and I was wondering if you'd like to dance with me?" There, that's how a normal person might ask someone to dance, isn't it?

Wes opens his mouth to respond when Eric cuts in.

"I'll dance with you."

I tamp down the desire to growl at him. "I wasn't asking you."

I turn back to Wes, giving him a sweet smile.

"Are you sure?" Eric interjects, forcing my attention back to him.

Him and his stupid little smirk. He thinks he's so funny. Funny looking maybe. Well, I used to think he was funny looking—short, wiry, bright red hair. But he has sort of grown into his looks. He's still a head shorter than Wes but he has filled out quite a bit and his face is symmetrical or whatever. He has a nice looking mouth—but I only notice that because I'm constantly looking at the stupid little grin he always has because he's constantly laughing at his own dumb jokes.

"Yes, I'm sure I know who I was talking to." I glower at him before looking back to Wes. "So, dance?"

He looks between Eric and me for a second.

"Uh, sure I'll dance with you."

I beam at him and grab his hand before he has a chance to change his mind. "Let's go they just started a new song!" I turn and head to the dance floor with determination, Wes following behind, my hand firmly wrapped around his.

I lead him to the middle of the dancefloor. The band is playing a slow song. The sky is black and strings of lights hang overhead as a warm summer breeze tickles across my skin. I wrap my arms around his neck, resting them on his muscular shoulders and he places his hands lightly on my waist. It's the perfect romantic moment for him to suddenly realize how wonderful I am and that we should totally be together. Seriously, fall in love with me already!

We sway gently to the music, surrounded by several other couples. Wes's movements are small, little steps, a slight roll of his shoulders. It's basically high school dance style slow-dancing, but that's okay because Wes is dancing with me and everything is magical. I take a step closer and swing my hips a bit to entice him to loosen up a bit. He gives me the cutest little smile and then looks out into the night as the music plays on.

And I think he just tightened his hands around my waist more? Could have imagined it, I'm choosing to believe otherwise.

While he's not looking at me I take the time to appreciate his gorgeousness from up close. I haven't been this close to him since that time in eighth grade when he helped me up onto a horse—and then had to promptly get me back down again because I was terrified. His neck is thick and muscular like rest of his body and tanned from working hard outside all day. His face is basically the definition of male beauty and what every sculptor who attempts to capture the perfect male specimen would aim to achieve. But they couldn't possibly do him justice, so they should stop trying.

His chin is strong with a little cleft in it. His nose is exactly right with just a slight curve on the left side from when his nose was broken during a football game his senior year—he still completed that pass, by the way. His eyes are baby blue, framed by the cutest blond eyelashes. His forehead is broad and masculine and his blond hair is short but when he lets it get a little longer it starts to curl.

"You're still working on the ranch for Gracie's dad right?" I already know for a fact that he is, but hey, got to start somewhere.

"Yeah, of course." His eyebrows knit together slightly, like he's confused by the question. Bah, of course he knows I know this.

"Just making sure, haven't really been around the ranch much the last year since Gracie was gone at school."

"Oh right, yeah. Gosh, it's crazy that you two are old

enough to be in college now. Did you go to university too?"

"No, I stuck around here."

"I know how that is. But it's nice to be home, yeah?"

I nod. "It is."

We dance in silence for a minute, we are at arm's length again, even though I swear I closed some of this distance earlier.

"So, are you still working at the diner?" he asks.

"No, I got fired."

"Fired? Doesn't your family own it?"

"Yeah. My mom fired me after I dumped the entire contents of a large strawberry milkshake over Jimmy Rogers's head. Some may or may not have splashed onto Emmie Miller's face as well. Mom claims the 'accidental' nature of it getting on Emmie is up for debate but I staunchly maintain my innocence."

Wes's eyes widen. "Wow. Well, I'm sure whatever Jimmy did, it was well-deserved."

"Oh it was. He and I made out in the bowling alley parking lot—" okay, we did a little more than make out, but I'm sure my future husband doesn't want to hear those details "—and then he asked me to go out with him that Friday night. I told him I couldn't do Friday since I was working, but he said he had a family party Saturday—it was this whole thing. So anyway, come Friday night he walks into the diner with his arm around Emmie looking all smug and when they asked for a strawberry shake with two straws so they could share I lost my shit."

"Rightly so." Wes nods approvingly. "Sounds like Jimmy has some growing up to do. Don't waste your time on guys like that, when the right one comes along he won't treat you like second best."

"You are so right." I smile sweetly.

Now all I need is for him to realize he's the right one. I've known it for years. We are destined to be together. He's reserved and sweet and I'm—well I'm not exactly those things, but we'll complement each other, opposites attract and all that. I know he'll be the perfect husband and father—not that I'm looking to get married and have kids quite yet—I'm only nineteen, almost twenty, but someday I will be ready and I want him for my partner.

The song ends and Wes drops his hands from my waist and puts them in his pockets as he takes a step back. He stands there awkwardly for a second giving me a shy smile and I'm just about to ask if he wants to dance some more when Eric swoops in between us.

"I'll take this dance."

What the actual fuck?

He grabs my hand then wraps his other arm tightly around my waist so that our chests are almost touching. The next song is more upbeat than the last and he starts swinging me around and doing spins and shit. He's only a couple inches taller than me, but with these four-inch heels he is firmly in shorter-than-me territory and it feels awkward as fuck dancing with him after having to crane my neck to look up at Wes.

"What are you doing?" I screech as he dips me so low my head almost hits the dance floor.

He leans over me, his face close to mine and looks at me with a mischievous glint in his honey-brown eyes. "Fuck me, but I think we're dancing, Rosenbaum."

I roll my eyes as he lifts me up out of the dip and spins me around again. It makes the skirt of my knee-length dress twirl around and, yeah, okay, that's kind of fun.

"No shit we're dancing. I meant *why* are you dancing with me."

"Oh. I didn't realize I was supposed to answer the question you *meant* to ask instead of the one you *actually* asked." He starts doing this shuffle step so I have to follow him back and forth and then side to side. I think we've taken a tour of the entire goddamn dancefloor.

"You're annoying."

Taking both of my hands he turns me around again, this time whirling me in close so my back is to his chest and our arms are crisscrossed across my stomach.

"I think you meant to say charismatic." He spins me out away from him so we are facing each other again.

"I actually meant to say you're a pain in the ass."

"Charming."

"Infuriating."

Eric just smiles and pulls me in closer, slowing his steps, one hand firm on my back and the other laced through my fingers. "To answer your question of *why* I'm dancing with you, when you so eloquently pointed out to Wes and me that we hadn't danced with anyone all night, I thought you were offering to help alleviate us of our loneliness."

I try to hold back my eyeroll again, but dammit I can't. "I wasn't—"

"Right. You were just offering your company to Wes, then?"

I narrow my eyes at him.

"Oh come on. It's obvious you have a crush on Wes. So what, are you finally making your move on him?"

"Something like that. Not that I want to talk about it with you. But since you're obviously so interested in my life, I'll have you know that Wes and I would be perfect together. He just needs to open his eyes and look at me. I mean, hello, I'm right here in front of him."

The song ends and Eric dips me low one more time, holding me there for a moment to lean in close again. So close I could count the freckles on his nose if I wanted. His gaze flickers down to my mouth for a split second.

"Yeah, must be frustrating."

Printed in Great Britain
by Amazon